In Too Deep:

'If you have been introduced to a Black and Tan about to be assassinated, or a girl about to feed her grandfather stewed cat, or a lonely man set on designing his final resting place – a grave "Fit For a High King" – or a priest who has behaved improperly with a woman and is thinking of suicide but may decide against it because he is In Too Deep to despair, chances are you're in O'Callaghan country, Co Cork… Classy, and bleakly atmospheric.'
– Sunday Tribune

'A masterful storyteller… O'Callaghan flexes his literary muscle with the grace of a dancer… (He) is the sort of writer who places heavy significance on the surreal and mythic power of everyday occurrences… That's what makes this book such a pleasure.'
– The Stinging Fly

'The characters and scenarios raised, though eclectic in the terms of location and of character emphasis, are really like the representations of a painting in language at once chromatic and vast… [these stories] are like finding amber on a beach.'
– Ireland's Literary Free Press

THE THINGS WE LOSE, THE THINGS WE LEAVE BEHIND

First published 2013
by New Island
2 Brookside
Dundrum Road
Dublin 14
www.newisland.ie

PRINT ISBN: 978-1-84840-267-6
EPUB ISBN: 978-1-84840-268-3
MOBI ISBN: 978-1-84840-269-0

British Library Cataloguing Data. A CIP catalogue record for this book is available from the British Library.

Typeset by Mariel Deegan
Cover design by Andrew Brown
Printed by Bell & Bain Ltd, Glasgow

New Island received financial assistance from
The Arts Council (An Comhairle Ealaíon), Dublin, Ireland

10 9 8 7 6 5 4 3 2 1

THE THINGS WE LOSE,
THE THINGS WE LEAVE BEHIND
and other stories

Billy O'Callaghan

NEW ISLAND

Praise for Billy O'Callaghan

In Exile:

'The landscapes and seascapes of Ireland form both backdrop and foreground in this collection of stories by award-winning writer Billy O'Callaghan. Ranging from the wildness of Cape Clear to the violent streets of Belfast, they speak of an Ireland that in some respects is long gone but in others has a modern resonance... Written in language at once lyrical and economical, *In Exile* presents a cast of characters, rich and poor, passive and violent, who are all in a sense yearning to return from exile to a place, a relationship, a particular stage in their lives.'

– The Irish Emigrant

'Traditional and hard-edged yarns about down-at-heel characters, wasters, mean, uncouth, insensitive... O'Callaghan is an award-winner, and he will win many more...'

– Sunday Tribune

'O'Callaghan writes evocatively of a way of life that has become memory rather than reality... he demonstrates an affinity with people and place which is tender but never trite, and invariably rewards the reader with a surprising twist.'

– The Irish Times

'The artistry... is spellbinding. O'Callaghan has injected his characters with enough resignation to make their failures believable, but enough emotion to convince us the failures are tragedies, not merely bad luck.'

– The Hudson Review

In memory of my uncle, Jerry Murphy,

*who took so much laughter with him
when he went.*

About the Author

Billy O'Callaghan was born in Cork in 1974, and is the author of two previous short story collections: *In Exile* (2008) and *In Too Deep* (2009), both published by Mercier Press.

Over the past decade, more than seventy of his stories have appeared in a wide variety of literary journals and magazines around the world, including: *Absinthe: New European Writing*, *Alfred Hitchcock Mystery Magazine*, the *Bellevue Literary Review*, *Confrontation*, *Crannóg*, *The Fiddlehead* (Canada), *Hayden's Ferry Review*, the *Los Angeles Review*, *Narrative*, *Pilvax* (Hungary), the *Southeast Review*, *Southword*, *Verbal Magazine* (Northern Ireland), *Versal* (Holland) and *Yuan Yang: A Journal of Hong Kong and International Writing*. He has also written for the *Irish Examiner*, the *Evening Echo* and *The Irish Times*.

In 2010, he was the recipient of an Arts Council Bursary for Literature. His stories have won and been short-listed for numerous honours, including the George A. Birmingham Award, the Lunch Hour Stories Prize, the Molly Keane Creative Writing Award, the Sean O'Faolain Award, the RTÉ Radio 1 Francis MacManus Award, the Faulkner / Wisdom Award, the Glimmer Train Prize and the Writing Spirit Award. He has also been short-listed in three consecutive years, 2008–2010, for the RTÉ Radio 1 P.J. O'Connor Award for Drama.

THE LAST DANCE

It would not matter
If all those years were today.
It would not matter
If you were here now
– I still could not capture you
As you are.

Whatever remains of you
Is distorted by sideshow
Shadow, and that dance
We never danced
You dance for me
Though I hardly see you.

– Andrew Godsell (1971–2003)

CONTENTS

Acknowledgements   xi

Zhuangzi Dreamed he was a Butterfly   1

Farmed Out   13

Are the Stars Out Tonight?   33

We're Not Made of Stone   45

Goodbye, My Coney Island Baby   61

Lila   79

The Matador   97

A Game of Confidence   119

Keep Well to Seaward   141

Throwing In the Towel   175

For Old Times' Sake   179

Icebergs   195

The Things We Lose, the Things We Leave Behind   213

ACKNOWLEDGEMENTS

I wish to acknowledge and express my appreciation for the financial assistance of the Arts Council of Ireland/*An Comhairle Ealaíon* for the generous bursary in 2010, without which it would have been very difficult to complete this book.

Special thanks to Eoin Purcell and all the staff at New Island Books for making this book possible, and for their show of faith in me at a time when it was most needed. Special thanks are also due to my agent Carrie Howland, of Donadio & Olson, for her hard work and unstinting devotion.

I am also grateful to Jack Power, Ann Riordan, Emma Turnbull, Chang Ying-Tai, Martin McCarthy, Frank Hanover, Noel O'Regan, Simon Van Booy, Ann Luttrell, Patrick Cotter, Yann Donnelly and Irene O'Callaghan for their encouragement, friendship, conversation, inspiration and, when needed, assistance during the writing of this book.

I would also like to thank my large and supportive extended family.

Finally, inevitably, my love and thanks to my endlessly encouraging parents Liam and Regina. They know a thousand stories, and share them all with me when I ask – even the ones they should know better than to tell.

A number of the stories in this collection (some in early incarnations) previously appeared in the following places:

'Zhuangzi Dreamed he was a Butterfly' appeared in the *Kyoto Journal* and, as an earlier draft, then entitled 'A Warm Day,' in *Prole*.

'Are the Stars Out Tonight?', then entitled 'The Speed of Light', appeared in the *Los Angeles Review*.

'We're Not Made of Stone', then entitled 'Forty-One Is Not Old', appeared in *Confrontation*.

'Goodbye My Coney Island Baby' appeared in the *Linnet's Wings* and, as an earlier draft, in *Waccamaw*.

'A Game of Confidence' appeared in *Alfred Hitchcock Mystery Magazine*.

'For Old Times' Sake' appeared in the *Menda City Review*.

'The Things We Lose, the Things We Leave Behind' appeared in *Art From Art*, published by Modernist Press.

Additionally, 'Icebergs' was a finalist for the *Glimmer Train* Open Fiction Award.

Zhuangzi Dreamed he was a Butterfly

Over these past few weeks, I have come to understand that there is no substance to time. None. One minute I am thirty-four years old, doing all the things that people of my age do, all the things we can get away with, and the next I'm fourteen again, huddled beneath the sheets and wishing that the whole world was nothing more than a fetid dream. To the vast majority of us, time travel seems ridiculous until we actually experience its turmoil.

Hiromi, my wife, says that everyone has their own particular way of dealing with grief.

We're born, we live, we die. Those are the facts, and good or bad doesn't enter the equation. People have been challenging this born/die theory forever, and the cycle has yet to be beaten, but knowing this in no way stops us from trying. Aiko was born, lived, died, and if the game had possessed even a single loophole I'd have gone all in with every cent in the bank that she'd be the one to find it. Our little girl. For six years she ruled Hiromi and I; always, it seemed, with a smile, always happy, but always in control. Six years, a span of time practically eternal in its passing but which feels trifling now that it has spun itself out. I've begun to think of time as an actual clock, and whenever I consider it now I tend to focus on its internal workings, the weighted springs, the greased cogs, everything working in minute perfection with everything else, but everything also an accident waiting to happen. When you think about it, there is just so much that can go wrong. If any one of those tiny workings should crack or split apart, then that's it; as fast as a finger-snap the whole thing comes grinding to a halt. One small break and all of time stops.

We know that it can happen, that it will happen, but until the moment of impact we never quite allow ourselves to really believe it. I didn't, anyway. All manner of menace surrounds us, stacked head-high and just waiting to topple. If it's not the ever-imminent threat of nuclear war then it is the six-mile wide meteor hurtling its way earthwards with every intention of doing to us what its illustrious cousin did to the dinosaurs. These and a million other worries hang above us like a piano on a string, and yet we wade ever onward, content in our glorious, purposeful oblivion. We know what's coming, but the inevitable lies somewhere beyond our scope of acceptance. It's how we are able to endure, I suppose, and it is how we careen, in a stunned, wide-eyed stupor, from one disaster to the next. The truth is that we control nothing, not our own lives, not the lives of others. Balance is yet another of our delusions.

A doctor told me once that reality is just a concept. He smiled when he said it, so I smiled too, though I hadn't felt much like smiling, either then or since. But he was serious. And the example he offered up to prove his point was a coma victim. Our concept of their reality is that they are locked in a bed, those poor bastards fresh from a car wreck or a collapsed building or a bullet in the eye. As far as we're concerned, that's it for them until they either wake up or die. But studies have shown that other things are going on beneath the surface of their placid sleep. More than lily scents and cool white light, more than machines that scat bebop and ripple sine waves across their screens. Not always, but in certain cases. Dreams, for want of a better word. The subconscious remains unfathomable to scientists; it operates in the same theoretical realm as the notion of an infinite space or the age and design of God. To these unfortunate creatures, the coma cases, it is possible, more than possible, that dreams have become reality. A question of concept, the doctor said. What their minds see is what counts as real. He was a psychiatrist, of course, and our business during those sessions was to discuss other things, but he did say it. A question of concept.

I thought about this for a while, slumped in a large tanned leather armchair and staring out of his office window at a colourless sky, and found that the words didn't fit quite right. I wanted the situation clarified. If reality were truly that fragile, how could the tangible be explained away? How did the mind differentiate between dreams and the physical world?

The doctor's initial reply was to stare at me, his mouth bending new shapes out of that smile. Arcs, a wavy line, and then something that was just about triangular. By that point in our sessions, the rules of the game were starting to make sense, so I wasn't too surprised at his reticence. But just when I'd begun to accept that this was yet another example of how he suggested ideas rather than explained them, he tapped his left temple and asked what did I think touch was if not a sensual reaction, some surge of endorphins invading the tender nerve endings? His long white finger continued to tap, and suddenly a light went on somewhere and I understood that the brain controls everything, all the senses, every taste, smell, touch, sight and sound that the world can possess. Every feeling, too. Flushes of adrenalin, chemical discharges, neurons sparking awake like live wires to spit out some notion before slumping back down into the mire of rest. Our entire lives are played out in three pounds of lipids, protein and water, and with just a pinch of salt thrown in. This complicated alchemical concoction conspires against nearly impossible odds to produce seventy thousand action-based thoughts a day, every day for years, for decades. Our bodies are the least of it, all that bone and muscle and fleshy fat not too much more than a convenient vehicular pulp, the wrapping paper on a precious Christmas gift.

So, what is real? My head is swollen with six years worth of memories of Aiko, and new ones, it seems, are brought to light with every passing day. I'll be staring at the page of some book, or shaving, or kneeling in the second to last pew of the church across town, or eating soup, or just holding Hiromi's hand the way I sometimes do when words feel like too great a challenge, and in those moments I'll find some new, unbidden recollection blooming in my mind. How I cradled Aiko in my arms when tears rather than sleep were the order of the night. How I walked with her to school, or to the store, or walked with her just for the sheer invigoration of our tandem movement, slowing my step to keep apace with her, she skipping along in an effort to keep up. Her tiny hand had a heartbeat, and it tickled and squeezed its marathon pulse into mine even as her concerned face studied the passing cars and we looked for a safe part of the road at which to cross.

I sleepwalk through life now. Occasionally, I wake and register some small detail of the day, or I'll catch the demand of some question asked and try, if I can, to answer, but the greater part of who I am confines itself to memories. Aiko's death has made two of me. One part is the true me, the part willingly lost heart

4

and soul to the past, before the sky fell in, and the other is the husk that has been left to drift at the whim of the wind. Everyone assures me that this is a natural way to feel, but their lives still pitch along on an even keel, they still believe in thinking the best of situations. Their guillotine is still poised.

Hiromi doesn't say much. Her stillness, her comfort with silence, has always attracted me, but I'd never noticed its predilection for melancholy. Maybe I'd been too stringent in my point of view.

The grey around her eyes feels like a duty now, and she wears it as such, but it is not offensive. She is still a beautiful woman and I suppose, in time, she will learn to sleep again. I wish for the closeness we'd once enjoyed, but life has a way of widening voids, and maybe it is enough to know that we'll love one another until we die, inasmuch as it is possible for either of us to love, broken as we are. Her hair has grown out of the pageboy cut that she'd sported through most of the early years of our marriage, but such surface shifts no longer matter. We speak in whispers, even when we are alone together. To an outsider, it must seem as if we are keeping secrets and don't want to be overheard, but that's not the reason. Our usual voices feel too loud, somehow. We have both sensed it. And there are times, when I take her in my arms, that I wish she'd smile, for her own sake more than mine, but I understand why she doesn't. Time hangs immense before us; the clock has been cracked, but now the seconds beat with greater vigour. And every one of them feels spilt, wasted.

We'd spent that evening, the one that has come to define our lives, sitting around, doing nothing. Waiting, it seems, when I look back on it now, but I know that's not right because how can it be? How could we have known? I was on the couch, halfway into my second beer. There was a game on, though I don't remember who was playing. In my mind I can see the screen, but the details elude me. Hiromi was in the kitchen, making meatballs for spaghetti. She's a great cook with food she knows. She does a mean stir-fry too, and very passable quesadillas. When the phone began to ring, I think we each thought the other would pick up, so the sound lingered, metallic and shrill, the sort of noise perfectly conceived to bear bad news. Then it died in mid-ring and I knew that Hiromi had it, and I slumped down into the couch and let the game back in, the baying of the crowd and the commentator's singsong clucking. Layers of white noise.

Ten minutes later we were at the hospital. My hands were clenched into fists, and the air tasted of rust in the high back of my throat. Hiromi was crying, even though we had no details yet. And the same white noise was everywhere: in the car, running through the corridors, in the waiting-room packed with people. Faces bobbed into view, white lumps that kept trying to speak and breaking off, because words had no way of expressing what needed to be said.

Aiko had been spending the evening after school at a friend's house. On a play-date. There is an organisational term for everything these days. We knew the family, in that way of next-street neighbours knowing one another. A name, a face, a wave, a smile. Strangers, really, but acceptable ones. Mike and Linda Finlay, and their lovely daughter, Helen. The Troy connection, Linda had explained once, at a friend-of-a-friend's fund-raising barbecue. In aid of Alzheimer's, I think, though it might have been Parkinson's. A delicate, thin-boned woman, easily five years younger than Hiromi and me, she bubbled with those soft, condescending chirps of a laughter that instantly defined her as a type. I'd just stood there, unable to really join in but settling for a smile just to assure them that I got it, that I wasn't stupid even if I did happen to be one of the very few men at the party not wearing a university tie.

The girls were playing hide-and-seek, their entertainment of choice whenever they got together, and it seems that at some point in the game my daughter had slipped away and hidden in a neighbour's driveway. 'Being too clever by half,' Mike said, the words leaking out of their own accord. Not meaning anything by it, but saying it. Hiromi was sobbing into a handkerchief and didn't hear him, but I heard. For a split second I wanted to take his head and smash it into the nearest wall, but that flare of anger quickly burned itself out, and I lowered my eyes and let it go. We bear our guilt in different ways. And Aiko had broken the rules of the game, stepping beyond the boundaries. Crouched behind the Lexus, she could see through the property's dividing hedge to where Helen stood, hands over her eyes, trying with some difficulty to count backwards from twenty-five. I wasn't there, of course, but I had witnessed this when play-dates rendezvoused in our front yard, and so can picture it with gruesome clarity. That gasped drone pummelling the first syllable of each uttered number: 'Twenty, nineteen,' and then a pause as, eyes still clenched shut, the hands were freed and fingers put to work. 'Seventeen, fourteen, thirteen, twelve.' On and on, and close enough.

We followed a male nurse down a tangle of corridors and through set after set of double-winged doors that whispered open and hushed shut. Some had 'No Entry' or 'Authorised Personnel Only' signs pinned to them, but those signs didn't seem to apply to us. It was all very dreamlike. After twenty steps, Hiromi and I were lost, disorientated. After a hundred, it felt as if we had touched down on another planet. Our shoes squeaked on the linoleum floors, and neither of us dared speak. The nurse was tall and very thin, malnourished-looking, with protruding cheekbones, a pair of round, wire-framed glasses pushed right up against his eyes and a finger-smear of a moustache greasing his upper lip. He wore green scrubs, and I noticed as we walked that the hems of his trousers were bloodstained. I was still considering those stains when he opened the door to a small, empty, windowless room and gestured us inside.

'Wait here, please,' he said, without looking either one of us in the eye. 'A doctor will be in to see you soon.'

Afraid and confused, we obeyed. Once the door closed, the light felt strong and raw and the floor was immaculately clean, cream-coloured tiles polished to an almost reflective gloss. Hiromi kept close beside me and slightly to the front, her body half-turned into mine, her shoulder pressed into the channel between my body and right arm. Her mouth was shifting, but even when I lowered my head I couldn't catch the words. I think she was praying. If she was, then God owes her for the wasted breath.

We were deep in the bowels of the hospital, but even without the confirmation of a visual I could feel the day's light dribbling like a wound and the first tempered lean of darkness. Because of the watch on my wrist I was able to monitor time's passing, but the sensation I had of real time was something far more powerful. When we work ourselves back to an instinctual level, we are not so far removed from nature's shift, from the moon cycles and the tides and the waning of the sun. The problem is that we are not hard, like rock, or strong like the trees. We can't always cope with being dragged this way and that. We might not look it, but we're fragile, and we break easily. I felt night coming on and later I felt it slip away and the first resonance of a new day waiting to break. And when a doctor did eventually appear, I knew what he was going to say before he said it. Not the words themselves, but what lay between the words. He explained how severe Aiko's injuries had been, a ruptured spleen, punctured lung, crushed upper vertebrae and extensive brain trauma. The medical staff had done everything possible and she'd fought hard through nine hours of surgery. But the bleeding in both the Parietal and Occipital lobes could not be stanched.

'Not Aiko,' I said, my voice helpless above a whisper. 'Not my baby, please.' He looked at me, then nodded and looked away. I could see by the set of his shoulders his struggle to add something more, but there was nothing else, and all he could do was nod again before leaving the room. Hiromi held my hand and wept. I knew she needed to be held, but couldn't bring myself to do it. This was a moment beyond redemption. My watch put the hour at just after six, but my body already knew that.

Another long march followed. This time the pace had less urgency. I don't remember any doors, or anything about the floor or the walls, or even who it was that brought us on this second traipse, though I do seem to recall the steady clatter of our combined footsteps as a sound too much for dawn. An image stood clear in my mind, of the male nurse from earlier in the night, with the blood staining the low legs of his scrubs. Life and death ought to know more dignity than that.

The lights in hospitals are too severe, they separate the whole world into one thing or the other, pallid glare or pitted shadow. There is no room for collusion, and nowhere to hide. All the staff required from me, the attendant nurse said, was a nod. Just pull the blanket back, and nod my head. She was middle-aged, creased with a permanent exhaustion but still playing the game of pretty, with stone-washed bangs spilling out from beneath the rim of her cap and her longish mouth reshaped by clumsy lipstick. She held a clipboard over her left breast, over her heart, and institutionalised to such work as this, her made-up eyes shone like wet tarmac. 'Just do it,' she said, so I did.

Beside me, Hiromi gasped, then began to laugh. No one was expecting it, but that's what she did. The soap-white body on the trolley was unrecognisable as Aiko. Unrecognisable as human. There was a small, terrible face abraded nearly to nothing, and a head bloated to a grotesque degree and strewn with ropy mud-brown tufts of hair. Tiny, naked shoulders poked above the blanket, shoulders that claimed to have in their infancy known my kisses.

'That's not her,' Hiromi said. Stunned by the twin jabs of relief and terror, she turned to me and repeated herself, announcing to any who could hear, the attendant nurse and the other staff members lingering in the open office just beyond. 'That's not Aiko. There's been a mistake.'

The seconds piled up, and all concept of reality fell away in chunks. I swallowed hard, and held her by the arms. 'It is,' I whispered, putting my mouth against her ear. 'Look again.'

How can you pick up the pieces after something like that? The answer is, you can't. All you can do is put one foot beside the other and try your damnedest to stay upright. That's the best we can hope for. We live our lives around the edge of a gaping hole, but we have to live. And when it's time, we get to heaven any way we can.

What works for Hiromi, I think, is prayer. She's let God in, and that's her crutch. For me, it's that psychiatrist's comment about reality being restricted to what our brains can countenance. That's become my gospel, and I'm holding on, learning to live inside myself. It's not always perfect in here, but it's peaceful. When I close my eyes, I no longer see darkness, or feel afraid. I find myself in a field on a sunny day, somewhere in the countryside, out where there are hills and rivers and where the sky is empty and huge. I am exactly where I want to be, with Hiromi sitting cross-legged in the warm grass and with Aiko beside me. She has on a light cotton dress the exact flowering colour of dandelions and her knees are scabbed from running. My job is to pluck small daisies; hers is to hold her hands in a cradling cup so as to horde our collected treasure, and to keep her pretty face locked in the grin that can move entire worlds out of their orbits and reduce nuggets of coal to their diamond core. The acrid musk of baked earth complements the scent of her skin and hair barely an hour on from a wash and still fresh, the honey tang of cider infused with something newfangled and screaming of the exotic, Echinacea or jaborandi, the sort of thing Hiromi would buy as much for the musicality of its name as for the shampoo label's sworn therapeutic properties. Beside us, the remnants of a devoured picnic, sandwiches, fruit, the last wedge of cherry pie, the legless carcass of a chicken, lie spread out on paper plates across a red and white check-patterned blanket, and my small transistor radio is tuned to an oldies station, playing the Beach Boys, Van Morrison and Creedence Clearwater Revival. Hiromi and I sing along to 'Brown Eyed Girl', my song for her, for both of them, and with Aiko joining in on the sha-la-las, we dance sitting down, helpless beneath the elemental nature of the melody and Van's voice hard as quarry scrapings and at the same time all the way soft. I can feel the sun's heat on the skin of my arms and the back of my neck, and 'memory' is nowhere near grand enough a word for something as deeply-etched as this. This was a real day, one we lived and smiled through, never guessing at its perfection.

A doctor's duty is to heal the sick. Some injuries and diseases are just too deep-seated to be properly cured, but most can at least be managed. Well, my pains and problems are deep-seated. I have responsibilities, especially to Hiromi, and I deal with those as best I can because it's what men do, even broken men. I know there is no cure, because time that's been laid down can never be undone. But in these past few weeks I've learned that it can be finessed, perhaps plastered over with layers of better pasts. Reality is a concept, Maya, a state of mind. Acceptance of this has let me learn to slip beneath the pain, shuck my skins of suffering and make a quest of searching out other better states. And the reality I choose, my paradise moment, finds me down on my knees in the burnt summer grass, inches from the solid, still unscarred shape of my little girl's skull, the clammy silk of her skin, the dark corkscrew wisps of her floating hair that greet my nose and cheeks whenever I lean across to plant a kiss on the back of her neck or in the high dead centre of her forehead. In this eternity, my taste buds still buzz from the joys of egg salad and cheese and pickled cucumber sandwiches, and the ice-cold cans of ginger ale and lemonade, and best of all the fresh-baked cherry pie, cherry being our absolute favourite apart from my own occasional yearning for pecan and banana. We are all here, Hiromi, Aiko and me, together, all within an arm's reach of one another. We are a family, still innocent and unbroken, and this is real. Here, there is no pain or grief, only laughter, only the smell of a late July day in all its full-blown glory. I have everything I want, and I am happy. Having followed my road to its end, I recognise this now as heaven. I'd been through here once before, and almost passed it by.

Farmed Out

THERE ARE NO introductions, no handshakes or words of welcome. They stand watching the bus ease back out into the empty road and turn off towards Dunmanway, left and out of sight at the bottom of the street. From the footpath, Thomas considers the village's quiet thoroughfare. The low white sky bulges with a certainty of rain, giving Enniskeane a bruised, tormented look, the dirt road pocked and turning muddy, the tired fronts of the few shops and public houses, the lonesome grey-green hills beyond.

'You have the letter?' says McNamara.

The boy nods, takes a folded envelope from his pocket and holds it out to the farmer, then sets to studying the scuffed toes of his oversized hobnail boots. A cold wind is blowing in from the west, adding something odd to the stillness, and blue glints of steel toe show through the broken leather, the only honest colour in the day.

McNamara clears his throat several times as he reads the letter, his mouth shifting at a pace with his mind, his eyes pinched in an effort to make sense of what the words are trying to say. But there is no meaning beyond the order of the facts: Thomas's full name and details, height, weight, age, situation. And, of course, an address to where the unmentioned donation should be sent. The letter is signed by a Mr Doyle, no first name. Not the headmaster, one of the administrators, the one McNamara spoke with the day he'd visited, the one who had shown only bottom teeth when smiling and who'd suggested a figure without delving into specifics.

'Come on,' the farmer says, bunching the paper in one fist. 'We can't waste the day standing here.' Then he turns and moves off down the street, and Thomas, clutching to his chest the brown paper parcel that contains his single change of clothes and his few personal possessions, is forced into a half-run just to keep pace.

The cart waits on one of the narrow cross-streets, lashed to a large Connemara gelding. The hum of a lone recorded fiddle moans from beyond the wedged-open outer doorway of a nearby public house, Corrigan's, and hangs heavy on the afternoon, and Thomas sets a hand palm-open against the horse's side and feels through the velvet hide all the warmth of old blood. A heart beats somewhere far away, vibrating up through the spokes of the ribcage. Not knowing the horse's name, the boy presses his mouth close to the animal's ear and mutters something that is all sound but no real words, and the Connemara raises his head from where he has been nuzzling through the dirt of the road's verge and gives up a sound of his own.

Four miles outside the village, the farm spreads out over the upper half of a west-facing hillside. A fur of rain has settled during the journey out, and there is little to see of the fields that fall away in two directions beyond the vague darkness of a few bent and scattered still-bare oaks and the haw and bramble ditches that divide up the land. At the head of the nearest field, the gate has slipped its top hinge and hangs wedged solid in the mud. McNamara stops the horse, and they sit and gaze back down over the valley.

'Twenty-two acres.' His voice is a low, scratched bass, caught between a whisper and the growl of a bark, the sort of voice that will resonate inside a room but is thin as the air itself out here. The cold wind diminishes everything, even the hills, and Thomas has to lean in close and concentrate on what is said before the words are swept away.

'Twenty-two acres and every one of them needs working. We have a bed set up in the barn. It's warm and dry and you'll be comfortable enough. And you can eat over in the house with us. Do the work you're given, boy, and there'll be no problems. You understand what I'm saying?'

Thomas nods that he does, clears his throat and then nods again. He is wet through and can see the rain as smoking sheets out across the fields to the west, smothering detail and obliterating the distance. But the air is fresh and cold on his face and in his mouth, clean as water. Compared to the dormitory, compared even to the cabbage and potato fields behind the school, this is freedom.

McNamara steers the cart up a long, rutted laneway so overgrown on both sides that man and boy must lean together in the cart to spare themselves a clawing from the ropes of heavy briar. At the top of the rise they pass a cottage on Thomas's right, a small, unattractive home with lime-washed walls stained grey and in places green by the elements and a thatch in need of renovation. As they pass, the red front door swings inward, but no one appears. The cart trundles on, McNamara gazing only ahead.

They stop in an open yard just beyond. The rain, soft and dense, clouds the latening day in whispers, and Thomas climbs from the cart and looks around, thinking of ghosts, of entities attached either to him or to the place, there and felt but not quite seen, watching with intent. The yard is penned in on two sides by empty concrete cowsheds, and on the third side, set a little apart, a large, deep, open-faced barn with an oddly pitched roof and walls of plywood and mismatched sheets of salvaged corrugated iron.The fumes of silage and beast pool together, cloying and sour on his tongue, and he steps behind the horse's haunches and spits, but the taste lingers.

In the barn, the air feels different. Sweet now, and heavy; the throaty sweetness of baled hay. In one corner, away from the corroded farm implements, the harrow, two hanging scythes and a few spades, a passable effort has been made at creating a living space. There is a makeshift bed dressed with a grey sheet and a coarse pink wool blanket, and to the right, against the wall, a small timber tea-chest locker with some cupboard space below, and on top a drawer that can't be shut and can't be all the way opened. Perched on top of the locker is a candle lantern missing the glass pane on one of its four sides.

McNamara waits, arms folded across his wide chest, and watches Thomas set his drenched parcel of belongings down on the makeshift bed, and with all his weight on both hands test the shuck mattress. There is some give, but not much. The mattress is soft and well enough stuffed, but has been spread out on a stack of timber pallets. Conscious of the farmer's attention, he perches on the bed's low corner and picks open the knot of his parcel, his numb fingers fumbling with the string until it comes apart. He folds the sodden brown paper, careful to match up the ends, then lays out and packs away his clothes, the few garments he keeps as best wear, for special occasions and attending Mass. A shirt that has lost its blue, a thin grey wool sweater and beige corduroy trousers.

There is a book on the bed, a slim brown paperback western, and protruding from its dog-eared pages, a dirty white envelope.

'What's that?'

'What? This?'

Thomas picks up the book.

'The envelope.'

'It's just some photographs.' Anxious to please, to be seen as hiding nothing, Thomas slips his thumb into the envelope and holds out three pictures. McNamara considers the boy for a moment, then takes the pictures in his thick fingers and studies them one by one at a long arm's length.

'That's my mother,' Thomas whispers.

'Your mother?'

The paper is brittle, the black-and-white images grainy and poorly done. Time and other factors have stripped them of their definition. The subject of the pictures is every imaginable sort of spectre, three head-and-shoulder shots depicting a woman who could be any age at all. Each captures a different pose, but all are marred by the same essential flaws, the face plain and vague, without character, the eyes dead, as far removed from the world as it is possible to be.

'I see the resemblance,' the farmer mutters, just for something to say. 'Better put them away safe, otherwise they'll be fodder for the rats. I want to show you the fields while we still have a bit of light.'

There is always work. Cattle needing to be brought in at night and milked before proper dawn has broken, eggs that must be gathered, chickens fed and coops cleaned. These are year-round duties, as is attending to the numerous fences, boundary walls and outbuildings, which stand in varying degrees of dis-integration. The details of field work shift with the seasons, though with ground to be tilled, grass to be sown, hay to be threshed and stacked, the land's demands do not slacken. And if the best chores are those that break the monotony of routine, some roof or sty in need of urgent repair after a storm has blown through, or a morning or even a night spent on the birthing of calves, then the worst, by far the worst, are the jobs that combine tedium with severe manual hardship.

Over the past few years, through private arrangement and once through public auction, McNamara has acquired, at an outlay of pittance, four of the seven fields that border onto his own land. Four fields, ranging in size from an acre to an acre and a half, that perch on the brink of ruin, their soil overgrown and choking on rock and ragwort from having been left to lie too long fallow. Once the day's pressing duties are completed, Thomas finds himself immersed in the task of nursing these fields back to usable shape. It is a mammoth challenge for one pair of hands, for one shovel, and after a while it feels less like work than a war of attrition. Stone gives onto stone, and every cleared yard seems to reclaim itself overnight, new rocks swimming from deep to pock the freshly turned surface, sudden wispy sprouts of clover bearding the broken dirt. The chore advances at a crawl, with progress evident only by the great pyramidal rock cairns that stack up along the perimeters and which, at some later time, will be utilised in the construction of loose-built boundary walls.

On the days when the rain lashes everything to slush, he often spends hours out here, plucking rocks from the mud until the skin of his hands is raw and etched nearly black and every muscle in his neck, back and shoulders have snagged themselves tight as a drawn noose. Rocks tease the surface like fish in a pond, appearing and then slipping back below, swallowed once more by the depths. And the mud gets everywhere, into armpits, between the legs, into all of the body's naturally protected spaces, and the only way to endure such toil is to disconnect. While his fingers trawl the quagmire he lets his mind slip free to wander, and to fill itself with thoughts of the friends he left back at the school, and the Christian Brothers, and most often of his sister, Margaret, two years older than him, who works in a hotel now in Wexford. The last time they'd met, she had given him the pictures of their mother. He'd just turned seven, and for twenty minutes they were allowed to sit together on the bench inside the school's high wrought iron double gates. She wept the whole time, knowing more than he did, and because it had rained either earlier that morning or else during the previous night, the teak laths of the bench were damp. Embarrassed, he had watched a pair of crows light from a copse of half-stripped alders beyond the gates and struggle against the breeze to cross the sky, but he let her take his hand and keep it in her lap, clenched in her own hot grip, and when the time came to say goodbye she kissed him so hard and for so long that his cheeks were warm and wet from her tears.

Whenever McNamara needs a few minutes of respite from his own work, he comes down and surveys the situation, and he paces the fields, slopping through the mud and poking at the surface with the prongs of a pitchfork, biting the pulpy inner wall of his cheek in thought. There is never any praise, never anything in the way of compassion, even when the rain falls in torrents and the wind has an edge that pierces bone.

'Are you working at all, boy,' he likes to say, not even making a question out of it. Thomas, standing a few paces back, clears his throat and shrugs or hangs his head, because there is no good answer, not for a man whose idea of comfort is a minute's rest over the shaft of a shovel. Words would be a mistake.

The days on the farm are long and full of demand, even in winter when some days never find anything more than a dull swab of light. Hour seems chained to hour, and there is always something else in need of attention, some waiting chore to hurry him along. During the weeks following his arrival, he exists in a state of perpetual exhaustion, but tries not to let it show. McNamara has not repeated his initial threat, but its implication looms. Thomas works hard, does what is asked of him, knowing there are plenty more where he came from, plenty who'd leap at the chance of escaping the school, and the Brothers. But as the months pass, and as a hard winter gives way to an immensely wet spring, the drudgery of the work begins to erode such fears, and by the first summer nothing else but work exists. He rises with the first crowing of the cockerel, pulls on his clothes and boots and hurries across the yard to where the cows are lowing, waiting to be milked. And yet another day breaks around him, mimicking all that has gone before.

The only break in the tedium is Sunday morning, and a few begrudged hours of respite so that he might walk into Enniskeane to attend first Mass. In a corner of the yard beside the barn, he washes from a large barrel, stripping to the waist and scrubbing his face and body with the stagnant rainwater and a bar of brown carbolic soap. On those mornings when the temperature fell below freezing, he'd take up up a rock, or some scrap iron, and smash through the thumb-thick skin of ice that had formed across the water's surface, devout in his belief that cleanliness really was next to Godliness. But even after summer closes in and the nights have turned warm, that water retains a dark, wintry chill. He washes quickly, his skin burning with the cold, then dresses in his good clothes and walks the four miles down into Enniskeane for Mass, following the narrow boreen eastwards into the rising but only rarely glimpsed sun. In the village, people stare and then ignore him, even the other children, the few he sees on entering the church, and he finds a place at the back, three or four pews in, and goes through the motions of kneeling, standing and receiving the Eucharist, keeping his head bowed at all times, avoiding eye contact so as not to cause offence. He says a decade of the Rosary, keeping score with the Hail Marys on his fingers to avoid miscounting and falling short, and then he adds his own special prayers, for Margaret, asking God to keep her safe and happy, and for his mother and father. Afterwards, he lingers among the congregation for as long as he dares, because it pleases him to feel part of a crowd, even one that acts as if oblivious to his presence, but by eleven o'clock he is back in his work clothes, elbow-deep again in mud or silage, or tending to cattle or some broken outbuilding roof or crumbling wall.

By the end of his second year on the farm, three of the four fallow fields have been cleared and returned to usable shape. New seed is planted, and McNamara increases his herd of cattle from twenty-five to thirty-eight, with intentions, he says, toward an eventual fifty. Extra cows mean extra work, but the land itself, once properly salvaged, is easily enough maintained. The workdays are still long and full of endless demand, but the details have come to matter less for Thomas. Time exists only to be filled. The two years have dulled little of McNamara's outward bluster, but the aura of threat has softened somewhat, and apart from the occasional screaming nightmare, Thomas no longer lives in dread of being sent back to the school. Once darkness comes in, and after he has washed and eaten, he stretches out on his bed in the barn and reads until exhaustion drags him into sleep. Margaret sends him books a couple of times a year, used and often ragged copies of the slender paperback westerns that she knows he likes. And that is enough. He has never been anywhere, and can barely imagine a world beyond the little he knows, but these books are like a fire to his mind. The pages are yellow and bear a musky smell of smoke and dust, and the gaudy covers depict granite-jawed types set against a background of desert, canyon and cactus, often but not always astride a galloping Appaloosa and wielding Winchester rifles or huge Colt revolvers. The collection forms a small stack on the locker beside his bed, standing now at an even dozen, and he reads and rereads them, working his way continuously from top to bottom, sometimes finishing a book a night, but more often stretching them over a few nights, taking the stories slowly, trying to absorb and picture them.

After a long, wet spring, summer breaks late and lingers through all of August and most of September, the air hot and dry and smelling of the sea whenever a breeze stirs the day. There is enough to do, and the work begins at five, or even a little before, and endures until the first stars break through, on towards eleven. The fourth field is left to wait, the ground being so dry, and this is weather for threshing, and for drawing in the two back acres of harvested wheat. By the end of the month there is a slight shift, a slip in temperatures and a wind, the first they have felt in weeks, that warns of worse to come, and then October dawns to howling gales and cold, violent downpours. For most of a week the hillside suffers, and even when the rain eases the dark sky seethes. Thomas busies himself as much as possible around the yard, taking advantage of the cover, but it is dangerous ground because McNamara haunts the out-buildings, face wrenched into a scowl, big shoulders bent against the wind, frustrated and angry. Whenever his gaze falls on the boy he grunts profane instructions, to clean out the henhouse, to get some firewood chopped or churn the slurry, to stop being such a lazy little bastard.

'I'm not feeding you for the good of your health, boy,' he says, and he moves into the cattle-shed doorway again to consider the bruised blue screed of rain cloud battening down the western distance. 'There's still that fourth field. You're here to work, and don't forget it.' He lets his glare linger, then turns away and is gone again, leaving a hole behind him in the day except for the sound of his boots sluicing through the pools of filthy water. Thomas finishes what he is doing, washing out the milking boxes or cleaning down the walls for a coat of whitewash, then hurries off to attend his latest task.

On the Thursday morning the wind shifts, and a new calm descends. The rain still falls and the sky remains heavy through most of the day, but on towards evening the cloud splits. Thomas spends the greater part of the afternoon on one of the shed roofs, trying to pin down sheets of corrugate that have lifted in the wind, and it is quite late when he discovers that one of the cows, probably spooked by the recent storms, has wandered off from the herd and is missing.

His first reaction is to panic. McNamara has burdened him with the responsibility of the cattle's well-being, and this cow, one of the late-season calving stock and nearing full term, is of considerable value to the farm. He tries to calculate how much light remains in the day, but his thoughts are in turmoil. A band of cloud lies yellow and dimming in the west, bulked with yet more rain, and darkness will bring terror for the animal. Deciding that a stop at the cottage would waste too much time, he starts out across the fields, letting the fall of the land lead him, mumbling prayers as he walks, a litany that feels separate from himself and quickly takes on the soft outward caress of mantra. The words spill from him, whispers at first, then as vibrations close to sound, their rhythm finding steady time above the slam of blood pulsing in his ears. He tells himself that he'll find her, that he knows this land better than anyone, and that even if darkness comes down he'll be okay because out here the night holds no terror. But for twenty minutes he stumbles into nothing but empty fields, and with footing difficult and in places treacherous his mind is tormented by images of the cow thrashing about in some dyke or snagged in a tangle of downed barbed wire. The land rises behind and on his left, and the evening has taken on a sense of compression, but then he clears a brow and sees her, standing calm and still beside an overgrown boundary wall at the bottom of the most recently reclaimed field, staring westward. He almost calls out but catches himself, slows his pace and eases through a gap in the ditch. After a minute or two she notices him, but does not move, and he approaches slowly, mumbling a gibberish canticle that works well with animals. He steps beside her and begins to stroke her neck. She moans once but still doesn't flinch, and his heart pounds in

24

his chest like something soft and trapped, clattering against the walls of a drum.

When he can steady himself, he slips a thin noose of rope over the animal's head and coaxes her into walking. The ground beneath their feet is soup, the natural incline draining everything through this part of the field. They struggle up the slope, side by side, labouring into every step, then begin to veer right, towards the open gate. He keeps to the cow's left, level with her bowed head and leading only occasionally with the lean of his body against her shoulder, thinking of little beyond the next step. He regrets leaving his staff back in the yard with the rest if the herd, the stout, supporting five-foot length of knuckled blackthorn that would have made this climb a lot easier, but its loss is a small thing. He has fought this field to a standstill, has salted its dirt with blood and sweat. And now, when he is most in need, it is doing right by him. Tears of relief burn his eyes. The rope is coiled around one hand, but as a gesture, nothing more.

He presses on, leaning sidelong into the pitch of the land and feeling the ground beneath them pull away from every step, but he can't stop, knowing the importance of making it back to the yard before night comes fully down. Already the air has dimmed to a sickly twilight, and vast yellow and dirt-brown continents of cloud heave with the menace of further rain. He can see the ditch ahead and fixes on that, and the open gate that will lead them to ground of less severe gradient.

The hour has an eerie stillness, a sense that the storm's respite will be brief, and though facing the incline refracts distance they same way water does with depth, he has to trust that every forward step is a step closer to safety. He keeps up the nonsense sounds, the soothing coax that sometimes slips into three or four bars of song, anything with melody, anything that comes to mind, and overestimates the distance to the gate at fifty paces, then forty, just to set a goal. Forty paces, and the gap of the open gate is close enough that even in the dying light he can identify the puncture wounds of his own incoming footsteps in the mud.

Then he wades into ground no longer quite solid enough to hold his weight, and he goes down. The mud slops cold and wet and very soft against his back and the words of whatever he is singing jar against his breath, and for a second or two all he can see is sky. He even begins to smile, because it is bad but not so bad, but then the cow begins to flail in search of balance, lowing wildly and tossing her head, and when her legs give, all her weight comes down on him, twelve hundred pounds of heaving, bucking meat pressing him deeper into the pulped ground.

Time loses all shape and substance against his struggles to escape. He attempts to drag himself free, pleading with and beating at the cow in an effort to encourage some movement, until weariness overtakes him. He closes his eyes, tries to suck air in through clenched teeth and has to settle for the grainy wisp that cools his mouth but achieves little else. There is no pain yet, but his breathing is constricted by the weight of the animal lying sideways across him in collapse, pinning down his chest, stomach, groin and thighs, her massive girth trembling with fear. One of his arms is trapped, but he stretches out his free arm, his left, over her back and shoulder and strokes the fleece of coarse, matted hair. Even when she turns silent, he can feel her heat and the chase of a heart that is either hers or the unborn calf's. After the efforts at escape, there is a kind of joy to be had in giving up. He understands on some level that he is being crushed, and that he'd be either dead already or else lying here in an agony of splintered bones, awaiting death, if not for the softness of the earth. With his eyes closed, there is only sensation: the weight, the tightness of his chest, the heat above and the chill of the mud against his back.

Wanting some restoration of order, he begins to count breaths. It is not a measure of actual time, but it helps, lends him focus. And after a slow fifty he opens his eyes again and finds that the cloud mass has darkened to a step removed from night and grown devoid of feature. Dusk and the sky's ashen screed fuse in a fog of blindness. And off across the fields somewhere to the east, a curlew screams. The sound stabs and leaves a shard of itself echoing in the late hour until he shifts his head and the mud sucks him down a little more and clogs his ears with the sigh of waves.

The sense of calm surprises him. Everything has its own way of ending. And even as the crushing intensifies and the mud coats his ears and cheeks and closes in a cold film across his throat to further constrict his intake of breath, the panic doesn't overwhelm him. The sounds of the world begin to exist only internally, even the patchwork song that, to appease the animal, has again begun to dribble from his lips. He listens to the words from deep inside and realises without surprise that they have become prayers set to melody, and they help or perhaps are mere expressions of his calm. And as he prays, his thoughts are with Margaret and the pictures of his mother, and he feels sorrow for one and regret for the other even as tears build in his eyes. They burst, exploding the sky, and it is full seconds before he understands that it has begun to rain again. A slop of mud squeezes into the corner of one eye, and he has to strain very hard to lift his head. By turning to one side and then the other, he gains an inch or two of elevation, but such respite is temporary.

He forces himself to concentrate on Margaret, that day she visited and held his hand, but earlier days too, better ones. She cries easily, but it is her laughter that he wants to remember now. Yet even as he tries to focus on those good memories, the darkness, possibly in collusion with his prayers, awakens other thoughts, and his serenity is broken by a vision of Brother Thady, thin and long-faced, middle fifties or even older, with his small red mouth, sunken blue-grey cheeks and the rheumy eyes of a nightwalker. He had taken Thomas to one of the rooms used for storage at the back of the school and made him unbutton his shirt, remove his trousers and lie down on his back on the hard flagstone floor. The cold of the mud has some of that same coldness, and the coldness of those bony hands fingering and grasping at his chest and stomach, pinching his tiny nipples and poking at his naval in a way that itched and then quickly hurt. Hitting him, too, when he began to cry, hitting him again hard enough to make his nose bleed when he tried to squeeze his eyes shut. And later, after washing their bodies clean with the same piece of flannel cloth and a basin of cold water, holding him tight, wiping away the tears and kissing him for a long time on the mouth, telling him what a good boy he was, what a beautiful boy, and that Jesus loved him and would forgive him all his sins, no matter how terrible.

Only now does he think about the possibility of rescue. The cattle are in, but McNamara often checks the yard and barn before going to bed, and Thomas begins to hope that his absence will be noted. There'll be the usual display of anger, the shouts and threats and name-calling, maybe even a hard hand across the head, but he'll explain what has happened and if necessary beg forgiveness, a second chance, and he knows that whatever the farmer might say there is still that fourth field to be salvaged, still work that needs doing. The sky has been overcome by night, the early, cumbrous dark of wet nights, and the rain falls soft but steady. McNamara will find him, but it could be an hour yet, even two, and he knows that he must stay awake. Again, mud seeps into the corners of his eyes. It stings, and hurts worse when he swabs at them with his free hand, but the pain at least helps to keep him alert and lets him know that while an end might be approaching it has not arrived quite yet.

More faces crowd his mind, a parade that disintegrates even as it looms. He knows it is his past unwinding, full of shapes he wants forgotten, and his way of repressing is to conjure up the west he knows only from his books. Wild and baked to dust, full of braves and gunslingers, full of men and women too who have seen the sky from the gutter and who understand what is right and what's worth fighting for. People of the soil, like him, living small and barely perceptible lives. He leans back his head to ease the stiffness in his neck, and the mud closes in across his forehead and cheeks and fills the craters around his clenched eyelids. The angle keeps his mouth and nose clear, and he breathes in small sips of an air that has taken on the sour mineral tinge of rain.

Across his chest the cow lets out a long, sorrowful low, then lurches with sudden violence in one final attempt at rising. The weight shifts, and for perhaps five or even ten seconds, Thomas is free. He lifts his trapped hand and flexes the fist, waiting for numbness to abate, but then the cow's legs give out and she spills across him again, her bulk snapping his arm at the wrist, crushing his chest and driving him hard into the hillside. Something jars loose inside of him, some cog jerked from its workings, and all thought withers as pain whitens his mind. He gasps, lacking the air and power to scream, until runnels of mud fill his mouth, his throat, everything, strangling him, and he goes under.

The day breaks cold after the recent rains, the air clean and still. Hunched in his overcoat, his breath trailing cobwebs of fog, McNamara crosses the yard, his big frame canting slightly leftward, like a sailor too long at sea. The sky is wide open, a skin of granite in the half-light. When he reaches the sheds he finds the cattle huddled together, still waiting to be milked, and a flash of rage blooms and then subsides, overtaken by a deep unease. And the barn is empty.

For the next hour or so, he walks the land. There is no need to call out. The fields hide nothing from him. The sense of unease becomes more pronounced, tightening his chest, and his mind dredges up the memory of his brother, Seamus, who'd gone missing in similar circumstances and was found late the second afternoon by some men from Enniskeane out running a drag hunt, hanging from an elm in the small glade of woodland at the bottom of the valley. When they brought him in, his bloated tongue bulged bluish from one corner of his mouth and his eyes had almost lifted from their sockets and refused to stay closed, even beneath the thumb-pressed weight of half-crown coins. One of the men in to work the harvest who'd seen things like this before put his mouth to Seamus's ear and mumbled an Act of Contrition, then examined the neck and blackened throat and, without meeting anyone's stare, said that it had not been a clean end. Often, if the rope was long enough and the knot placed behind the ear, the neck would snap, but even if it didn't there was a thing, an artery, running down one side of the throat that usually gave against the pressure. But Seamus had lumps of flesh imbedded behind his fingernails from where he'd clawed and struggled to reverse the strangulation. McNamara himself went through his brother's pockets, which were sodden and filthy from the body's natural purging, and in the days and weeks after he'd searched every corner of the cottage. But no note was ever found. That had been the most difficult thing to bear, that lack of explanation.

He sees the cow from a long way off, but the sense of relief is momentary. Her slumped girth is a misplaced detail in the expanse of field, and unnerving in its solitude. Knowing she is close to calving, he quickens his pace. Footing is bad on the way down, and he angles his body side-on to the hillside and chooses his steps with care. Gravity presses down on his neck, hips and shoulders, and he can hear the strain of his own laboured breath but resists the pull of thought. Within a minute he is at the gap in the ditch, the partially opened gate that holds firm against his entire weight, its bottom rung so deeply rutted in the mud from where the land had slipped during the recent rains. He starts forward, then stops. Twenty yards away, he sees the arm straddling the cow's back.

The sun has come up in the low east, but remains hidden by the sweep of land except for a suggestion of yellow along the sky's edge, and the fields down towards the bottom of the valley are still banked in gloom. When he closes his eyes, his breathing has the roar of the sea, and he waits in that darkness, slumped against the gate, until the air settles and his mind grows still. Then the cow, sensing his presence, moans. The sound is flimsy but reassuring. He wades through the mud and goes to her, drops to a crouch and begins running a hand from her ear slowly down her neck. Her hide is slick with mud and rain, but when she lifts her head her black eyes are wide and alert and fix on him with a kind of pleading. Trying to ignore the arm and what lies beneath, he whispers words of comfort until she grows quiet, then rises again and starts back up the field toward the cottage. Later, once he has cleared his workload, he'll visit the Sergeant down in Enniskeane and they can go through the paperwork and decide between them what has happened here. But for now he will need to saddle the horse and find a decent coil of good strong rope, and he can only hope to Christ that the calf has not been harmed.

ARE THE STARS OUT TONIGHT?

WE SPENT MOST of the summer denying the inevitable, and then this evening Jenny joins me in the backyard, armed with a plate of Italian sausage and a six-pack of cold beer, and suggests that maybe the time has finally come for me to move out.

'It's what we both want, Bill,' she says. Not quite meeting my eye, but not looking away either. 'And it's the right thing to do.'

I take the beer from her, tear a couple of bottles loose from their cardboard carton, uncap them and hold one out for her to take. Her clenched jaw realigns the features of her face, making her young again, twenty, twenty-five, making less somehow of time's veneer. She has her hair down and smells of lavender shampoo, and something about that combination causes me to recall the warm taste of the skin along her collarbone and neck, and holding the tight, soft lobe of her ear between my teeth. She is young again, until I look too close. Then her eyes give away the lie. Sharp and furtive, darkened by the hour's lateness from their usual milky coffee calm to the blunt black of jet, they scan the garden's corners and hint at a different story.

The sun is going down but the day's heat lingers, a stifling, hard-baked heat that hurts just a little to breathe and makes your limbs heavy and good for nothing much more than sitting. In the east, the first stars are already in evidence, the first of the limited few that ever make it through suburban Cork's light-polluted veil, four or five scattered pin rips fire-white in the darkening sky. I drink my beer, and for these few seconds let all my worries go, knowing they will not go far. By this point in my life I have almost stopped drinking, cut it from what had grown close to being a problem down to a glass or two of wine with dinner if we happen to be eating out, and the occasional beer at barbecues or when people come over. A lot of drinkers need a cold turkey way out, but I am one of those who find rationing to be an effective enough measure. With a bottle I can take my time, savour every sip, soak up all the benefits without any of the negative equity. Having something cold to hold on to at least lends me the pretence of normality, which is something I think we all need on some level. But this particular night, I don't hold back. Maybe I can't. There is the sense that, having lived for so long on the edge of something, the hand at my back has just knocked me off kilter.

'You can stay until you find somewhere,' she says. Letting the garden's depths hold her entranced, the dropped and melted ice-cream colours of the primroses in their silted flowerbeds all the way down this side of the dividing fence, and then the drooping cherry blossom that she planted five years earlier out on the common ground beyond our back gate in full, certain flouting of the law. 'Get somewhere nice, set yourself up properly. There's no great hurry. You don't have to settle.'

I think about it, and nod.

'Fine,' I say. 'I'll start looking for a place tomorrow.'

'Thanks.'

'For what?'

She shrugs, and for just a second seems set to cry. I understand why. Her face, inches from me, holds its hard profile, and her jaw line jogs again in a little flexing motion beneath skin that looks suddenly pale. I watch, wanting tears. But they don't fall.

She is seeing a friend of ours, Jack Leary. That's what has prompted all of this. She doesn't say so, but she doesn't need to. Relationships keep peculiar balance. It takes a while for two people to get used to sharing time and space and air with one another, but once it happens, any intrusion, even the suggestion of one, rocks the equilibrium. The surfaces might seem undisturbed, but the currents shift hard beneath our feet.

Actually, their fling has been going on for quite a while, time enough to no longer count its shape in weeks or even months, and she swears like she means it that this time, with him, it's all the way real. But that's one of the features of love affairs. They all have at least a little of that quality. I know it better than anyone. Still, she's right about us both wanting this. And Jack is one of the best, really, the kind who'd always help you out if you were in a hole. He's pretty well set up, too. Works in finance. That's one of those vague blanket terms that slightly embarrasses him, and at parties you'd hear him from any corner of the room, offering clarification, a gurgle of laughter thickening out a voice already helped along by liberal doses of neat Scotch.

'What I do is facilitate procreation. My job is to make money out of money. I put two tens together in a room with some mood music and hope they can produce a little twenty. Essentially, I'm a pimp.' He considers the work absurd, yet time has proven him surprisingly efficient at playing the rules. He has a talent for limiting himself to the basics, and is better than good at what he does. Numbers, he says, are really nothing personal. And he has been sleeping with Jenny since at least the day of his divorce. I've always thought that it must be a question of need on her part because, to look at, he doesn't stray within a bargepole's length of handsome. Apart perhaps from a mouth made heavy by a tyre-thick lower lip, the problem isn't anything specific, just a general lack of cohesion. Into his early forties, he is already grey-faced, and all the edges are beginning to show. He's tall, six-one, six-two, and that should be a plus, especially for Jenny, who has always liked climbing things, but he wears it badly, and gives back maybe a couple of inches in one of those hangdog stoops that tend to accompany certain combinations of height and shyness. I like him, always have, but in truth it is an affection borne of pity. His bones show even through his clothes, and we all know who he is from the things he sometimes says once the drink starts getting to him. Just hints, and then he seizes up, but that little is always enough.

'It's funny,' I say, after a long swallow of beer, 'but after all this time, this feels so sudden.'

She nods. I catch the gesture more as a feeling than as actual movement. But it is there.

'And you're sure this is for the best?'

'I am.'

A part of me does feel that it's wrong to give up without so much as the show of a fight, and I know I could, if pressed, come up with something that would leave a mark, probably using our daughter, Nell, as leverage. But the easier option is just to let it go. The marriage is over, has been for some time. We've done the shouting, the crying, we've thrown the blame around and put up with the pretence, and now there is only this: acceptance.

It all feels a little like how I imagine it must be to find yourself washed up on a deserted beach after a violent storm at sea. Glad to have made it through, but beaten, body and soul, and also a bit afraid of what might lie ahead in the silence.

We have been married a little over twenty years, but have known one another a good deal longer. The first time I kissed her, she had just turned sixteen. We were walking back from a school dance and I could taste cherry on her breath, and it was there between us the whole time. As we turned onto her road I stopped her, making use of the shelter offered by a high wall. She closed her eyes and I followed, and afterwards she held my hand whenever she could, not caring who saw, not caring even about her father.

Now we sit side by side on the teak bench seat that I stripped and varnished only weeks ago, and we are calm in a kind of shared stasis, but clear inches apart, no longer touching. I finish a second beer and start straight in on a third, and try to enjoy the little that remains for what it is, knowing I'll miss it, all of it, even the bad stuff. Jenny drinks at a more considered pace, but seems equally at ease, now that she's said what in her mind needed saying. She has on faded denim shorts that stop in a fringe mid-thigh, and an old oversized Bob Dylan t-shirt, black faded to grey, that she has fallen into the habit of wearing to bed but which actually belongs to me. To prying eyes, what we have going must seem like domestic bliss.

I smile, just wanting to feel it on my face and to assure myself that I still can, and when I glance again at Jenny I find her watching me. She doesn't ask, and I hope she doesn't know, but I can sense her want. She drinks from the bottle, holding it a long time to her mouth, and I only now notice that she has painted her nails. This is something she very rarely does, and something I have always liked, though as with so many things, I have left the sentiment unsaid. And understanding that it is too late, I take her free hand in mine and let our fingers entwine. With the sun gone down the air has thinned. It is not cold, but the loss of heat awakens a kind of primal defence mechanism, a tightness that anticipates the state of abandonment. She watches what my hand is doing to hers, then without a shift in expression looks away.

Ahead of us, a few more stars have appeared. They are there, waiting, and all we need to do is choose a place in the darkness and stare until they fall into view. That's how it is with stars. Spread out across the sky, these specks of light mean nothing to some people and everything to others, but for all I know the few I see may be dying or already dead.

'I'm sorry,' I whisper, and Jenny clears her throat in a delicate way and, without looking back at me, murmurs that she is sorry, too. This time, there is no need for her to repeat that it's for the best or that it's what we both want.

Minutes later, Nell's arrival is announced in song. One of those high-pitched country numbers that's all sex. That's the way things are going now. I've seen them, the long, blonde, leggy types in flimsy white sleeveless blouses and jeans that put their asses on a plate. 'The night is so long and I miss you.' Johnny Cash used to be country, and Merle Haggard and Willie Nelson, grizzled types who looked like they drank from fruit jars and had kept on long after the line was crossed. They did the heartbreak numbers too, of course, only their voices, hard and old as dirt, earned them the benefit of the doubt. But country changes, just like everything else. Everything burns out in time.

Neither of us turn when the patio door hisses open on its rail, but Jenny sighs and takes her hand back, as if we have been caught doing something wrong. Stripped of her touch, a void opens up in me and there is a sudden and actual sense of loss. I'd known this was not a game, but now the words feel carved into my flesh, so that there can be no further mistake: It's over.

Then Nell appears on my right and drapes an arm across my shoulders. She continues to sing, the melody thin and flighty as a wheeze beneath her breath, yet even made small the words retain their clarity. The song's narrative doesn't stretch the imagination, but that's not what this is about. She breaks only to plant her kiss, high up on my cheek just beneath my eye, then starts off again, determined to reach an end. She smells of lavender too, only on her it has the utmost innocence, a child's scent without any chemical insinuation, and this time when I smile, I mean it. But the underlying melancholy doesn't shift.

'Ooh, beer.' She helps herself to one of the two remaining bottles, and drinks in a clumsy, unpractised fashion. She is nineteen, and pretty, even to an unbiased eye. Not tall, but assured. Confident of who she is or wants to be. At that age, such decisions matter. Her hair is the colour of wet sand, a shade of blonde that relies on the blessings of the sun, and until this summer she'd worn it long, sometimes to her waist, always to at least her elbows. But in June she'd arrived home from her first year in college with a new look, a neck-length bell-cut that has transformed her practically overnight from girlhood. The style seems to emphasise the sculpture of her face, and ties me nearly hypnotised to her gaze.

'Studying?' I ask.

She pulls up one of the plastic folding chairs, gives me a hard look and does something with her mouth. 'Very funny. No, actually I'm meeting Paula for coffee. She wants my advice on something but has to work until nine.'

'Work? What a novel concept.'

'Dad,' she says, 'if you really want to get into comedy, try at least getting to grips with the fundamentals.'

'I'm just saying that work is how most people are able to pay for coffee.'

'What kind of thing?' Jenny asks, from about twenty miles of distance.

'What?'

'You said Paula wants your advice on something.'

'Oh, yeah.'

'What kind of thing?'

Nell takes another sip of beer, closes her eyes, and sighs in a manner that is almost hilarious because it's like watching children play house. 'That's all she said. A thing. But with her it's nine out of ten times a boy.'

'And you're the expert, is that it?' I ask. I'm being an asshole and I know it, but can't seem to help myself. And I more than earn the glare.

Nineteen is such a strange, beautiful age. Life is at high tide, and nothing is absolute. At nineteen your horizons have yet to burn. Nell has a lot of Jenny in her. Maybe she has a lot of me too, but if that's there then I don't see it. Maybe I choose not to see it. She could be miming Jenny with the inside-out openness of her smiles, and when she laughs the sounds she makes are very small, wispy flurries that feel like roars compressed, and her eyes narrow into helpless slits and her shoulders shake with such violence that at first you are not quite sure she isn't crying. These qualities feel fuelled by DNA, but I know them to be details absorbed, consciously or otherwise. And like Jenny, she uses silence as a thrown punch.

She leans back again into the chair, letting it click two notches down into its incline, kicks off her sandals and stretches out her bare legs. 'I shouldn't be late,' she says, lapsing back into that breathy put-upon voice that sounds at once forty and childish. I'm not sure if she means she doesn't expect to be late home tonight or that she shouldn't be late in meeting her friend, but decide not to ask for clarification.

There is one bottle left. I want it, but I don't want to be selfish about it. I reach for it and snap off the cap, and almost offer it to Jenny. But she is in her trance again, fascinated by something the cherry blossom can be doing only in her mind. So I drink. It doesn't matter. We're beyond selfish now.

Nell has been ours since the age of two. Jenny wept when the doctors spoke of fibroids on the walls of her uterus. I just sat there and held her hand, and did my own crying that night in the shower, where no one had to see or overhear. There were treatments available, but the likelihood of us ever conceiving lingered in the low percentages. And numbers beat us. 'I'm damaged goods,' she said, one of the mornings after. I leaned in and kissed her and felt the pillow against my cheek and ear wet from her tears, and I told her that we were still young, kids practically, and that we had options. I didn't blame her at all, I blamed myself. Sometimes you just know.

'Is this what getting old is all about?' Nell asks.

'What do you mean?'

'I mean sitting in a garden on a warm night, waiting for stars to appear.'

Jenny crosses her legs, turning herself away from me. 'Ask your father,' she says. 'He's the one who likes looking at the sky. I just come out here for the beer.'

Our daughter is smiling again. She is dressed casually, in a light blue cotton summer dress deckled with green and yellow flower patterns. It's a coin-toss of a dress that somehow manages to remain modest while still showing off a good deal of skin, not too low-cut but low enough and falling to midway across her thighs, higher when she sits or sprawls, and I know she has put care into its choosing. But at this moment, I'm not sure that I have ever seen anyone so beautiful. Her eyes gleam in the dark, and I wonder if the whole Paula story is a ruse. We have given her no reason to lie, but she is nineteen, and that age craves the clandestine. She has spent her first year at college in Dublin studying Agricultural Science, but since June she's been talking about switching courses and pursuing a degree in English Literature. I was annoyed by her attitude until I gave it some thought. And I think she's right. Everyone makes mistakes, everyone is allowed the odd wrong road. I haven't made it easy because she needs to learn about responsibility, and I don't want her to be fooled into thinking the world will always turn just for her. But she knows that, whatever happens, she has my support, and my love.

She leans forward and hands me her bottle, which is still half-full. I take it and do nothing else. She has very slender fingers, very delicate hands. The bracelet Jenny and I gave her when she turned eighteen hangs from her wrist, an unbroken series of linked gold hearts that she only ever wears on special occasions.

'What's the fascination?' she asks. 'Are you expecting something big to happen up there?'

My gaze draws itself to the heavens. Mars is a gleaming redness in the south, but about to fall from the sky. Saturn is up there somewhere too, if you know where to look. For me, there is something hopeful about their presence, their existence.

'Something big is happening,' I tell her. 'Stars are tumbling through space at speeds that seem reckless and even impossible until you realise how ordered the whole thing is. The patterns don't break. Cosmic forces are at play, all the elements of the universe are waging war just to keep a balance. I think the least we can do is bear witness.'

'Well,' she says, after considering the matter for an entire minute. 'It looks like a lot of nothing to me. I don't expect to be too late, okay?'

'Have a good time, sweetheart.'

'Thanks, Mom. I will.'

I go into my pocket and take out a crumpled twenty. Nell smiles again, lands another peck on my cheek mere millimetres from its predecessor, and relieves me of the note.

'What do you mean, getting old?' I say, pretending to take offence.

She shrugs.

'Need I remind you that I'm only forty-five?'

'When you're nineteen, Dad, forty-five is practically ancient.'

Without thinking, I reach for Jenny's hand again. It's a reflex action. And probably without thinking, she once again lets me take it. 'Since you asked,' I add, just as Nell turns to walk away, 'getting old isn't all about expecting something big to happen. It's about assuring ourselves that the best things in our lives don't change.'

Jenny tightens her grip in mine, but nothing shifts on the surface of the night. In our family, we are all conversant in lies.

'You've had too much beer,' our daughter says, from the doorway. 'Take him to bed, Mom, before he accidentally says something meaningful.'

And then, as before, there is only us. We continue to hold hands, and the night is still warm, but retains its vague, instinctive discomfort. Everything has been set in motion, we've talked it all through and the decision, once announced, has the permanence of stone. Tomorrow the world will spin us loose of one another, but for now we're hanging on. Both of us.

'She's right about one thing,' Jenny says. 'You have had too much. And you've gone and painted too bright a picture. How can we tell her now?'

I finish the bottle I am holding, Nell's bottle, the one she handed to me. I hit the end suddenly, and it is like being pulled into a vacuum. I am slightly drunk, and also not nearly drunk enough. I look at her, then look away. The same few stars are shining, and everything is still. The sense of permanence feels absolute.

All I can do is shrug.

'There's nothing to tell. She's a bright girl, Jenny. She knows when things are right and when they're not. I'll start looking for a place tomorrow, but finding somewhere good might take a week or two.'

'I already told you, there's no hurry.'

'I know. Thanks.'

I hesitate then, because thanks is not quite the right word, and something almost happens. I come very close to lifting her hand and kissing her knuckles, her fingertips, the ropes of vein that lie like web beneath the skin. Instead, I clear my throat.

'I'm not going to make a show of looking around, but I won't hide it either. A week or two will give us all time to start getting used to the idea. And Nell is old enough now to understand. She'll cry, but she'll need to cry. Because it's a big deal. But in another month she'll be back at university, tucking into Joyce and Dickens.'

'She'll feel abandoned.'

'Then it's up to us to show her that she's not. That she's the only one of us who's not.'

'Let's go inside,' Jenny says. Her expression has stiffened again, her mouth slightly ajar, her eyes staring. In profile, there is something hawkish about her face, a tensile quality for which I am to blame. I've neglected her, and for that I am deeply sorry. Her hand in mine is all bones. Maybe it's the beer that makes me want to put things to rights, maybe it is a selfishness fuelled by the dread of the turn my life is taking. But it's too late for that, and we both know it.

She looks at me. I nod, and begin to gather the empty bottles. My arms are full when, inside the house, the phone begins to ring. I let her go ahead, knowing that the call will be for her.

WE'RE NOT MADE OF STONE

AFTER SO LONG and so much effort, they decided, without discussing the matter, to give up trying. This made life easier, if a little more empty. Margaret took up sewing; James became more serious about his reading, with intent toward perhaps writing something himself, one day. Their apartment sat on an incline and was small but cosy, consisting of an acceptably snug bedroom, windowless bathroom and a living/dining room-cum-kitchenette area with a narrow brick balcony feature that afforded views west across town over staggered rooftops to the remnants of countryside and a fast-receding ribbon of woodland. During their first few years together, the place had worked for them as a love nest, a little safety deposit box against the world where they could snuggle up together and feel safe and even worthwhile. Now, it simply worked as home, though in the smaller definition of the word, an agreeable piece of living space that fit their needs well enough without really fulfilling any cravings. They had a floor above them and three below, and on winter evenings they liked to sit by the fireside, facing one another but only rarely speaking, and when summer came they threw open the doors and let the air in.

Initially, because he'd been rather lax in his reading habits and had lost some muscle in that department, James favoured plot. His tastes were broad but, by and large, hardboiled. He enjoyed stories with guns, and with a lot of running. Later, though, perhaps by the end of the first year or the middle of the second, he found himself turning increasingly to less hectic and more character-driven work. A natural progression, he decided, not worrying too much about it. And this new devotion to reading replaced many things, for both of them. It encouraged a kind of silent comfort that would otherwise have been pretty difficult to achieve. She sewed, he read. No longer kids, each dreamed their own private dreams.

They had just entered their fourteenth year of marriage when Margaret discovered that she was pregnant. A Sunday morning in early April, with rain pecking at the glass and the light the colour of day-old fireplace ash. The news came as a shock, and then a good shock. They stood for a long time in the kitchenette, holding hands and trying to smile a great deal. James kept one hip pressed against the counter's edge, so that he could hold himself ever so slightly off balance. Sundays were his lazy days, days when he didn't have to feel guilty about doing nothing. They stood, smiling and holding hands, and each fancied or imagined that they could see a blush of absurd happiness in the other's face and so tried hard to match it with a similar blush of their own.

'At least we've been sensible,' James said, the words typical of him. He had always been the sort of man who tried to be practical whenever he found himself edging against some moment of particularly torrid emotion. As a trait it was neither a positive nor a negative, or perhaps it contained elements of both at once. 'We have some savings,' he went on. 'Enough to get by if we don't get too carried away. And we're pretty well set up. Our age doesn't have to be a downside. We're past the panicking stage, and that must count for something. I'll bet a lot of couples would trade their dancing legs to be us.'

Margaret wanted to believe him. She was shaking, but from deep inside. In her bones. 'I love you,' she murmured, pressing her face against his chest. Some of it was gratitude, an appreciation of his happiness, but at least a part of it was despair. Because this felt enormous, a life-changing event.

She was not a beautiful woman. Never had been, even on her best day, but at least at eighteen or twenty-five she'd felt presentable. The passing years had played a part in her deterioration, but there was more to it than age. Her face was turning grey. Not her hair: her face, her actual flesh. Like something had gone rotten on the inside and was beginning to show through. And her skin felt tight, the way it would after exposure to too much heat. She meant what she said, about loving James, but she was not at all sure that what she meant by love was equal to what the rest of the world meant by the word. And James held her, but didn't say the same words back. That didn't matter though. She had long since given up expecting to hear them from him. What they had, what they'd always had, was enough, because it had to be enough.

He was wearing yesterday's wool shirt, and the fibres held his musk in a way that was not pleasant. She felt an urge to pull back but couldn't, because his big hands held gentle but secure against her hips. Trapped, all she could do, short of insulting or embarrassing him by making a fuss, was pray that God would grant her the small mercy of not having this stench forever attach itself in her mind to what was supposed to be one of the most special and precious of moments of her entire life. Held in place, she drew back her lips and settled for breathing in little sips through clenched teeth.

She had recently turned forty-one years old. James was older by three and a half years. He worked a steady, unspectacular six-day shift at one of the large Home Improvement warehouses out on the Kinsale Road, a nine-to-five routine of manual labour, but of the bearable, forklift-truck variety. She filled some part-time hours with a little light typing and bookkeeping, working from home for a small brokerage house on the South Mall. Neither one of them had longings to set the world alight with their fire. In truth, neither one of them had ever felt much able to muster a significant spark. Without a lot of thought, and without any in-depth discussion, they had dedicated the majority of their fourteen years of marriage to enduring the myriad complications of life. Until this morning's bombshell, they both believed, and accepted, that things for them had reached something of a plateau.

Over mugs of cocoa, James talked. He had a lot to say, but she knew that few of his words were of a substance that could be relied upon beyond this day, or this week. He talked about how they probably ought to start looking around for a bigger place, how he was going to put in for a promotion down at the warehouse, how at the very least he was long overdue a raise. She knew he meant the things he said, but only in the moment. His voice had a smokiness about it, the way it sometimes got after he'd had a couple of beers. They sat facing one another across the small fold-out table, the one with the sky blue and white speckled Formica veneer that had come as part of the apartment's original décor and which had been long since ringed by a multitude of too-hot coffee mugs. He held her hands and leaned in so that their faces were only a small distance apart, and, wondering just how close he'd need to get before she would be forced to suffer again the acrid reek of his body stench, she brought her teeth together and let him talk, encouraging him with the occasional nod of her head or shrug of her shoulders not because she was interested in what he had to say but because it was easier to do this than to do nothing. And when, after a while, the cocoa had turned cold in her mug and his words lost their smokiness and instead began to take on the tenor of a stone inside a tin can, she gently but firmly pulled her hands back, rose with an apology that needed neither words nor explanation, and fled for the sanctuary of the bathroom. When she emerged, several minutes later, having done nothing more than perch on the rim of their small bath and practice her breathing, he had talked himself out, just as she'd hoped he would. He got up from the table and moved to his armchair in front of the television set, but instead of reaching for the remote control fell headlong into the novel he had going, some middle-period Saul Bellow, with all suns blazing and rules still existing to be broken. She brought him a beer and he thanked her, but in his usual distant way. She set a glass down on the floor beside him, knowing he wouldn't use it. He cracked open the can, took a deep shut-eyed swallow, then returned to his place in the story.

None of this felt quite real. That night, lying in bed listening to the scrape and rumble of his laboured sleep, she tried to imagine the child inside her body, the size of an orange, perhaps, but made of flesh and blood, and alive. She waited, wanting to feel something, anything that would mark her out as being in some way different from before, from yesterday, or six months ago, or any single day of the last fourteen years. But she was just herself, nothing more.

Three weeks later, she suffered a miscarriage.

It came on suddenly, while she was in the kitchen stuffing a small chicken for dinner. James was at work and not due home for several hours. She felt an urge to vomit, and a series of violent cramps twisted her down onto the floor. Her initial instinct was to try to make it to the bathroom, but then something broke inside of her and such thoughts fell away. There was a lot of blood. At first she was too terrified to cry, but after a minute or so the tears came and the details of the day were lost.

She lay on the floor for a long time then, trying not to think, and kept her eyes clenched to spare herself the trauma of having to see. But she didn't need to see. It had all been so fast, like a magic trick, there and then gone.

When she could, she phoned James. Twenty minutes later, he arrived home to find her still sitting in a slump on the cold tiles. She was either still crying or else had begun to cry all over again. The tears came in heaves, like small, wet, strangling convulsions, but they found a rhythm that fit well with what had happened. A sense of emptiness pervaded, a degree of desolation for which she felt quite unprepared.

James said and did all the right things. He held and kissed her, told her, in a whisper that sounded strong and assured only because it had been so reduced in scope, that everything would be fine, that he'd look after her now. She was what mattered, he said, only her. It was a lie, but one that was at least well-meant, and she felt unspeakably thankful for that and clung fast to his body. His stench did not trouble her now. In fact, it carried with it a kind of comfort, an assurance that not everything had changed, that some details remained the same and always would.

When her legs could bear her weight without crumpling, he led her slowly to the bathroom, helped her out of her clothes and gently washed her body. Her skirt was ruined, the bottle-green worsted number that she'd saved for two full months to buy and which had been her single most precious item of clothing.

'It can always be washed,' James told her, but she just shook her head, knowing that she could never again bring herself to wear it. She stood and let him peel away her garments, and watched as he unbuttoned his own shirt one-handed, clumsily, so that he would not get too wet. Then he helped her into a sitting position in the bathtub and began to douse her body with the spray from the removable shower-head. The water was hot and felt good against her skin. Her inner thighs were coated in a blackish rheum that seemed to bear no relation whatsoever to the little life she'd been carrying for so many weeks. She watched the blackness turn a syrupy red and then pink in dilution and spin in a slow vortex down the drain. While James's caressing hands were thoughtful and thorough, helping rid her of the mess, his upper teeth pinched at the flesh of his lower lip in a way that was almost boyish, or would have been, were it not for the weary blueness tincturing the skin around his eyes. She watched him work until some part of her mind was struck with sudden understanding, and then she could no longer bear to look, and so she missed the point when he too began to cry, missed it because of the silent way in which his tears started to flow. And even when she opened her own eyes again, she did not immediately notice, not until he drew his hand away from her leg and wiped his face, first one side of his nose and then the other, with the back of his wrist. By then his hands were clean, the yellowish skin around his hard fingertips had already begun to prune. It was over, or as good as over, though for quite a while afterwards their tears continued to fall.

Forty-one was not particularly old. The gynaecologist who told her this was a young man, early thirties at a push, but with the kind of handsome features that kept the years off. A Mr Elango. He was Indian, though of extract rather than by birth, as his smooth accent readily attested, and he had a brigh, open face with sallow skin and large, wide, honest eyes. His hair was clipped in a jet-black crew-cut style that would have looked okay on a fourteen-year-old. Margaret listened in silence, understanding that he was, of course, correct in what he said. Forty-one was not old, or did not have to be. The problem, though, was that age had already turned her to mud, age and the turgid lifestyle of all comfortable ruts. The details had for quite some time been keeping an irregular schedule: she'd already been three months along before even fully acknowledging the pregnancy. So while forty-one might not have been considered old any more, it was still knocking on the door of old the way she wore it.

In that small, anaemically decorated office, James sat beside her, not quite holding her hand but holding himself in a way that seemed to suggest that he either wanted to or felt it was expected of him. She understood. He had always struggled with public displays of affection. His mouth moved around little sighs, and he clearly wanted to offer some words of comfort, but could not decide quite what to say. So he kept silent.

And in the weeks that followed, that silence held. According to Mr Elango, a great many women suffer miscarriages, especially on their first child, and that even at forty-one there was still time for them, more than enough time. Of course, losing a pregnancy was traumatic, and some women found great difficulty in coping, but it was important for them to understand and accept that there was no question of blame. Sometimes such things simply happened.

The emptiest part of the day, the stretch between late morning and early afternoon while James was still at the warehouse, was best for thinking. With James at work she'd sit at the kitchen counter, sipping coffee or a glass of warm milk and very often crying, though not with any great intent. The day of the miscarriage never felt far away, and she'd play out that morning's scene over and over in her mind, looking for a cause, some mistake she might have made, an inadvertent nudge against the counter, standing too close to the oven or just standing for too long. Anything. And sometimes she pretended nothing had happened and that she was still pregnant, or that it was a year on, or five years, or twenty. Entire worlds opened up to her then, and she'd indulge in fantasising whole lives for the unborn child, boy or girl, with an emphasis on the key notes, the moments of joy, heartbreak and sorrow. Problematic situations drove the fantasy: a daughter seventeen, eighteen, falling pregnant; a son getting in with the wrong crowd, doing drugs, or sitting her and James down at the kitchen table, and breaking the news to them that he was gay.

At first, all of this seemed like harmless indulgence, but as her skill in conjuring them sharpened, the fantasies began to dominate her thoughts. By comparison, her own life felt staid, insipid, empty. Several times a day she'd catch herself laughing aloud or smiling until the muscles of her face ached, and she wept away entire mornings, entire afternoons. The extremes, the black rains, the delirium of laughter, left her hollowed out and weak as a drugged kitten. It worried her, but she couldn't bring herself to stop.

Finally, she mentioned it to James.

They were beside the unlit fire, late in the evening. A radio was playing, just to keep out the silence. She lay down her sewing. Across from her, James was in a book and took a long time to look up. When he did, finally, he held his place among the pages with an intruding thumb, his way of letting her know that this would be no more than a brief interruption. He was not angry, merely impatient.

'I can't believe there is any harm in it,' she said, trying to smile but not quite finding one to fit. 'In fact, I'm sure it's quite natural.

And I know it's not real. That's probably important. Knowing that. Because otherwise, it becomes something else entirely, doesn't it? But as it stands now, it's an indulgence. That's all.'

'It could be delayed shock,' he said, after a dozen seconds. 'Or the onset of depression.'

She shook her head. 'No. It's not depression.'

'It could be. Depression comes in many forms. We don't always realise that. Some people live their entire lives crippled by depression without even knowing it. The signs can be subtle. And we're flesh and blood, you know, Maggie. We're not made of stone. When something like this happens, we're bound to feel an effect. Different people deal with things in different ways.'

He eased the book shut, but his thumb still held the place. She was glad of this, the small generosity of the closing gesture but also the fact that he was clearly not preparing to stray too far from the story. A simple stroll was fine, but she felt lazy. She was not ready in her mind to go taking on the mountains. Not this evening. From where she sat, she could see the book's cover, inverted in his lap. The double R, coupled with the glint of the reading lamp's cast, caused her a little trouble in deciphering the name, and then suddenly she got it: le Carré. She wondered if his choice of reading was unduly affecting him.

'You're making too much of this,' she whispered.

He stared at her. She knew what he was looking for. Sometimes she revealed truths by a shift in expression. She wondered if she was giving away anything now, or even if there was anything to give, this time.

'Just the same,' he said, 'I think you should see someone. I'd feel better about things if you did. You're probably right, it's more than likely nothing at all, just a normal part of the grieving process. But a chat can't hurt. And if you won't do it for yourself, then do you think you could do it for me?'

That was a twist, like being caught in a snare. Struggling only made matters worse.

So she went, made a call the following morning to her doctor, received a referral, and eleven days later, on a whitewashed afternoon with a sky too cold to do anything more than glow, took a taxi to a nondescript Western Road address and climbed four floors in a walnut-panelled elevator to lay out her innermost secrets before a total stranger. She'd spent days rehearsing a litany of backup deceptions, but the soft white embrace of the plush, faux-leather reclining chair was designed with abject surrender in mind, and she simply fell into place, too exhausted to put up a fight.

Her psychiatrist sat at a reasonable remove, perched on the edge of a low-slung bucket seat, notepad in hand, silver or perhaps platinum pen at the ready. She was a middle-aged woman in a purple blouse with puffed sleeves and a buttoned-up collar, shin-length navy blue skirt and sensible black patent shoes. Her face was long and slender, full of sheer angles, with small, fixated eyes and a mouth like a paper cut, and she wore her hair, which had been bleached a shade so blonde as to be practically stripped of colour, clipped into an expensive-looking but quite ill-suited angled bob with a low split fringe.

'Talk about anything,' she said, not smiling, hardly even appearing to care much, one way or the other. Margaret nodded, but because the whole business seemed quite sordid, this notion of buying an hour of someone's time, she had some initial difficulty in verbalising her thoughts. But it soon became apparent that this would be strictly a one-way dialogue, and some inner barrier gave. The time passed quickly then. She lay back, closed her eyes and talked away the entire hour, in a voice that felt separate from her own and which, by its intensity, discouraged interruption. The fantasies were the problem. Everything else was mere dressing.

'Well?'

James went in and out of his beer can again while waiting for her to say something.

'Well, what?'

'The doctor. How'd it go?'

Froth lay like feathers on his upper lip, held by a day's stubble.

'Firstly, she's not a doctor.'

'No? Where does she get off asking one-eighty a pop, then?'

'Some doctors go by Miss or Mister. It's a rank thing. Don't ask me why because I haven't the faintest idea. It didn't dawn on me to find out, though to be honest, I wish I had now that I think about it. And secondly, it went okay. As okay as can be expected, anyway.'

'Did something happen? Or is this one of those deals where you're not supposed to say?'

She shrugged. 'Nothing happened. And there's nothing wrong. I told her everything. About us and the miscarriage, about how I've fallen into this habit of fantasising. Everything.'

'And?'

'And nothing.'

'For a hundred and eighty euro? Nothing?'

'Going was your idea, James. Not mine.'

He held up his hands. His surrender gesture. 'I know. I'm sorry. I didn't mean anything by it. I just wondered if she was able to offer any advice? I know it's only the first session, and some people need months of therapy before...'

'She said I'm fine. Well, maybe not fine but as good as can be expected, considering everything that's happened. She said I might be a little bit depressed but that it'd probably be far worse for me if I wasn't. And I don't need months of therapy. In fact, I'm finished. This was strictly a one-shot deal.'

'Who says?'

'We both did. We discussed it and agreed. My shell might have a few dings but it's not cracked yet.'

James swallowed from his beer can again.

'So you're really okay?' he asked at last.

She smiled. 'Better than most and at least as good as the rest.'

It was the truth, but not the whole truth. There had been talk of more appointments, appointments without end, actually, and whatever had broken was not even close to being recognised yet, much less fixed. But sometimes the clichés had it right. Time, that most holistic of approaches, could bring its healing powers to bear on her. It was less expensive and far less invasive.

Not that night, but one of the nights perhaps a week or two later, James moved against her in bed. She'd been on the edge of sleep, that calm place where it was okay to drop off but fine too just remaining awake.

At first, she smiled. She liked his touch, the way his hand slid across her midriff and held her in a snug curl around her ribs. If had been just that, or even just sex, then it would have been all right. She could feel him against her, his hips grinding gently against her thigh. When his face pressed in she closed her eyes and waited for his mouth to meet hers, but instead she felt the scrape of his unshaven cheek against her chin and the corner of her lips, and then his breath sighing into her ear: 'Let's try again, Maggie. Let's make a baby.'

She turned cold. She didn't speak or try to push him away, but he seemed to sense the change because he stiffened and then drew back. A moment later he was sitting up on his side of the bed. From her place on the pillow she watched him, the way the quilt tented over the poles of his knees, the way his shoulders rounded and his head hung a little forward, silhouetted against the slightly tempered town-lit window.

'I'm sorry,' she whispered, without moving. 'It's too soon. I can't. Not yet.'

With a kind of wonder, she thought about how much easier lying became with practice. In the space of mere weeks, she had learned the basics and was now ready to explore the limits, maybe even to break them. Beside her, James seemed suddenly very much like a child, like the boy from her fantasies. His innocence and ready acceptance felt incomprehensible to her.

'I'm afraid,' she said, in the same soft hum. 'Because what if it all goes wrong again?'

He nodded. 'It's all right,' he told her, whispering. 'I understand.'

She reached out a hand and began to stroke his arm from shoulder to elbow and back again. His flesh was cool to her touch, but he didn't pull away, didn't react at all. She was surprised to find herself feeling a little sorry for him, and she was struck again by his boyishness, at least in this darkened form. She moved closer and kissed his arm, her pursed mouth jabbing at his skin with little pecks. He had strong arms, toned from hauling boxes all day. His forearms were matted in thin, dark hair, but above the elbow the flesh was clean and smooth.

The following morning, after he had left for work, she called Dr Morley for an appointment and had him write her out a prescription for the contraceptive pill. Dr Morley had been their family physician for the past eight years, though until the miscarriage he still needed to read their details from a manila folder in order to know who they were, by condition as well as by name. Since then, her status had been upgraded somewhat. He was a difficult man to age. He could have been forty, or old enough to be her father. Some men had such faces. Too brusque when young, too boyish when old. He wore wire-rimmed glasses, but only to read, or as an affectation. There was something ever so slightly effeminate about him, even though he sported a wedding ring. When she entered his office he smiled and called her Maggie, perhaps in an attempt to emphasise their newfound informality. But only James had ever called her Maggie, and to hear it from the doctor felt like trespass.

He sat poised above his pad, but took a long moment to consider her request. She met his gaze with stoicism, choosing not to offer anything in the way of explanation. Finally, deciding that it was not his place to press the issue, he scribbled the prescription, folded the piece of paper with meticulous neatness and held it out to her. She reached for the note, thanked him with a nod, then stood and left the room without speaking another word. There was nothing to say, nothing that needed discussing, either with him or James or anyone else. Two nights later, in bed, after they had turned out the lights, it was she who made the first advance. In the darkness, she felt James lurch against an intake of breath and then slowly relax. He didn't ask for details, so there was no need to fill in the blanks, and as long as the lights were out it could be just like before, or like any way they wanted it to be. The pieces and colours could be added, or if not added then at least imagined. Fantasised.

'You're sure,' he said, not quite asking but still trying, in the best way he knew how, to come across as considerate even as he hurtled toward a brink. She smiled against his cheek and murmured that she was, quite sure. He smiled too then, and there was no reason for him to doubt the illusion that his mind had created, no need to question. She wrapped his body in her arms and lay snug and happy beneath his press, forty-one years old and knowing not for the first time in her life but for the first time with absolute certainty that while forty-one didn't have to be considered old, neither was it necessarily obliged to be young.

'I love you,' she whispered into the darkness as her husband's body thrashed and heaved towards its climax, and she settled, with contentment, for silence as a neat and acceptable reply.

Goodbye, My Coney Island Baby

The late afternoon is cold and threatening snow, and the streets of Coney Island are deserted except for an elderly black man walking a ridiculously small dog out along the boardwalk and a few drunks in a doorway arguing in mute slurs over a bottle. Peter hurries by without making eye contact. The wind gusts around him, tugging at the hem of his overcoat, and he is glad that he has thought to wear a scarf but knows he could have done with gloves, too. His pockets provide nothing in the way of heat.

He follows the main thoroughfare south, moving at a solid pace, until he reaches an outlying bar, a little nonentity of a place that keeps its lights turned low and won't spoil the mood with awkward questions. As he enters, a few men at the counter strain into begrudged half-turns and stare at him, their slow eyes playing games of focus with the dusty, pressing light. But he ignores them.

Susan is perched in a little semi-private alcove with a view across the floor to the doorway and the two large fogged-glass windows, but she is lost in thought and does not immediately register his arrival. She has already been here nearly an hour, long enough to have grown accustomed to the bar's weighty gloom. From a distance, she looks tired and put-upon, the wrong end of middle-age. It is a delusion, but only of sorts. A glass waits between her hands, containing a thimbleful of bourbon that she has sipped to taste and then promptly abandoned.

Peter moves to her side, startling her. Her mouth turns in a little explanatory way and holds there.

'Hi,' he says, the word all breath.

'Hi back,' she replies, and pushes deeper into the booth so that he can sit on her right side. Their bodies come gently together, their shoulders and arms and hips and thighs, and she is overtaken by a wave of elation that feels at once both absurd and entirely genuine. If it should all end suddenly, these would be the moments she'd wish to hold dearest to her heart. After seventeen years of carefully planned twice-monthly collisions, they know each other's bodies inside and out, but the way he sits beside her always feels like the definition of intimacy.

By contrast, his kiss is a perfunctory thing, barely a step removed from a handshake. Publicly insecure, his face stabs at hers, their mouths meet for a dry instant and then as quickly slip apart. In place are the nuts and bolts of a smile, but nothing has been assembled, and after a few seconds his gaze begins to stray, pulled by a need to survey the bar, an old paranoia but a difficult habit to break. Susan considers the labyrinthine scrolling of his ear and out of duty or want tries to smile for both of them, and to hold fast to the myriad flavours of his fleeting kiss.

He orders a drink. During the summer he is a staunch beer man, but once the wind begins to blow his tastes turn Scottish. Old blood, he explains, whenever he feels the need for wisecracks. He orders a fresh bourbon too, without asking, and sets it down alongside her barely touched first.

Their routine feels carved in marble. Order is important, to Peter more so than to Susan, but to Susan too because she wants Peter to be happy, or at least at ease about what they are doing. Without the small, refined details he would turn to dust.

'Thanks for waiting,' he says, as he settles against her body again.

She smiles, does something fresh with her shoulders.

This, like much of what is going on here and what will go on later, never varies. Same words, same acts, same feelings. Beautiful routine. He lifts his glass, and the lines at the corners of his eyes momentarily pinch and deepen, then soften once more. When the glass makes it back onto the table, he has become a different man, the man she knows and wants him to be rather than the lurching shell who spends eight or ten hours a day working a desk and the rest of his time working his way home.

'Isabel's got cancer,' he says, almost absently.

'What?' For a second or two, she holds on to the desperate hope that she has somehow misheard.

He looks at her, nods his head, then lets his gaze fall again across the table. There are a few pale spatters of paint staining the upholstery across from them, ancient milky teardrops dating from some prehistoric time when somebody actually cared a damn about the way this place looked.

'In the kidneys, they're saying. The prognosis is not all that great. They're not saying so, at least not outright, but I think the doctors are already expecting the worst. Hearing words like "aggressive" and "metastasis" doesn't exactly fill you with confidence.'

Susan sips her drink, holding her lips tightly to the glass. But the bourbon has lost its heat. 'That's awful,' she says, her voice sounding reedy and flat as paper. 'Jesus Christ, Pete. I'm so sorry.' Not insincere, just worthless.

There is more to be said, but for now the stillness feels absolute. Peter has been living with this news for a while, though he is only now speaking of it, perhaps is only now able to speak of it, but even weeks or months along, a kind of numbness pervades. He has the dreamy look of a boxer who has known too many blows to the head, or of a drunk who has finally given all the way up on the pretence of sobriety. He speaks slowly, leaking air.

'The treatment will be hard on her. Chemotherapy is poison to the system. And even on good days the side-effects don't bear thinking about. Isabel has never been what you might call a great patient. I can't see how she'll cope with something like this. But I suppose when your back is to the wall you either fight or you curl up your toes and call it quits.'

In this poor light, his skin has the flushed-out texture of tissue paper and hangs from his bones, lending a maudlin heft to his nose and cheeks. The way he takes his Scotch in small, repetitive jabs reminds Susan of a mother bird vomit-feeding her young. On any other day, she'd be asking him now about work. They have been peddling the same sentences for seventeen years, venting a mutual air of unhappiness by exchanging titbits of office gossip; who's doing what to whom, who's climbing or the outs, taking turns condemning all the tedious workplace politics. The subject matter might be stale, but such talk offers safe ground and clearly marked boundaries. At their age, Susan in her early forties, Peter a fraction older, their sense of longing has shifted. Life has become less about thrills than comfort.

But work seems inconsequential now. The news of Isabel's cancer has changed the ambiance of things, ruptured the idyll. Peter rolls his empty glass in half-turns between his palms, and looks ready for more. But Susan has had enough.

'Let's go,' she says, fighting off the press of tears. 'Let's take a walk.'

The glass between his hands stops turning. His face moves to within kissing reach, and she notes that his pupils, because of the bar's gloom, are significantly dilated.

'It's bitter out.'

She hitches her shoulders. 'Just out to the end of the boardwalk. I love Coney Island on days like this, with the wind keeping everyone else away.' A smirk crimps the corners of her mouth and her voice slips into softness. 'Come on, Pete. There are ways of keeping warm, you know.'

He meets her gaze, then sighs, one of his beautiful little foibles, a great heaving gust that suggests a spine-deep level of exhaustion. She enjoys the sound of it, mostly for its yielding quality. After a moment he sets down his glass and rises from the booth. The surrender is slight but absolute.

Out on the pier, there is no shelter, no protection. The famished wind tears at them. The cold is dense, even painful. They push on, holding one another, lending and finding support, until the end is in sight, and then they stop and lean against the protective railing. Pale flecks mottle the surface of the slate-coloured ocean and a great furred bilge of surf breaks in thick, repeating rheum across the deserted length of strand northwards as far as the eye can see. Further out, a sense of weary calm prevails, though this is perhaps an illusion, some trick of distance coupled with the tawny compression of fading day. Susan tightens her grip on Peter's arm, and together they listen to the bleating wind and the delicious crashing of the water against the stanchion posts below. They fit comfortably together. Around them, the hotdog stands and ice-cream stalls sit shuttered tight and padlocked, battened down for the season, but even in a dormant state, even with a lack of calliope music and the running laughter of tearaway kids, there remains a kind of residual joy to be had from this air, as if all the good of better decades has somehow impacted on the ether of the place.

Happiness engulfs her. Only its magnitude surprises. The news about Isabel is truly terrible, the fact of the cancer itself, of course, but more than that the sheer aggression of it, how intent it seems on working to the bone, on finishing what has been started. Yet such details feel oddly separate from her. It is all somehow impersonal, like a story accidentally overheard, or news received from far away. On a day such as this, out of season and with the elements given fullest reign, Coney Island seems like the edge of the world. This place has long since become a sanctuary from the muddy floundering of their first-and-foremost lives, a place of decaying and perhaps deluded pleasures, yes, but one that grants them a necessary protection. Here, twice a month every month, they are afforded the opportunity to be strangers together, strangers who play at being something more than that, taking advantage of a rare shot at freedom to sit and whisper small-talk, to hold hands and exchange wishes. Such realities as cancer and betrayal and loneliness and pain have no place out here; they simply do not belong. Coney Island has none of Manhattan's vast claustrophobia. Out here, there is still sky to be had and freedom to be imagined.

'I think about it,' Peter admits. His eyes fix their direction southwards beyond the brackish jut of Breezy Point and search for answers along the washed-out horizon line. His voice is hoarse, broken, and the words hit in thumps against the taunting breeze. 'How it'd feel to just toss it all aside and get out while I still have some life left open to me.'

Susan slips her free hand inside the lapel of his jacket and seeks by touch his beating heart. There's not much to feel, except the warmth. Then she presses her mouth into the snug of his neck just beneath his right ear and whisper-sings the teasing prompt: 'But you stay.'

He makes a small snorting sound, one familiar to them both from years of practice. The note of amused resignation. 'Yeah,' he says, with a heave of breath, 'I stay. We dream, don't we?

That's how it is for the likes of us. We find a thought that helps to get us through, and cling to it like moss. And we bear the clouds for the occasional glimpse of sky. There are some who can wake up one morning and just start running, clear across the world, the way Gauguin did, or Brando, or Marco Polo. Wives, homes, jobs, all shed like a worthless second skin. But I don't have in me whatever it is that they have. Where I am now is where I'll probably always be. I'm not a brave man, Sue. If I was, I'd have left Isabel years ago, and I'd have found a way of talking you into leaving Mike.'

The wind digs in, and when they can no longer take standing still they walk again, just for the sense of movement. Going as far as they can go, out to the very edge of the pier. The boards underfoot are coated deep into their grain with algae a shade of green so dark as to be almost black. The ocean spray dusts their faces, and every drawn breath salts their throats and tongues. Its sheer enormity is splendid, but also intimidating. All those thousands of miles of surface, all the uncountable leagues of depth. And all the secrets that lie hidden. Susan thinks about how it would be to float even six feet beneath the surface, just at that point where the day's light no longer penetrates and where even the strongest winds fail to reach. Barely a single miserly fathom down, you breach the ceiling of a whole new world, one running to a well-ordered cycle of feeding, multiplying and dying, and utterly oblivious to the world toiling above. Slip six feet beneath the surface and good and bad cease to exist, and tide alone is the only god capable of disturbing the accepted reverie.

She closes her eyes and feels for Peter's hand, the cool, damp assurance of his skin, the pulse insinuating from somewhere deep inside. They stand here, holding hands and holding on to one another, each thinking thoughts that approach the same subject from different angles, and then finally they turn and walk back down the pier to find a hotel.

Their room is small and intensely white. Everything: the walls, the curtains, the bed sheets, even the last of the evening light that pours in through the large old-fashioned sash window, shares the same brittle quality. There was a time when the hotels along this stretch of coast were genuflections toward true luxury, but what survives is basic, perfunctory, clean in an ugly, careworn sort of way, good enough for those with needs measured in hourly lots, but sorely lacking if your desires run to anything more refined. And this place, like all these places now, cuts cash deals. Credit cards complicate matters, and only serve to cause embarrassment. Peter settles the account in advance, paying for twelve hours more than they'll need. While Susan sits cross-legged in a hulking bottle-green leather armchair beside the lobby's blazing fireplace, hands folded primly in her lap, he counts out the notes, signs the register and tries to avoid eye contact with the elderly, pencil-thin manageress.

Thirty-five dollars buys them time in the company of four walls and a bed. The view, apparently, is complimentary, utilising its fifth-floor vantage to peer out across a scrub of wasteland at the ropey upper spindles of a lopsided and long-abandoned rollercoaster. Beyond, dissected by the undulating landscape, the top half of a candy-coloured Ferris Wheel perches prehistoric and shell-like. The ocean, unseen from this angle, nonetheless dominates, its relentless abandon present in every pore of the fading day.

Peter removes his overcoat, undoes the two holding buttons of his sports coat and immediately turns his attention to an antiquated thermostat. 'See if I can't get some heat going,' he mutters, as much to himself as to Susan. 'It's like Dakota in here.'

Susan, moving past him, nods in a distracted manner. There is a white plastic kettle on the bureau and, alongside, some sachet servings of instant coffee and two plain white porcelain cups upturned on almost-matching saucers. She fills the kettle from a tall glass gourd, taps the switch and sets the water whispering towards a boil. Outside, the sky is an enamel of cloud polished by winds and cold to a bright sheen. She turns back from the window to find Peter perched on the far corner of the bed. He has already removed his shoes and trousers and is unpicking the buttons of his shirt, his fingertips awkwardly working a downward traipse. For an instant their eyes meet, and she either catches or chooses to imagine a bright flash of something pass between them, something with the same brilliant rawness as love. Sipping a breath, she proceeds to undress too, kicking out of her shoes, wrestling loose of her grey wool sweater, hurrying to catch up.

The kettle switches itself off with a click. Naked from the waist down and with her blouse partially undone, she tears open two sachets and concocts cheap, foul-tasting coffee. The cups rattle on their saucers as she carries them to the bed. Peter takes a sip and cannot avoid a wince, but he doesn't push the cup away. She perches on the edge of the mattress. Not so long ago, their hunger to be bodily together would have stood no such trifling distraction as coffee, but a great deal has changed in seventeen years. Time educates even as it erodes.

Peter finishes first. He sets the cup aside, stands and continues to undress. He is meticulous in his movements, folding his trousers and shirt back into their tightly pressed creases and draping them over the frayed back of a puce suede wing-chair. Susan notes with some amusement how slow he is in removing either his shorts or undershirt. Even after the hundreds of intimate occasions they have shared, he remains bashful about his body. And the past five or six years in particular have seen him gain considerable weight. He has tried dieting, exercise, even pills, but there seems no obvious way of stanching the decline, and his stomach, which had been flat as a stone wall when they'd first started in on one another, now hangs bloated inside his vest. His health is showing signs of strain, too, with a general increase in fatigue, sweating and, following moments of even moderate exertion, a notable shortness of breath. Sensitive to his feelings, and partly fearing a glimpse of what the future, near or distant, might hold for them, she turns her head slightly away so that she doesn't have to see.

He slips beneath the covers and gasps. 'Jesus,' he says, his voice like a slow puncture, 'this bed could stop a beating heart.' He pulls the blankets up over his shoulders and nestles deep into the soft pillows.

Susan smiles to herself, finishes her own coffee and returns the cup and saucer to the bureau, then gets on with peeling away the last of her clothes. She does not stop at her underwear. To her, these are mere garments, no different from the rest. She has weathered better than Peter, but this hardly matters. Even back when everything had been fresh and new and exciting, when modesty might have been an issue, her nakedness had never bothered her. From the first time they'd come out here and taken a room, she understood how much he cherished her, how highly he prized every bump and crease. And even though she is past forty now and finally beginning to show signs of wear, she knows that his feelings for her have not changed. He'd told her once, at the high point of some collision or another, that she was his goddess, and even though the words, delivered in a strangled gasp, sounded like a line from some fourth-rate piece of drive-in trash, she could only smile and thank him for saying it, recognising it as just the surface of what he really meant to say.

Such words, such intent, filled her with a confidence that has never since diminished, and no one had ever given her so much. No gift, not even diamonds, could have stood comparison.

In their hired piece of privacy, she unclasps her bra and slips from her panties, taking her time for his benefit, knowing without having to check that he is watching and giving him every chance to be ready for her. The chill of the room coats her skin, the thermostat still sluggish about its duty, and the coldness in the air puckers her small, dark nipples and rashes her slender body with goosebumps. She moves to the bed and slips beneath the blankets. Peter makes room, letting her take the small warm pocket of space that he has created.

Twenty minutes later, they give up trying and settle instead for the sort of dozing slumber that still allows room for words. They have been through disappointment together before, not often but often enough, especially these past couple of years, and they have both learned to accept rather than to attribute blame. Susan lies on her back with her head resting against Peter's right shoulder. The time is just after six, and another day has somehow drained from her life and the life of the world. Her skin is clammy with cooling sweat from the exertions of their attempted lovemaking, and the white linen bed sheets cling to her feet, thighs and low stomach in a tangle that feels at once sordid and lovely. She stretches her limbs, pleasuring in their aching tightness, then closes her eyes and swims a little while in that dark place.

'You're my best mistake,' she murmurs, wanting to say something that she could never imagine saying anywhere other than here, in this bed, now.

From the rut of his doze, Peter twitches, a motion driven by a certain heavy kind of breath. Around them, the silence is not total, not with the wind beating occasional beads of sleet against the glass, but a stillness pervades, as though the planet has become snagged in mid-turn. The sense of this holds even when he clears his throat and, softly, begins to speak. Words are just words, uttered and spent, but in the bed and around the room nothing moves, nothing except hearts in their beating.

'You think we're a mistake, then?'

She smiles. 'Of course I do. We both know marriage is a sacred bond. The Bible, chapter whatever. Even a bad marriage is sacred. Even a boring one. Maybe a boring one most of all.'

'And what about love? Do you think they factor that into the equation? Like time off for good behaviour?'

'They?'

'Whoever gets to call the shots on this kind of thing.'

'You're talking about God.'

'Or the Gods, if there's more than one of them.'

'You think there might be more than one?'

Her laughter is sudden, unexpected, a gush of sound that leaves behind its mark. He lets it wash over him, through him. 'I'd hope so, sweetheart,' he says, baring his teeth. 'For their sake.'

Games like this know a kind of intimacy, too. Maybe, after a certain point, a better kind even than that offered by the physical. But she understands the situation. During the years of nights when the apartment she shares with Mike seems too small for who she is or wants to be, there has been ample opportunity to contemplate all of love's problems and consequences. Cut adrift on her side of that sad marriage bed, waiting without expectation for the drag of sleep, loneliness overtakes her and she has to fight in her frozen state to resist the otherworldly darkness suggested by the inch-wide chasm that gapes between the wardrobe doors. It is how a god must feel, cursed into solitude, if the ancients had it wrong and there really is no bacchanal. Alone and abandoned. Lost, and endlessly falling.

'Love?' she murmurs, without opening her eyes, 'That's just the excuse we use, to justify all that's rotten.' Not believing it, not wanting it to be true, but saying it.

This stillness soothes the body in the way that the wind at the glass soothes the mind. Even the sheets, worn tawdry by so many visiting lovers, feel good against her skin. But when she opens her eyes again, everything has changed. A proper and thorough darkness has stolen in. She sits up in the bed, sighs, and rakes the fingers of both hands back through her hair.

The room has taken on a midnight feel. She gets up and moves to the window, but there is little to see beyond suggested shapes. As she stands there, gazing mainly at her own weak reflection, her mind conjures up an image of the ocean, the bluish night surf breaking moonlit over some luminescent strand. It is a romance, nothing more, an indulgence, sweet but inessential. She considers the glass, and the darkness beyond, Coney Island's fringe, with all of Brooklyn's lights burning at her back, then draws the curtains and switches on one of the two bedside lamps. Dressing by touch is easy enough, but the glow of lamplight on her skin has become the traditional closing act of their trysts. In the bed, Peter sits up, packs his pillow and her own behind his back and settles into watching her.

'Come back to bed,' he says, as she pulls her panties up over her slim thighs and fingers her way to comfort in the crotch area. Pearl lace: a catalogue-bought anniversary gift from Mike. 'Isabel is being kept in overnight. They're inserting a morphine line. You could phone Mike, tell him you have to work late. An audit that's running long, or something.'

She continues to dress. His words, too, are part of the tradition, spoken out of duty but better left unchallenged. Can't they just stay a couple of hours longer? After all, the room is paid for until tomorrow.

'Keep an eye on the time,' she tells him. She sounds tired, and is, but it's not the kind of weariness that sleep can ease.

They have often spoken of running away, of dropping everything and just skipping out. Get a place somewhere up in Maine, maybe, one of those little coastal towns that melt in summer and get locked down come October and the first snow of the season. The perfect nest for two migrating birds. But it's just talk, the stuff of fancy.

She pulls on her skirt, clasps it at her hip, then dallies with her bra, straightening out the straps. Nakedness becomes her; lamplight, too. Clothes change her demeanour, add a hint of spite. She knows that if she were to put him to the test, he'd crumble like stale cake. Still, it's tempting, if only to trigger a flush of upset into his restfulness, but his stack of suddenly remembered excuses would cost them the next ten or twenty minutes and leave a bad taste. She sees clean through him, which is probably why they work so well together. Between them, secrets have never stood a chance. Dreams are fine in their place, but acceptance is the key to survival. Some people see a glass as half full, others see it as half empty. But there is a third group, a small, almost unnoticeable percentage, who want nothing more than the opportunity to quench their burning thirsts.

Coffee acts like a truce, or the replacement for words as a small, temporary goodbye. She boils more water. The cups are dirty, but clean enough to use. Partially dressed, she crawls back beneath the sheets and waits for the bed's heat to close her in its arms again. Time has changed them from the people they had once been. And yet, they fit together easily now. Perhaps they have grown towards one another, like flowers to the sun. For them, familiarity has bred a kind of contentment. Though it would have seemed impossible back when they were young and in need of greater thrills, a cup of coffee holds value now.

There are many ways of making love, and no time spent together ever feels wasted. Susan drinks her coffee, with her shoulder resting against Peter's. And when her cup is empty she leans across and opens his mouth with a kiss generously devoid of expectation. Smiling against her lips, he sets his own cup down and pulls her body onto him, holding fast.

Down at the station, the train is already at the platform.

They board quickly so as to escape the weather, which the darkness has somehow worsened. The wind is hard, dashed with cold snarls of sleet. Susan glimpses her reflection in another lit-up window and makes a pass at patting down her hair, but the task is a mammoth one.

A few passengers are already ensconced in the second carriage from the rear. They lift their glances, but only for an instant, then slump back down into the torpor of old paperbacks and badly folded newspapers. Peter leads the way, keeping his stride detached. He surveys the carriage and elects a single seat that backs on to the pull of the train. For a moment, Susan stands there, almost beside him, gripping a handrail. Nothing passes between them, not a word or even a glance. It is a break made clean with practice. And, finally, obedient to ancient instructions, she wanders along the aisle and pushes through the door. The next carriage seems more brightly lit. She hesitates at the entrance, then drops down into the first available window seat and settles herself for the ride back to Manhattan.

The totality of the station's outer dark presses against the window, and the carriage's illuminated glare etches ghostly, washed-out portraits of her past and future selves across the dust-encrusted glass. She stares until the sadness of both close in, then lowers her eyes.

She has long since given up asking why they can't sit together. It hurts her, though she understands the reasons. Peter is the type who takes caution to an extreme. In a working environment, such a fastidious nature is held in high regard. And if, away from work, it can at times stand too fast in its devotion to the empirical, it remains just one yardstick in the measure of a man. Valuable, yes, but not definitive.

They work in the same building, for the same company, though in offices some four floors apart and facing in opposite directions, and their paths have little or no job-related reasons for ever crossing. On the rare occasions they do happen to meet in a corridor, each is careful in showing ambivalence toward the other's existence. A nod is acceptable, a fleeting smile, too. But no lingering sideways looks, no conspiratorial body language. Such dedication to secrecy, the fortunes worth of attention spent on detail, has played a significant part in keeping them safe and undiscovered through all the years of their affair.

'You just don't see the menace,' he has told her, more than once. 'A single slip and everything we have will come apart like a cobweb.' And because she knows he is right, she always nods and cedes the ground to him without bothering to mention that actually, taken strand for strand, the tensile strength of cobweb surpasses even steel.

She owns two photographs of him, neither of which he knows about. She keeps them in a shoebox on the top shelf of her wardrobe, mixed in with decades of holiday snaps, ticket stubs from concerts and shows, and other assorted keepsakes. The pictures are neither concealed nor displayed, which is the best way to hide anything, and she knows them by heart, every shade and detail. Both were taken right here on Coney Island and date from a period quite early in their relationship, probably late in the season of their second or third summer. Nothing special, just a couple of dollar-a-pop Polaroid snaps that she had coaxed a boardwalk vendor into taking.

The first picture shows the two of them together, walking arm in arm; the second captures Peter alone. He is wearing navy Bermudas and a short-sleeved cotton shirt, white with red trim, open to mid-chest. She has on a light blue flower-patterned summer dress with yellow flecks and shoulder straps. A quick calculation would put her at late twenties in age, but the sun is shining and time has washed away enough of the reality to lend her an aura of youth. She is slim and girlishly pretty, her laughter branded from deep, the best she has probably ever looked. And beside her, as close as close can get without crossing a line into bawdy, Peter stands fit and strong, with the swarthy, brooding complexion of a movie type. Pacino, maybe. Accidentally handsome. The miracle is having a photographer here to record the scene, surely one of their time's proudest crescendos, for posterity. In the instant that the trained lens snatches its image, she is looking for the camera and almost finding it, but Peter is already halfway into a profile pose, his strong chin slightly raised, eyes clear and hard, ever vigilant of the borders. The impression they create is of a perfect, happy couple.

The second picture is like an alternate reality. Shot mere seconds later, it captures a portrait of heightened grief, the dead-weight freefall after an impossible high. Desperate to have a snap of her man alone and unhindered, Susan plays a little connivance and slips from frame on the excuse of wanting to check out a stall or to purchase a soft drink or an ice cream. The result throws the composition off balance, catching Peter on the high point of a spill, his strong upper body leaning into too hard a tilt. His expression has shifted, too; the youthful assurance gone, replaced by a kind of middle-aged dread that rusts edges and widens folds. The sun still yellows everything and the background remains unchanged after barely a dozen steps, but the sense that dominates now is one of overwhelming loss. In the span of thirty seconds, twelve whole years have been sucked from the world. This second picture is not what she has anticipated but exactly what she wants. Because alone, Peter seems worth less, somehow. And it is a vindication, of sorts, a truth that has been at last exposed.

Beyond the window, a station sign boxes itself into her field of vision, two black words on a plain of white: Coney Island. She mouths the name, certain of its magic, and a snatch of song suggests itself, heaving with barbershop harmony. Not caring what the few other passengers will think, she begins to hum the melody. For a moment, her breath rolls and tumbles, catching the lilt, finding a kind of freedom. Then, abruptly, she lapses back into silence and closes her eyes until stirred by the first pull of the train's engine. She listens to the noise, the soothing piston shots of metal and motion built to honour the laws of gravity, dragging her slowly homeward. But homeward is the real world, full of work and worry, full of Mike with all his tedious love, full of Isabel and her cancerous fears, full of take-out meals and wines from places far away. This place, and these last few hours, are what help to keep her alive, but a heart needs more than dreams to go on beating.

LILA

THIS MORNING, Lila Stankovic and I shared a carriage on the L. I was at one end, with my back to the journey, penned in among a crush of bodies. Space is at such a premium at that hour, and I usually bear the twenty-minute cross-town ride either slumped in some dream state or mentally catching up on work I've left undone. I tend to notice only what is exceptional among my fellow passengers, the disfigurements and small familiarities, the snaring morsels of detail. Lila had either boarded early enough to score a seat or else lucked out on finding some gentlemanly type willing to surrender his, because she sat there, three-quarters of the way along on the aisle's left side, with her slim, bare legs crossed beneath a demure apple-green wool skirt and her head bowed over a rumpled paperback.

I knew instantly that it was her.

In the two decades since moving to Chicago I have thought of her often, the way we all do with close friends who for a time mean more than the world itself to us but then, for whatever reason, fall out of our lives. Yet in all those years it never once occurred to me that she'd have aged. My mind preserved her in a perfect, permanent state, keeping her forever sixteen and alive and fresh in spite of all the nastiness that passed her way, and still somehow capable of dreams, still somehow certain that better days lie waiting in her path. The face that has always come is the one I held and kissed and could have drawn by heart if my talent had ever stretched even an inch in that direction. The Lila who aeroplane-danced through gales of laughter while the Stones kicked loud and overblown from my beat-up turntable speaker, who stretched out beside me on my bedroom floor to read comics and old, inherited sci-fi novels, and sometimes, closing her eyes so she would not have to see my face, to whisper the secrets of her heart.

Her hair was different, cut up from elbow-length into a short, stylish fashion that better fit a cosmopolitan existence, but it retained its natural shade, the colour of field dirt on a hot afternoon, brunette baked by a long summer's worth of sun and breeze down to a kind of muddied gold. From twenty paces she might still have been the late teen of my memory instead of fringing on the great collapse of forty, and I had to suppress the urge to holler out her name.

We were best friends, Lila and I. More than that, I think, looking back. We came from the same small County Cork town, fifty miles or so west of the city, with a pencil-line of ocean in sight. Back before the boom, when rural Ireland was still defined by its own inflicted limits, it was a beautiful place and a beaten one, a good and even glorious place to be until melancholia set in. Through the running years and on into that difficult time when running feels no longer quite enough, when the freeze of isolation begins to harden the edges of every thought, we had little else but one another.

I have a thousand memories of her, some beautiful, others heartbreaking. But one dominates everything: an evening in early June soon after we had both turned seventeen. I remember that we'd taken a walk, at her prompting, four or five miles out of town to Scannell's Point. A day or two earlier, some fishermen had reported basking sharks in close to shore, a certain sign of heat. We'd both seen sharks before, but Lila wanted us to see them together. She made some ham and cheese sandwiches and a flask of tea that I carried in a rucksack with one broken strap, and it seemed to matter to her that she and I could be in one another's company, away from the rest of the world, with nothing to distract and no one to judge.

We reached the beach a little after six. The water was calm and dark, and the sun had slipped behind a head of land, leaving the sky full of blood away in the west above the cliffs. We couldn't see the sharks because of the shadows striping the water, but it didn't matter too much, and after a while Lila even suggested that it was better this way, that it was enough just knowing they were out there. She took the rucksack from me and moved away. I peeled off my t-shirt to enjoy the slight coolness of the still air but continued to scan the ocean for a few minutes longer, still hoping to catch a hint of something, and I gave up only when she called out to me.

When all else is lost, we have our memories. The details of that evening are burnt into my mind, sitting with her in the soft sand, eating our sandwiches and passing the flask's cup back and forth between us, taking alternating sips. She liked her tea sweet to the point of cloying, with three or four spoonfuls of sugar, and I drank only to pleasure in the sharing. God, I can taste it in my mouth even now, wonderful and terrible, flushing my senses, the corrosive feel of the granulated sugar on my back teeth. Beside me, she ate her sandwich in delicate bites, chewing slowly, with her lips pinched shut, and I stole glances at her profile, understanding even then, I think, that this would last with me forever. She had on a stonewashed denim skirt that hugged her thighs, and a sleeveless yellow blouse with the top two buttons untied and pink false-pockets sewn over her small breasts. The flesh of her bare arm was cool whenever it pressed against mine, and she smiled a lot but kept her eyes low and, after the sandwiches were gone, we kissed for the first time apart from a conditional kiss she'd made me give her when we were ten, after we had agreed on a suitable trade for one of her speckled marbles. This was different. This time there was no discussion, no negotiations. She turned into my waiting stare and something in her dark eyes lured me in. Her mouth was warm and soft, and when her tongue brushed against the tip of mine I felt her sigh. My hand moved upward from her hip and slipped beneath her blouse and I cupped her breast and felt the cool softness of her flesh, plump against my palm and fingers.

A minute later, just when I was stirring towards a little more, she brought us apart again.

'That's enough,' she said, and turned her attention to the small waves breaking in white spumes against the beach.

'Just a little longer,' I gasped, and began to kiss the crook of her neck, my hand still inside her blouse, my thumb taunting the tiny bud of her nipple.

'Please, Bill. I said "enough".'

Something in her voice, a coldness that seemed new, made me pull back. I looked at her, and she met my stare and softened only after several seconds had passed. She rubbed my arm from shoulder to elbow. 'There'll be other nights. Don't worry. But I need to take this slow.'

My heart was racing, and the world seemed to have dimmed a notch in the time since I'd closed my eyes. My breath had the ragged, slopping sound of the tide, and every muscle the entire length of my body snared like a jerked noose. I was angry, but not just angry. My eyes fell to her bare feet, the skin pale as curd, her neatly trimmed nails painted a red the deep shade of rust in the growing dusk, and I bared my teeth in a hard smile.

'You don't take it slow with all the others,' I muttered, a crackle of laughter flushing sour in my mouth.

I didn't mean to say it. I have told myself often in the years and decades since that those words were not me. But I couldn't have hurt her more with a head butt to the face.

She made no reply, and we sat there, twenty yards up the beach from the lagging tide, and I could actually feel the small, irrevocable implosions rupturing the world we'd made around one another. The water, a darkness touched with red, put me in mind of rose petals strewn across freshly turned earth, and I tried to listen for her breathing, but there was nothing to catch, nothing above the banging inside myself, the deafening slap of blood in my ears.

Perhaps I could have tried for something then, risked whispering the apology that I truly would have meant and which she at the very least deserved. And it might even have been enough, it might just have saved whatever it was that we had going. But such words moved beyond me, and all I could do was sit there, helpless, even as she let down her hair and began to unbutton her blouse.

Once, a day or two before Valentine's Day back when we were either fourteen or fifteen, she insisted that we make cards for one another. There was no need to sign them, she said, and we weren't breaking any rules because we both knew how we really felt even if neither one of us was ready yet to talk about it. At least the cards would get everything out of the way and keep us from having to feel bad. I made no reply but did as I was told, and I spent most of that night decking the pulled-out centre pages of a copybook with little carefully drawn flowers and love hearts and even plundered a few lines from a particular Willie Nelson song that I knew she liked. Her card, the one that on the morning in question, came through the door an hour in advance of the postman, was much less of a production than mine, and on first consideration much less thoughtful. The message was a roses-are-red cliché scrawled in crayon, the letters staggering at random through the pack colours and hanging lopsided and babyish across the folded page, and on the front she'd drawn two stick figures shackled together by a nest of fingers beneath a large, pink, misshapen heart. The stick figures were unnecessarily named as 'Billy' and 'Lila', their respective sexes already implicit in the long, sweeping fishhooks of hair, the triangular red dress and, most worthy of mention, certainly most memorably, the two mismatched, asymmetrical breasts. I can recall feeling, just for a second, a bit hurt by the lack of effort she'd made, but the more I considered the card the more I absorbed and understood its sentiment, the acknowledgement that because of me she didn't have to feel alone. It was a thank-you, the most beautiful I have ever known.

I loved her for that card, and for so much more, but I hated knowing all the things I knew, and my insides broke like hammered glass every time she'd tell me, smiling fit to scream, that she couldn't come over this evening because she was being taken out. This had been part of her life, part of both our lives, I suppose, since the age of about fourteen, and I did what best friends are meant to do: I'd shrug and try to act like it didn't matter. But my eyes always gave me up. They'd fix on some distant point and refuse to soften, and she'd see and crack some terrible joke in an effort to restore our state of comfortable pretence.

Lila's story was an open book, or at least the clammy pages of one of those magazines that got passed around under classroom desks and later from cubicle to cubicle in the boys' toilets. Her father, a Yugoslav named Goran who'd come to town as part of a trawler's crew, was in Portlaoise on a repeat stint, two or three years into the sentence of eight handed down for one of those bodily harm raps, grievous or actual, the sheet bulked up by charges of assault with intent, the carrying of a concealed weapon and associating with known paramilitaries. For a while, her mother, Maggie, did what she could to keep things together, but burdened with the sort of debt that wouldn't yield gradually succumbed to the black pull of an unbreakable habit. A lot of what was done in that house were things no child should ever have to see, but from an early age Lila saw and was sometimes even made to see. Men came and paid, and if a few were not too bad, not the worst, then there were others who could only laugh by making Maggie cry and plead, and one who held her cheek to a hundred and fifty watts of naked light bulb, removing a thumb-pad's worth of skin and flesh and getting to within half an inch of costing her a left eye.

Everyone talked, pity vying with revulsion at what the neighbouring women knew and thought they knew, and for those kids who'd spent the bulk of our school years calling Lila every disgusting name they could think of, mud stuck. Now, at fifteen, sixteen, seventeen and desperately hoping that this was a case of like mother, like daughter, the bad boys jostled to get in line and take a turn with her, their words suddenly sweet and coaxing, full of promise. Lila was such an intelligent girl, the best of us really, but needing something I could never understand, aching, I suppose, for acceptance and for what she could persuade herself, even for a little while, was love, she went with them. She sat beside them on walls, sharing cans of Coke and, when they could get it, beer, holding their hands and afterwards going into the woods or the wheat fields with them, letting them press her up against a tree or pull her down into the long grass, closing her eyes only so that it would be easier to believe their whispers.

Strands of light still lingered in the sky when I followed her down to the waterline. The sand felt very fine away from the reefs, but was possessed of a coarseness and condensed strength down where the waves had run in, and a slash-wound in the low west mined the sky for hues of amber and russet; a vague, slanted final cough of day that spilt my shadow long and spectral away across the beach.

Lila was inside the tide, knee-deep and squatting down, with her back mostly turned on me, her skirt pulled up to her waist and her blouse, still wide open, hanging cape-like around her back. The ocean had grown dark except for the pinkish flecks that continued to dapple the surface. She knew I was there, but didn't turn, just continued in her stoop, one hand gripping a fistful of skirt hem against her hip, the other sluicing saltwater between her legs. I wanted to say something, but in that pose she looked both able and pathetic, and my throat closed up. I glanced around, stepped out of my shorts and, naked, started in towards her, drawing up just shy and a little to one side.

The air then was still, and the only sound was the gentle lapping of waves. Still nothing from her, not tears, not even the labour of breath. I'd jarred all sound from her and left her again only with this silence, and it made me want to weep, knowing what I'd done, what I'd caused. I dropped to my knees and let the water come to my waist. The cold tore through me, similar to cold I'd known from other summers and other swims but never quite like this, never as sharp and penetrating, and I wanted to run, to get out and throw myself down on the sand, but forced myself to remain. I knelt and washed, and a few feet away, just out of reach, she washed too, in retreated profile, calm as the ocean, the ends of her loose dark hair tipping the passing water, pulling like hooked line, taut and then askew.

I was thinking about the sharks, somewhere out there, circling, when she turned her face to me.

'You don't get to notice new details,' she said, her voice thin and small, barely audible above the slopping of the water. 'What happens is that old ones fade and get forgotten. It's an end to things, not a beginning.'

My throat hurt like I'd taken a punch there. 'I love you,' I said, the first time in my life that I ever spoke those words. I meant them, but wish now that I'd kept silent. Because in those moments, a phrase like that was nothing but an attempt to justify what I'd taken from her, what I'd made her give. 'You know that, don't you?'

For a second she held my gaze, then let it fall away. I watched as she continued to scrub herself clean, her fingers slipping between her legs and vanishing, kneading the flesh where I had been, and half of what bloomed in my heart was, again, anger. An end to things. Her words had blood in them. I decided that she would think so, that she'd earned the right, but it didn't have to be for me the way it was for her.

I loved her and ached for her, because she was who she was, sweet and lovely and fun to be around, but scarred too in all manner of brutal ways, and marked out in the eyes of most as damaged goods. Kids used and taunted her, but at home I was never once warned or even told to stay away. I'd like to put this down to compassion or free-thinking on the part of my parents, and I hope and believe that there were at least elements of both involved, but it is right to mention here that my mother drank, and this was certainly a factor, even if back then she could still keep her excesses to the hours of darkness. And my father drank a little too, mainly, I think, out of empathy. The old man taught English and History at a private school in the nearby town of Bandon, and was one of those wan, serious types, middle-aged by thirty, winding down by forty-five, who shouldered blame like duty. The nights not spent marking essays found him tucked into a library novel with two or three more stacked at one elbow and a glass kept always half-full at the other, and the only conversations he and I ever had were about books, the pulpy Raymond Chandler or James M. Cain paperbacks that he pushed on me until I learned enough to start grabbing them of my own accord, or his occasional thoughts on Hemingway, Lawrence and, in whispers, as if anyone who overheard would understand or even care a damn, Henry Miller. As parents, they kept me clothed and fed, kept me safe, and that, to them, was their duty fulfilled. Things had happened to them in life, and the marks they bore, had a sense of permanence. Their relationship was not quite a one-way devotion, but the balance was definitely tipped, and they found their best connect three or four inches into a bottle of whiskey or gin, because that was when my mother would soften, open up.

Apart from the nights, more than I care to count, that she spent in our spare room, with the door locked and the stab of her crying coming through my bedroom wall, Lila lived more or less alone. Her mother kept crazy hours, she said. And while it was a good deal better for her that way, there were times too when it was just hard to be in the house, hard to be on her own.

She never had to go into detail with me, knowing that I knew because everyone knew. On the nights she stayed over, I'd sit awake, listening without wanting to until the sound of her weeping fell away, and then I'd creep out onto the landing and tap on her door with something for her to read. Ray Bradbury, her favourite, or Ellison, who I liked but who she couldn't quite get. Science fiction was what mattered to us then, and I had a decent used collection, creased and yellowed paperbacks with gaudy, faded covers and badly dog-eared pages that made our hands feel dusty just to look at them, but which never failed to fuel the inferno in our minds. She'd take the book from me and try to smile, but when I'd turn to go she'd grip my hand and lead me inside. These are some of my best memories, and my worst. I have never since felt quite so close to anyone as on those nights, but neither have I ever been exposed to so much hurt. We'd squeeze together into the single bed and I'd hold her tight against my chest and feel her hot tears soaking through my t-shirt while I ran my fingers through her hair. Talking in whispers, having learned to ignore what could not be helped, letting her lead the way. Her brother, Charlie, two years younger than her, with mild-to-middling Down's Syndrome, had been taken into care soon after their father was put away for the second time. Occasionally she'd talk about him, dredging up recollections of how excited he'd get on long-ago Christmas mornings or that summer when, searching for nests, he had climbed the big sycamore in the Protestant churchyard but then couldn't get down. Charlie was raped in his bed by a dealer named Finnegan who'd come to the house in the middle of the night and on a whim decided to take what was owed out of the one ass that could be damaged most. Lila wrote long letters that she had to edit down into simple language before sending, and though her requests for visitation were repeatedly refused, she kept on asking. Most of the tears she cried were for him, because it was easier to cry for someone else than for herself.

Knowing the feel of her in my arms, our bodies pinned together in that single bed beneath piles of blankets or on summer nights the thinnest cotton sheet, is a level of intimacy I have never again experienced, not even in marriage. I love my wife, and for the past sixteen years there has been no one else for me, but that love is different, somehow. Not less, simply different in that it lacks the innocence of the earlier time, when the world was just beginning to bloom, and lacks, too, the openness. Lila could weep while I held her and be as if she were alone, be that completely herself, and I'd feel the broken rhythms of her sobbing penetrate my chest and later, after the tears were gone, the burn of her cheek pressed hard to mine. There were nights when one or the other of us, exhausted by such purging, would drift off into sleep, but more often than not we'd lie awake for hours, even clear through until dawn sometimes, facing one another in our clench, not speaking, not needing words. More than once, helpless to age and hormones, I stiffened against her, but in the darkness this was something we could both pretend to ignore. She had no fear of me. She loved me that much. And she knew me better than anyone else, or thought she did.

After she had finished washing, she stood and waded back up onto the beach. Still on my knees, I watched her move past me into the shallows, the surf breaking in pale flumes around her ankles. Once on the sand she stepped into her panties and resettled her skirt back into place. Then she turned and stood watching me, her fingertips working to close her body back into the blouse, picking the buttons together slowly upwards from her stomach. The squeezing twilight masked her details, but I no longer needed to see. I bore the cold a minute more, before coming out of the water and taking her hand. She looked at me, then lowered her gaze to my naked body. I could feel the stinging residue of the saltwater on my skin, and the heat of the day had been sucked back down into the ground. When she smiled something was missing, something that had always been there for me, and to let myself off easy I decided it must be down to the angle of her face, lowered like that, playing a dirty trick.

She waited beside me while I dressed, sometimes watching me, how my body bent into my clothes, sometimes gazing out to where the water had turned blackest, and where the sharks might have been lurking. Then, without speaking, she began to walk away, keeping to the rough line of footsteps we had made in coming. I pulled on my t-shirt and had to run to catch up. And once I was beside her she pressed herself to me, slipping her arm inside of mine at the elbow and leaning in to kiss my cheek just at the corner of my mouth. The tide was drawing in now, and our line took us so close to the water's edge that we could feel the faint spittle of its breaking against our bare legs. Behind us, the sky sealed in the last of the light, but the darkness that took hold was gentle, and on the side of the waves, she tightened the press of her body against me and let her head lean against my shoulder.

The road back to town seemed very long. We went slowly, pinned together, not saying much, neither of us really knowing what to say. My mind churned with apologies and questions, but for a while it was pleasant just to walk, until the sweep of the land turned us away from the sea and into a twisting incline. I stopped, unfastened the rucksack and pulled out the grey loose-wool sweater that I was glad I'd thought to bring. Lila slipped it on and it pooled around her, falling almost to her knees, and she stood like a child with her arms outstretched, smiling at me and at nothing while I rolled the cuffs back up over her hands. Then with a tiny whispered thank-you she nestled herself against me as before. A large crescent moon, still early in its first quarter and barely more than a sliver, appeared in the south, and stars began to show, hesitant at first and then in clusters. I looked for shapes, but not knowing where to search or what to expect, found none.

'One more year,' she said, 'and I'm gone.'

Now, I thought. Ask her. Tell her.

'Where?'

'I don't know. Dublin, London, America maybe, if I can get that far. The where isn't important. What matters is distance. I just need to get away.'

She glanced at me, then pulled her stare to the heavens. The few stars that had fallen into view were icy specks decorating the blackness. A copse of nearby alders temporarily hid the moon's shape but not its glow.

'I'm going to join the army,' I said, with too much force.

'Really?' Her eyes were wide and black, beyond reading.

'Or the navy. I need to decide. But it's been in my mind a long time.'

For almost a minute she made no reply. Her head found my shoulder again and we stood there in the middle of the narrow road, my arm around her waist, and watched the sky, waiting for something to change, or to change back.

'I think you're a fool,' she whispered, and I knew by the feel of her breath that tears were once more readying themselves to fall.

*

We rocked on, the L whistling its way above the bottlenecked Chicago streets. I had hold of a supporting bar and tried to focus on both my balance and my breathing. Ahead of me, she finished one page of her book and turned to the next, her slender fingers as nimble and familiar as ever to my stare. The nails were neat, trim, unpainted, and she wore no rings, nothing that might suggest a story lived. I absorbed her details, hungry for them, and it was easy because so little about her had changed. Her hair shortened and styled, perhaps some light puckering of the skin around her eyes and the corners of her mouth, but not much else, at least not on the surface.

Seconds built, full of the train's dull inner-ear heartbeat, a smooth enough sensation, but only by comparison, and yet it felt as though time were moving in reverse, taking us out of ourselves back to some better state. I kept hoping she'd look up, that our first moment of reunion would be made across the protectorate of a buffering crowd. Aside from a ream of questions that couldn't be rehearsed or even ordered without first knowing the answers, I had no idea of what I might say to her, what I'd do, but I knew she'd smile and that I'd feel like crying. We'd surely embrace, perhaps even kiss, and if I could I'd coax her into abandoning all other plans and disembarking at some convenient stop, to spend the morning over coffee, not only reminiscing but reconnecting. I think a part of me believed that if I stared hard enough she'd feel it as a touch, and would find me. But she just sat there, reading, carried by her book to some place far away, and all I could do was suffer and wait.

Then the driving heart shifted beat and everything dimmed and brightened again as we entered another station. The doors shuddered open on my right, and at the far end of the carriage, and a fresh horde of commuters pushed aboard, heedless of the little available space and showing the sort of determination that quickly displaced those of us already inside from our captured positions. Jostled from my moorings, I lost perhaps a minute of time, and when I regained a foothold among the throng I saw that another woman had planted herself in Lila's seat. Middle-aged, with skin the lightest shade of brown that could still be considered black, she patted uselessly with a small fat hand at the carousing plume of her pink-tinged hair and shifted and resettled her considerable bulk with an enthusiasm that brought a pinch of annoyance to the face of the old man seated alongside.

I was trapped. Even as the pieces fell into place in my mind, the doors came shut. I tried anyway, pushing forward between bodies, but the aisle was blocked, sealed against movement. I scanned the platform and found it thick with people, too, slow fusions of opposing tides. And then, just as the engine shunted and we were lurched forward into another slow crawl, Lila was for an instant there before me, close to the platform's edge and barely twenty feet away, still as gravestone. Crowds moiled all around her but she seemed untouched. Framed from my point of view in a square of filthy, scratched Plexiglas, she stood facing me, perfect and familiar, forever sixteen, but with her eyes turned away and smiling open-mouthed for a distant someone else. She remained like that, a photograph, even as a rumble swelled to a whine; long lost and now lost again, sucked once more into my past.

The day since has fallen mostly out of focus. At the next station, one of the line's main stops, the crowd thinned out, but even when seats became available I held my place, one fist wrapped white-knuckled around an overhead chord, not particularly wanting to stand but afraid, I think, not quite trusting myself, to move. Keeping my balance was difficult without the pack for support. And ten minutes later, when it was my turn to disembark, I buttoned up my overcoat, bypassed the rank of taxi cabs lining one side of the street, and walked the eleven blocks to work, even though the grey morning had given in to the first heavy downpour of rain.

Apart from a staff gathering at ten-thirty and a budget meeting immediately after lunch, I spent the morning and afternoon in my office with the door closed, leafing through the telephone directory and drinking cup after cup of the strong black coffee that my secretary, Margaret, delivered at more or less hourly intervals. For the first hour I think I actually believed it might be possible to track Lila down. But when the St- pages of the directory yielded nothing, I began to wonder if what I had was in fact only half a name, if Stankovic might have been shucked at an altar or tossed out by some Justice of the Peace. And from there, it was hopeless. Going cover to cover would, I realised, be a waste of time. Still, I tried, because there was little else I could do, but I knew that even if a name like Lila seemed out of the ordinary, the odds were better than good that she'd be listed under her husband's name, or that she would have made herself anonymous by the simple, solitary act of an initial. Either way, she'd have become what she always yearned to be: invisible, one of the crowd. A ghost.

I left work a little before three, a couple of hours earlier than usual. The late afternoon had slipped into an apathy typical of October. Dry for now, after the earlier rain, but with a cold wind blowing down from the north and a deeply ashen sky that churned and threatened. My coat, still damp from its morning walk, felt heavy across my shoulders. I took a cab to the station and bought a newspaper so that I wouldn't have to think too much or look at too many faces. I just scanned the headlines, not that interested. The banking crisis, yet another summit organised to solve the problems of the Middle East. Another suicide bomb in Riyadh, thirteen dead, dozens wounded. And closer to home, an eighth grade teacher in Missouri who suffered third degree burns to sixty percent of her body after being doused in methylated spirits and set alight in class by two of her students. The sports pages couldn't see beyond the White Sox, who'd just clinched a wild card berth in the playoffs with a shock sweep of the Royals. As an outsider, I'd never caught the fever of baseball, but I enjoy the ambience and every season try make it out to the Cell for a game or two at least, usually at my daughter's pleading. She's eleven now, a great kid. Dark hair, big, pretty, green eyes, a bit of a tomboy still but growing up fast. She's a big fan, has her bedroom walls decked in pennants and posters of all the big hitters. Her name is Lila, too. My choice. My wife doesn't know why. Nobody does. Sometimes, I'm not even sure I know myself.

THE MATADOR

IN THE EVENINGS, at one of the outdoor cafés with a nearly empty bottle before him, Enrique still looks good. It has to do with the wash of light, a shade of gold rusting shut, the late sun burnishing and enriching the crumbling brickwork fronts along the street's western face. Even after the air turns cool, he likes to sit beneath the orange trees, still and straight-backed in a hard chair, his trim body open slightly onto the inclining street, his legs crossed tight at the knee. With a bottle near to hand he can be calm and act as though he doesn't need the burn of the wine.

People know him. The waiters, but also several of the passers-by. Many have seen him fight, but even those who haven't know of his reputation. And of his misfortune. The bull that got him was a clear rank below his level. At the Royal Fair in Algeciras, warming up for Seville, the big one, the homecoming that never came, he'd stepped out of another routine pass and gone over on his ankle. That was all. A tragic accident, in a game that does not countenance margins of error. But sitting here, it can still seem as if nothing has changed. And in the dying light, he encourages the masquerade. Not to impress, but to feel whole. Now that he has entered his thirties, the signs of ageing are at last beginning to tuck at him, though this has less to do with time itself than with the manner of its spending, His flesh, greyed from late nights and days slept away, hangs stretched across the bones of his face, emphasising hollows, and his mouth keeps a hard clench, used to silence. Yet his build retains the leanness of old, strong across the narrow shoulders, the slim torso still suggesting speed, agility. It is only when he stands, and worse still when he walks, that the illusion comes apart.

He pours the last of his bottle, counts out the few coins that already lie bunched and counted on the red and white check-patterned tablecloth beside his glass, and finishes his wine. When the sun slips behind the cathedral the day seems to thicken, and the chill is gentle on his face and brow. These are his favourite moments, the middle ground between all that was and all that will ever be, when time is somehow checked and there is nothing to be done but let the heart go on beating. But it doesn't last. He becomes aware of the waiter in the doorway, Miguel, watching without pretending to see. Everybody knows, but they know only surfaces. Enrique takes his time over the last mouthful of wine, gives his breathing a chance to steady itself. Then he rises from the chair, holds up his hand in a 'so long' gesture to no one in particular, and walks slowly away, measuring each step as a conscious thought and letting the street carry him home.

Pilar doesn't hear him enter. She is at the stove, frying rice in the half-light and singing along to something in her head, a low husky sound that pulses with feeling without bothering to properly shape its sentiment. They keep two rooms on the second floor of a crumbling seventeenth-century building, a living-room-cum-kitchen and a small bedroom. The rent is low, partly because of the area, partly due to the apartment's state of general disrepair, but it meets their needs. He stands in the doorway and watches, and when finally she becomes aware of his presence she merely turns and smiles. A tight-fitting white blouse and a dark blue or black cotton skirt that falls to just above her knees help emphasise the subtle curves of her body. And she is barefoot on the tiled floor. The song continues to come, low and hesitant, in gasps as staggered as the breeze that sifts in from the street during the hot afternoons of summer.

'Okay?'

She glances back over one shoulder again, and smiles.

He closes the door and moves to the window. The view is mostly of rooftops, and a little of the sun's light remains as a redness in the west. The first stars have already begun to appear. To the eye, everything is still, though a fur of traffic noise insinuates the hour. He finds himself watching, waiting for something to happen. From here he can see a few other windows, but all are either shuttered or exist yet only as black holes, conserving their own secrets. He can still taste the wine in his mouth.

Dinner is rice with peas, and frozen shrimp. They sit facing one another at the small foldout table and eat slowly, by a stump of candlelight. Pilar talks as if a child were sleeping in the bedroom just beyond, her voice full of air and rubbed of its edges. He holds her gaze as much as he can and tries to concentrate on what she is saying, nodding his head in all the right places. In the candlelight, she is beautiful. She looks good in any light, but there is something about the yellow assurance of the candle's flame that heightens what she has. The hollows deepen, the surfaces shine, flecks of moisture gleam in her eyes and on her lips. She has taken her hair down, and it cascades in sable flumes across her shoulders and down over her small breasts. He wants to tell her, abruptly, that he loves her, and he almost does. But she is talking about the tourist who was killed this morning on the street in front of the Maria Luisa Park, and he holds back the words until his need for them passes.

'A Canadian. On holiday with his son. He shouldn't have stepped out, of course, but it's very sad.'

He nods. 'A high price to pay.'

'The boy was right there too, saw the whole thing. The radio said that he'd just stepped off the footpath to allow a group of students by. His good manners got him killed. It's very sad, don't you think? I only hope it was instant.'

Enrique chews his food with care. An uncle of his choked to death on shrimp. He'd been chatting and a piece went against his breath. His wife had done all she could to save him, even tried putting her fingers down his throat to clear the airway. For several years after, her hands bore the most terrible scars. Like she'd been savaged by a dog. And all to no avail. They said he turned blue and that the veins along his temples stood out like branches of a tree. For the Canadian, there would have been a second of understanding, less even than that, just as or just before the car hit. A realisation that this was what death looked like, felt like. He probably saw the driver's face, stretched like gum in a palsy of horror. The world turns slowly during such moments, vibrations seem to magnify.

'I doubt it,' he says, softly. 'Violent death is almost never instant. The newspapers never tell you how it really is. They simplify. "A man was hit by a car and killed." That's all they say. There's no room on that page for the screams, the howl of the brakes, the descriptions of bone poking through flesh and even clothes, or how the eyes fill up with blood. Because readers can only stand so much. We want to know, but once we do we're marked with it. So they spare us.'

'That poor child. Jesus.'

Pilar is a good cook, even with simple ingredients. Half a bottle of red remains from last night, and she watches him pour out a glass for himself. He knows that she prefers him not to drink, but she also understands his need. Just to change the subject, she asks if there was anyone she knew at the café, and he tells her no, not really, only Miguel. 'He asked after you.'

She chews some rice and nods, not looking up.

'I knew his wife.'

'I know.'

'Not that he ever thought too much of her.'

'Miguel's not so bad.'

'He's a hateful man. Those last months, when the cancer had Consuela nearly eaten away, he was out until all hours, drinking, whoring, Christ knows what.'

'Well, he says to say hello, so, hello.'

Across the table, Enrique turns his glass by the stem. At times like this, the man he once was feels close enough to touch. His fingertips and thumb twist the glass, and his eyes watch, with something like a smile forcing tight the corners of his mouth. He is almost handsome, a side-effect of his natural stillness. Pilar remembers him, too, from when he was famous. He either doesn't know she remembers or pretends not to, but a passing history exists. Little has changed on the surface, but there was something statuesque about him then, a sense that he'd been sculpted by immaculate hands. He still tries, but because of how much he needs to force, his bearing now seems false. Pity has widened the cracks. They have been together almost five years, and there are things between them that can never be discussed. Who she was, who he has become. But words are unnecessary. On a level, they might be perfect for one another, but it is a theoretical perfection only, compromised by timing. Their bests passed one another on the way to here, and now exist epochs apart.

They first met in one of the riverside bars. The world was younger then, and less understood. He'd entered, already somewhat drunk, with his arms raised and a bull's severed ear gripped for show between his teeth. Everyone cheered in answer to the roars that carried him in, even the tourists who didn't quite get what had happened or what was going on, and a lot of wine followed as he held sway, recounting feats, close calls, moments of terror. Stories that for a captive audience counted towards greatness. She remembered how he had stood in the middle of the floor with a bar towel while the fat owner, also drunk, played a charge, snorting and stamping one foot, index fingers acting out the part of horns. Another pass, and another, until sweat was in everyone's eyes and mouths ached from laughing, and until the shouts of encouragement came from places deeper down. And later, hours later, once the party had broken up, he took her by the hand and led her home with him, selecting her from among them all as if one was much the same as another because all he wanted that night, all he needed, was a body, warm and pliant, to hold and play against. In bed, still smelling of sweat, dust and recent slaughter, he was strong with her but not rough, not the way some were, and though he never once asked her name, he touched her body with his hard hands, kissed her mouth and afterwards held her tight to him and whispered the sort of things against her skin that she decided to believe he could never have shared with anyone else. The following morning, wrapped in one of his old shirts and a little bit in love, she sat and drank coffee at his kitchen table, spiking her cup with the last of his sherry, then slipped away while he was still sleeping, never imagining that four years would pass before they met again. And by then everything had changed. Gone was the fanfare, the authority. The colossus had begun to crumble, the strain now too much to bear. This time it wasn't a bar but one of the cafés in town, late morning, early afternoon. He had a table in a corner, away from the windows, out of the light. She sat at the counter on a high stool, tired to the bone from a night spent scrubbing down hospital walls, and watched him for several minutes, her mind full of that one earlier night's details. So much had happened since, but it felt natural that he should be there, in the corner, because a part of him had been with her always. And when she could bear it no longer, she left her coffee and came uninvited to sit with him, for the sake of companionship accepting the merest thimbleful from his bottle even though she was by then a year clean and almost as long sober. He looked up from the floor, his small eyes narrowed, struggling and threatening to break whatever trance held him so fast. She sipped from the solitary glass, hardly breathing, aching for him to recognise her but also praying that he wouldn't. Questions fell between them and lay unanswered, and after a couple of passes at talk and beyond the reach of anything except the bottle, he slumped back in his chair and let the stupor take hold. He drank in a way different than before, with an aggression that made her feel afraid for him, but the feelings when she looked into his face were exactly those she'd known with him asleep beside her in his bed, his black hair tossed from its precision, the press of his ribs showing as a whiteness through his sallow skin, the slender fingers of one hand tucked high and snug between her thighs. She waited until he finished the dregs of wine, then paid a taxi and took him home with her, and she laid him down and washed and dried his face and body. Tears came as her touch traced the scars, because the papers had only hinted at the true extent of his hurt, and she wiped them away only when her eyes began to burn and decided to accept that there were still things they could do and be for one another.

'I just can't stop thinking about the little boy.'

Enrique nods, plucks a shrimp from the nest of rice and slips it into his mouth.

'They'll be looking after him, of course. And someone is probably on their way from Canada as we speak. His mother, maybe, or a grandparent. A relative, anyway. But that's a long flight. I can't imagine what he must be feeling. What a thing to have to see. How does a nine-year-old even begin to come to terms with something like that?'

'It is, it's very sad.'

'And then there's the driver. You have to feel for him, too. Don't you? All the papers say it wasn't his fault, but he'll blame himself even if no one else does. When he got out of bed this morning, the day must have seemed so bright. And now he's killed a man.'

They continue to pick their way through the food, she going on in bursts about how the world stops turning all the time and how a person will imagine, wrongly, that the impact of it should be widely felt. 'We all like to believe we're in some way connected. But the truth is that you spin through your days, I spin through mine. We only notice one another in the moments of collision. Christ. I don't even know these people and I want to cry for them. But a month from now, even a week from now, I'll read something in the paper, about the inquest, maybe, and I'll be surprised at how quickly I've forgotten. It's happened before, and it will keep on happening. What do you think that says about me? About any of us? Because we're all the same, as much as we might like to believe otherwise. We're all boxed up in our own little catastrophes, and even though we tell ourselves that we care, the truth is that it's a pretence.'

He takes some wine and holds it at the back of his mouth.

'Jesus,' he says.

In the candlelight, her eyes gleam. A smile breaks, along with a hard breath, a kind of expulsion, but it just as quickly stiffens and he can see that she is readying herself to cry. The bone of her chin quivers, jogging once with some word that goes unspoken. His hand moves flat across the table. Her fingers feel cold against his, the skin dry as paper, and he knows that seeking out a pulse would do no good. Her heart beats slow and shallow.

'You can't get hung up on these things,' he says. 'You're right. We are all the same. A story like this gets to everyone. It's tragic. And it's natural to feel pity and compassion. But too much happens, and we can't spare the room in our heads for anyone else. If we held on to everything we'd be overwhelmed. We'd suffocate.'

'Can I have some of your wine?' she asks.

He hesitates, then grins and holds out the glass to her. He watches her drink, glad that he can help. He tells himself that if she finishes the little that is left he'll go out and buy another bottle. He won't even ask because she'll try to talk him out of it, saying that she has had enough in a mouthful, more than enough, and that they really can't afford the extravagance. But the sip she takes is a small one, and she holds the wine on her tongue for several seconds before swallowing, not really wanting it at all, wanting only to share in something of his, to taste what he tastes, to know the world in some small way as he does. Then she sets down the glass and lets him take it back.

The day that changed everything had been like any of a thousand he'd known. A little light morning cloud, but that had burned away towards noon. No rain, not even the threat of rain. No paired ravens or slipped breaths, no omens of any kind. He'd dressed slowly, as always, taking his usual twenty minutes, half an hour, keeping to his favoured order of garment and sipping water that was not too cold, not wanting to quench the first agitating sparks of fear lighting in his mind and deep down in his stomach. Sitting and counting beats until the time came to pray. He was twenty-six and knew the ways, the routine. That day, everything was right. Through the mass concrete, he could hear the muted tumble of the crowd spilling in, and then the drone as the opening picadors set to work. It was music from the other side of time, held back by the walls. And when the call came for him to go, the announcing word for the *tercio*, the final third, he did not hesitate. He shouldered his cape and stepped into the tunnel, bodily ready. The light fell beyond the gate, yellowing the ground, but here the shadow lay still and matted with a hot stench of dust and beast. The noise as the crowd worked itself to fever hit a dense, seamless beat that smothered every other detail, but this close to the ring he could feel, coming up out of the ground, the prancing gallop of the horses swinging hidden past the gate and, in chase, the explosions of the bull, a monstrous weight of vibration, echoing through him as thunder sometimes does when it breaks directly overhead.

During their first months together, trying to rest through the hot afternoons of August and September, Pilar told him often that other things mattered more. He was almost always drunk then, using the wine as an excuse but needing it too, and he'd throw open the bedroom window, draw the curtains to keep out the hardness of the light, strip to his shorts and stretch out on the bed. She'd nestle beside him to kiss his mouth and let the cool flat of her hand explore the smooth nubs of his chest where the bones stretched the skin, all the while explaining in stumbling whispers why she no longer valued that or wanted it, having had her fill, more than her fill, having suffered its brutal sides. And they'd sleep that way if sleep would come, in one another's arms in the cloaked light, breathing the hot air. More often, though, she'd undo the buttons of her blouse and the clasps of her skirt and lie against him or above him and they'd make what passed for them as lazy love, he only half awake, the wine a darkness of its own, and it was not easy but in moments also not bad, since neither one of them held any expectations now, just having a body to lie with, having gentle flesh to feel against their own. Sometimes, overwhelmed, he'd cry, and she'd cry too, for him, even as she kissed his tears away, but usually he'd just lie back and stare at the ceiling, the cornflower paintwork blistering with heat and age and splitting open like desert dirt, wondering if today could be the day he'd take his razor and finally open up his wrists or throat.

A misstep, and he'd gone over on his ankle, hung himself accidentally out to dry. Had he fallen, the doctors assured him in the days and weeks that followed, he'd almost certainly have died, he'd have been either trampled or fatally gored. But there are slow ways of dying, too. For a long time after, whenever he closed his eyes, there was only ever brightness, the white-brass glare of a late spring afternoon, the air on fire with light, the dirt of the bullring sallow as exposed bone. He carried no clear image of what had happened, only a confusion of sky and dirt and the vinegar stench of rage in an animal driven to a state beyond insane, the *banderilla* spears pinned to its haunches, dug barely flesh-deep and bobbing to every flexed sinew but holding at skewed angles even through the charges, the lumbering turns and the final terrible impact, their pink and yellow ribbons, like prayer flags, flapping absurd colours into the day. The pain was immense, even from behind a morphine wall, but it was the discomfort of the penetration and the certain dread of irreversible damage that scorched a permanence into his mind, the freshly suffered feel of the horn never further than a breath away, slicing through him, impaling him on that enormous rock-hard head, that hulking back with its ridge of high shoulder muscle resisting the desperate edge of his sword. He'd fought, the newspapers had later noted, even when all was obviously lost. Valiant in the face of a fluked routing. He'd stabbed and flayed, but the angle was wrong and his own twisted, writhing position left him none of the necessary leverage to land a telling shot.

Later, in the infirmary, after he'd regained consciousness, he lay on the table and even through the haze of drugs felt split nearly in two. The room was windowless and lit white, making a mystery of the hour, and after the noise of the bullring the silence had the heft of sudden deafness. Seeing that he was awake, a doctor had leaned in, a woman doctor, perhaps forty years old, dark-eyed and with a potential towards beauty, and told him how lucky he was to be alive, the first of many times he'd hear this said. He stared at her, wanting to answer, but his mouth flushed with two kinds of blood and no words would come.

It rains during the night and on through most of the next day. Pilar rises early, makes coffee and returns to bed. The morning is hot, so she stretches out above the covers in her underwear. Beside her, Enrique stirs and resettles. Just lying here feels good, and she likes to watch him sleep. Without the world to trouble him, his face wears an expression of youthfulness, even innocence, and seeing him that way lets her imagine that she is young and innocent, too. But only for a minute. The rain comes soft against the glass, and she closes her eyes to thicken the darkness and her breathing slows in tandem with its caress.

Some time later, she wakes to find Enrique gone. For a moment, she is lost, and a little bit afraid. In her life, she has woken too many times to such confusion, and even now, these few years on, the sensation lingers. The past throws a long shadow. She switches on the radio, closes her eyes again, and draws a deep breath. Music seeps into the room, a classical piece, indistinct and unfamiliar. She remains still, listening but also trying to feel for sounds beyond, for evidence that she is not alone, or that a world still exists outside these walls. But under the music there is only the soft, calming rustle of the rain. And finally she reaches for the glass of water that sits waiting on her bedside locker. The water is tepid but not unpleasant, and the earlier coffee makes it a necessity. She drinks, keeping to sips, until the glass is empty, then rises and begins to dress. Yesterday's clothes lie draped across the back of a timber chair in the corner, but they are clean enough still to wear, and she pulls each garment on slowly, not thinking much about what she is doing, still not really fully clear of sleep.

While she is tying the buttons of her blouse, the front door opens and shuts.

'Pilar?'

'In the bedroom.'

Enrique appears. 'You're up.'

'Thank you for the water,' she says, and smiles at him. 'What time is it?'

'After nine.'

'I was tired. I don't know what came over me. I didn't expect to sleep so long.'

He throws the morning paper on the bed. She looks at it, then at him, and awaits an explanation. They never buy newspapers. The little they have barely keeps them fed and housed, and what remains usually goes on cheap wine. Papers are an extravagance they cannot afford.

'What's happened?'

'Did you get the news yet?' He looks different. Sounds different. He stands in the doorway, watching her, his posture lean and again boasting the illusion of strength, his clothes, an old, grey shirt and faded jeans, clinging to his body, his black hair glued to his forehead by the rain. Years of training with bulls have turned his exterior to stone, with all suggestion of excitement or anger concealed, but there are certain tells still for someone who knows where to look. He waits until she is drawn into the front page, then turns and leaves the room. Within seconds there is the sound of water being run for coffee. She catches the small clatter of cups and, behind her, the radio spinning out its music, a string movement that climbs and dissipates and is occasionally cut apart by an invading flute or piccolo.

The child, the boy from the accident, is Swiss, and has been missing for nineteen months. Pierre Laurent, eight years old. Abducted from outside his apartment building in Lucerne. The dead man, named unofficially as Nathaniel Filbin, forty-four, is a divorced father of three and native of Toronto. No known convictions, though questioned twice, some five years ago, regarding an attempted assault on an underage male in the changing rooms of a public swimming pool.

In the kitchen, Enrique sits gazing out through the window at the dim sky, his hands spread wide and flat before him on the table. Pilar knows by the set of his jaw that he is thinking about the bull, and better days. Everything about his expression has tightened, even the intensity of his stare. The body does not easily forget its traumas. She pours the coffee, brings him a cup but remains standing.

'That poor child,' she says, again wanting to cry.

'It happens a lot,' Enrique replies, without looking up. 'A father, an uncle, a neighbour. There's help now, though. Doctors and such. People he can talk to. And he has his family back.'

She nods. The coffee is very hot, but tastes good. A residue of sleep still clings to her, and the thick, white cast of the morning light feels suffocating.

'But he'll never be the same.'

'No.'

They each drink a second cup of coffee, then Pilar scrambles some eggs. She likes to cook. Some of her earliest memories are of her mother in the kitchen. Dead from cancer at thirty-two, but looking already middle-aged by then, a short, thickset woman with a dour face and a voice that softened only when she sang. Cooking was for her a respite, and this seems an inherited trait. Pilar is nothing like her in looks, but has her voice, her gentle confidence with melody, and her ease beside a stove.

The eggs spit and crackle in the pan. Yesterday, the driver of that car had a killing on his conscience. This morning it seems as if he has saved the life of a child. Some of the things she says feel and sound good when spoken, but they are not always true. Promises, mainly, and assurances about what matters and what does not. She loves Enrique, but there are times when it feels as if she doesn't know him at all, or when the little that she does know feels less than it should. After all she has been through in her life, what they have together is enough. In him, she has a companion to sit with at dinner, to lay with after the lights go out and to wake up alongside when another morning breaks. He still takes her in his arms, but only rarely of his own volition, and when they kiss now there is always a shortfall, always barriers. She contents herself with what he has to give, yet cannot deny the occasional yearning for more.

Since the accident, he has avoided the bullring, hoping perhaps that the sense of it would fade. But everything remains as he remembers. Into summer, the crowd carries him along, making less of him, reducing him to another among so many, and he moves with the body of the pack, feeling the air hot and alive against his face, cloying with the stench of sweat and baked dirt, then slips loose and climbs nineteen steps to the whitewashed granite shelves that represent the cheapest seats.

It does not have to be this way. He still retains certain privileges, and could watch the fight from the exclusive seats, or even from the pen, with the men taking part. But he wants anonymity, preferring to spare himself the pitying stares of those who know him and, even worse, those who don't but who know of him. The men, the ones who must fight today, the *toreros*, the picadors, the *banderilleros*, would smile and shake his hand, showing due respect and perhaps even speaking in admiring tones of having seen him fight in Bilbao or Pamplona or Madrid. But something of their balance would be compromised, and they'd not be able to help viewing him as an omen. It would show in their eyes, and the corners of their mouths, a certain loathing infused with dread.

The crowd sifts in, the early-comers in droves, quickly half-filling the arena, humming in expectation of a good day, if not a great one. The line-up boasts a few recognisable names, men of competent ability though with reputations on the wane. Around Enrique, the terraced seating fills up fast. The spectators within his vicinity are mainly groups of men, most already drunk or still drinking, passing bottles of wine back and forth between them and swearing at one another though gales of laughter. But there are women in attendance too, and children, families enjoying a day together, and when the fighting begins, when during the second *tercio*, one of the picador's horses is caught coming out of a slow turn and is lifted and gored by the bull, these women and children roar as loudly as the rest.

A splice of shadow crescents the north eastern edge of the ring and recedes to nothing throughout the afternoon, and in the glare of sunlight the dirt has the tanned colour of old hide. Above, the sky is empty cobalt, sealing in the day. The final *torero* fights a young, cumbrous bull, and puts on a good show, beguiling, full of grace, always in control, his steps choreographed for maximum effect, fooling most and at least sating the rest, but never daring to stray between the horns, never risking his seams. After several minutes of torment, eight or ten passes, each acknowledged by a rapturous, unison *olé*, he draws the animal in close, forces the head down to open the vertebrae and with the practised skill and ease of an executioner buries his sword to its hilt, severing the arteries to the heart or even penetrating the heart itself. There is an instant of danger when the bull, in reflex, lifts and tosses its head, and the *torero* abandons his sunken blade and has to contort his body to avoid the sweep of horn, but then the beast's forelegs give and it collapses bleeding into the dirt, half a tonne of black hide and steaming meat, and the fight is done.

Afterwards, the bars along the riverfront are loud and uncomfortable. Enrique elects the one most familiar to him, a long, narrow, two-tiered tavern owned by a man named Velasquez, who is well known as a passionate follower of the fights. But tonight, Velasquez is nowhere to be seen. At the counter, spectators jostle for position and relive in lurid shouts the action they have just witnessed. Everyone's shirt is soaked through from the heat of the day, but a rotating electric fan churns the air, giving the illusion of coolness, and jugs of cold, sweet sangria line the bar, available to all who can pay. Enrique holds back from the crush until he can catch the eye of a waiter who knows him, then, opting for the relative seclusion of an outside table, settles down with a bottle and a glass and drinks to quench his thirst, trying hard not to feel anything for what he has just seen.

Pilar is at home, in the apartment, either cooking or mending the hem on one of her dresses. She had asked where he was going, what he had planned for the afternoon. The sort of question couples ask of one another. Not to interrogate but out of curiosity, a casual enquiry. A butcher was giving away parcels of tripe at one of the market stalls this morning, the stuff he couldn't sell, and so she had a stew in mind for tonight. All wrong for summer, of course, but the kind of good, rich food that easily keeps, should Enrique find himself delayed. He'd shrugged. Nowhere special, he'd told her. No plans. A drink at one of the bars. Maybe a walk. He wouldn't be late.

A normal Sunday in every respect, except one: just as he was leaving, he kissed her. Looking back, she won't be able to help but read that as a false note, a flag she'd not so much missed as elected to overlook. An act entire compass points out of character, it seemed to surprise them both, the way he'd turned into her and tipped her back in his arms, just inside the open doorway. And how he'd bent to her. Her lips and the tip of her tongue hinted of salt, and she relaxed only gradually, finally smiling against his mouth.

'What was that?' she whispered, putting a hand to the wall for balance.

'Nothing,' he said, suddenly embarrassed. 'A thank you. For the tripe. I haven't eaten tripe in the longest time.' He left her standing in the doorway, but glanced back as he stepped into the stairwell and found her still watching him. Her hair was down and hung unkempt around her shoulders, and everything about her body seemed on the brink of surrender, yet she didn't move and didn't call out, not even with a goodbye.

He goes quickly through the bottle, and after filling the final glass has to reduce his intake to sips, his money spent. The wine, cheap and good, would under different circumstances be enough, but this evening it limits its effects to surfaces, and the part of his mind that he needs rubbed out continues to retain an unhelpful clarity. From his table he can see the road, four lanes of fast-flowing traffic. The stretch here is straight and, this early, in the thickening dusk, not well lit. Bulls don't move as fast as cars, but hit just as hard. There are nights still when he wakes screaming, with the feel of the horn inside him, not the agony of it but that sense of intrusion, and the helplessness. The heaviest part of any life is the part already lived, and the past is going nowhere. He should have died that day, in the ring. Having dedicated so many years to the movement of the fight, it would have been a dutiful end. But the bull that took so much from him stopped just short of enough. On the worst nights, Pilar presses his head to her breast and holds him, murmuring that he is fine, that they are fine, that it is just a dream, a nightmare. He lets her, grateful for the embrace, his body trembling, the skin of his face drenched in sweat, and sometimes she can coax the tears from him until he is almost overcome. She has told him often that they will go on together from this, whispering, promising, but these are just words to be spoken because of how they hold back the darkness. In such moments, pressed to her body and feeling the punch of her heart beating against his eye, he recognises love for what it is, a two-faced thing, good on one side but selfish on the other, and he wishes now that he'd been able to give her more of himself, that she could have had the chance to know the best of him. She'll have the kiss, though, even after all the questions have been asked, and while it might not amount to much, it is at least something, and he hopes that she'll remember it well.

The waiter brings a second bottle and draws the cork, 'No charge,' he says, without offering an explanation. He doesn't sit but pours himself half a glass, then stands there, gazing out at the road, at the passing traffic, though with a different kind of longing. The cheers and noise from inside break to the next level, an indication that one of the bullfighters has joined the party, falling into this one probably on the way to the next.

'My wife is pregnant,' the waiter adds, just speaking the words aloud, not expecting anything of them. Enrique considers him, but there is little to see: a strained face, mouth taut, brow gleaming from the heat and the hustle of work. Then, awakening again to the demands of the bar, he drains his glass and hurries back inside.

Enrique continues on down through the bottle. There is a point where he feels as if he has had enough, but he stays because a little wine remains. In no great hurry now, he can relax and almost enjoy the evening. He sits upright at his table, his legs crossed tightly, and the air of the night is hot and still, infused with the sweet tang of the street-side orange trees and the hanging baskets full of gazania in explosive bloom. Cars sweep by at speed, a suggestion of their colour left to linger in the growing dark, and he can hear music from the bar, piped flamenco bolero, the guitar beading gypsy notes even through the heckle and chatter of the crowd.

He empties the last of the bottle into his glass and drinks it down. It leaves his mouth dry, but spreads a certain warmth in his chest. Then he stands, squares his shoulders, settles within himself. He feels steady, and for the first time in a long time, good. Behind him, the music shifts tempo, stirring itself to something more, and, as if in answer, his own pulse quickens, as it always did when standing behind the gate with the ground alive beneath his feet, waiting his turn to see the bull. He is almost sure that someone is calling out to him from the crowd, and perhaps it is one of the *toreros*, the one responsible for the second bottle and who wishes to shake his hand or have him share a few stories, now that the omens can hold no further sway. The shape of his name rises once and then is lost among the voices, and he takes a deep breath and without a backwards glance begins to walk away. Ten paces puts him at the roadside. The voice calls out to him again, his name for certain now, and almost recognisable, stringing laughter across frets of anxiety, but the increased noise of the passing cars reduces its magnitude and makes it a thing easily enough ignored. Staring straight ahead, he starts across the road, his pace steady and unhurried, taking him where he needs to be.

A GAME OF CONFIDENCE

THE BACK ROOM was small and cramped. Cigarette smoke clung to the ceiling in a soft, churning haze, bars protected the small, fogged-glass window, and the plaster had split in a dozen different places along the walls, exposing clammy, mud-coloured patches of brickwork. The lights were kept low, except over the green-baize-covered table. There, light was everything.

Tonight, three of the four chairs were filled.

'I'll take three…'

Kimble, who owned the game, the joint and the whole damned setup, dealt the cards. 'Three from the top.'

The third player, Wilson, the player with the window seat, sighed thoughtfully. 'Two, I guess.'

'Two.' Kimble's dextrous fingers flicked the new cards into play. 'And Dealer helps himself to one.'

All three players settled to their dealt hands. The odd man out here was Jake Tanner. He was a stranger to this game, middle-aged going on for elderly, slim-set and with the blanched pallor and pinched expression of someone never far removed from pain. He wore a cheap, worn-out, pepper-coloured suit, but seemed to fit well at a card table, and moved as if he knew the form. He considered his cards, then bunched them together and tapped their edges into place on the table.

'So, she says to me… get this, she says, "You don't know how it feels." Ha! Can you believe that. And she just as close as you like to tears, too. I'll tell you. Kids these days, they think they invented love. The way they go on, it's like they've got the patent on it, or something. "What?" I said. "You think I don't know things? Ha! I know things, believe me. I know plenty." She had the lip going, too. You know, quivering. The whole works. "Is that what you think?" I ask her. "That I don't know? Well, let me tell you missy," I said. "You can take this one to the bank and lock it up safe and sound. I know plenty."

Kimble rolled his eyes. 'We playing, or what?'

'What?'

'I said, we're here to play cards, old man, not to listen to you run your mouth off.'

'Is there a problem here?' Jake said. He moved slowly, laying his cards face down flat before him on the table. His voice was measured, too, soft but assured, and his rheumy stare never flinched. 'Because I've got money on the table just the same as you, you know. That buys me some entitlements, I reckon.'

Kimble took a breath and held it, hoping that his anger would abate. Rage and poker did not make for a healthy mix. 'Look, old man. All I'm saying is, you feel like making a speech, go find yourself a town council. I like a little silence when I play cards. If you don't mind.'

'Hey, I don't mind at all, sport. Wouldn't want to knock you out of your stride.' Jake smiled. His teeth needed work, or at least a good cleaning. 'Tell you what. How about we split the difference, okay? You keep all the silence you can carry over at your side of the table. But I quite like a little chitchat when I play. If you don't mind, sport.'

His hand chased a wrinkle out of the emerald tablecloth, then settled over his chips. The plastic disks lifted with his fingers and tumbled back down as a stack, over and over, making the sound of crickets at play, or the sound of rattling bones.

'So, it's down to me, is it? Well now, let's see. Yeah, I think a little raise might be in order. Pot's looking a tad on the thin side.' He glanced at Wilson, then returned to meet Kimble's stare. Wilson was at the table merely to make up the numbers; Kimble was the real challenge here. 'A hundred,' he said, and pushed a small bunch of chips out into the middle of the table. Then he smiled again. 'Now, tell me, gentlemen. Isn't that a whole lot better?'

'A hundred? Damn.' Wilson sighed again. 'Too hot for me. I fold.'

Jake smiled, without even looking at his beaten opponent. 'As you please, young fellow,' he said, going for a kindly tone and almost making it. 'Won't be the same without you, but I do admire a man with sense enough to know when quits is quits.'

'You're full of shit, mister,' muttered Kimble, but his words only widened Jake's smile.

'Hey, you got me cold, Mr Kimble. You're absolutely right, I'm plugged to the gills with the stuff. In fact, that's the reason I chew so much gum. Bad breath has become the bane of my existence. I've damn near worn my teeth down to stubs from all the chewing I do. But tell me, am I to take it that you're not quite so ready to make for the door?

'You like to talk, all right. But a hundred is pretty tall words for such a little man. Yeah, I'm in. And I'm staying in. This pot's not for sale.'

'Are you sure about that, sport? Because there's plenty more where that came from.'

'I'm glad as hell to hear that,' said Kimble, showing his own teeth now. He glanced once more at his cards, then leaned out and pushed a loose rabble of chips into the centre of the table. 'Your hundred, and let's say a hundred more. Just to keep things interesting.'

Jake whistled softly. 'Nice, kid. Now you're talking my language. It took a while but I knew the words would come in the end. Knew it just by looking at you. Well now, let's see. Here's your hundred, and… what would you say is a fair price then? For the pot, I mean. Another hundred? Or how about we make this really interesting. Let's try five. Five hundred.'

'What are you, old man?' said Kimble. He looked stunned, but Jake knew that his heart would be heaving in his chest. 'Some kind of nutjob? You swapped three cards and don't even have a pair showing. You really think I'm going to let you come into my club and bully me out of my own game with a lousy five hundred? Your five, and another five.'

'That's the spirit, kid,' said Jake, and his calmness now was more irritating than any other stunt he'd pulled tonight. 'Don't ever let yourself be pushed around.' His right hand rattled another stack of chips. 'So, what was I saying before? Oh yeah, my kid, Molly. Great girl, but, well, you know. "Let me tell you something," I told her. "There's more to the world than you, you know. What? Seventeen years old and you think you're doing business that no one else ever done before? I adore the very bones of you, Molly," I said, "but it might surprise you to know that…"'

'It's up to you, old timer,' said Kimble. 'Put something on the table. Your money or your cards. You decide.'

Jake smiled again, then relaxed slowly into laughter. 'Get on with it, huh? Well, there is a ballgame on, and I have a little, well, shall we say professional interest in the Giants. So, why not? It's still early out on the west coast. I might even be able to catch the final inning. Tell you what, Mr Kimble. I guess I'll settle for calling your five. I mean, there's no point in being greedy, now, is there?'

Wilson's Honda Civic crawled through the late night streets. The city was quiet. Dead, almost. The adrenaline of an hour ago had flushed itself out, and all that remained now was a lead-boned exhaustion. Soft jazz dripped from the stereo speakers, soprano sax flurries that probably sounded aimless to the uninitiated, but which, to his ears, seemed perfect in every note, every pause, every wandering line.

In the passenger seat, Jake Tanner was watching the streets. Even in profile, his demeanour looked shot. Only the illusion of life clung to him; he seemed to awaken only when the heavy night shadows were set to crawling by the occasional invading wash of a streetlight. And yet, words flowed from him, with a detachment that was quite disturbing.

'They always give themselves away. No matter what they're holding, you can always count on some gesture that will tip their hand. It might be nothing more than a chewing of the lip or a flicker of eyelid, or maybe they'll touch their nose or their ear, tap their fingers on the table. There's always a giveaway. Even as a casual observer, you might spot one out of every twenty slips, maybe even one in ten if you happen to be particularly sharp. But the biggest difficulty you face is always trying to interpret what you've seen.' He raised a hand, pointed through the windscreen. 'Take a left at the next set of lights. You need to cross over onto tenth.' He paused and waited for Wilson to properly navigate the turn, and there was only jazz to keep the silence at bay. He shifted in the passenger seat, then settled again to considering the rundown store fronts and black alleyways. An earlier thundershower had fixed the road and the sidewalks with an eerie glint, a sheen that emphasised all that was squalid about this part of the city. 'Look,' he said, 'this is not magic, not really. It's simply a matter of learning all the signs and understanding what each one means. The real trick is in knowing what to look for, without being seen to look.'

Put that way, it sounded reassuring. But Wilson could not relax. There were just too many possible pitfalls, and a single mistake could prove fatal. He glanced at the older man. 'But how can you be so certain? What I mean is, do they all give themselves away? Supposing you were to come up against someone who knows the game, really knows it. What happens then?'

Jake shrugged. 'If they really know the game then they won't be sitting down across from me. Or not for long, anyway. Not for more than a couple of hands. They'll know better and so will I. I've been doing this for more years than I can count, and I don't make mistakes. Like Walter Brennan used to say in that old TV show: "No brag, just fact." If you aim to last in this business then you learn to make the read. Everything depends on that. Poker's not a game of chance, not if you play it right. And if you do happen to come up against a brick wall or a straight face and for whatever reason can't make the read, then you get the hell out. Fast. Otherwise it's suicide. Only a fool tries to beat the odds.'

'And this one? I mean, you are sure, aren't you? Because you have to be. There's too much on the line. You'd goddamn well better be.'

'I've seen him play, kid. No problem.'

The Honda switched empty lanes again and drifted a few blocks further. Wilson had his bearings now. 'So,' he said, at last, 'how much did you take him for?'

Jake cleared his throat, fixed his gaze hard on the street just ahead and to his right. A homeless man stood bent over, peeling sodden newspaper pages off the sidewalk. In a few seconds they came abreast of the man and then they were past. Jake glanced at the wing mirror, but with the glass set to the wrong angle he saw only darkness.

'How much, I said.' Wilson had a way of sounding angry without even raising his voice.

'I don't know,' said Jake, feigning disinterest. 'Altogether? Something like two grand and change.'

'What the hell's with you, Jake? You were supposed to hit him hard, clean him out. What good is two grand?'

'Do we have to listen to this shit?'

'What?'

'This,' Jake said, gesturing towards the radio with the toss of a hand. 'Fucking Jazz. You'd think a fancy stereo system like this could do better than some asthmatic horn. Or are you just getting a kick out of tormenting me?'

'You ignorant bastard.' The anger was still close to Wilson's surface, but was finally showing cracks. 'That's Coltrane. 'My Favourite Things'.'

'Figures,' Jake muttered. 'And if you're not happy with the way I work, you are more than welcome to just stop this car right now and go get yourself another chump to roll for you.' He let his voice purposely spin out of control, then paused and drew a gasping breath. 'I told you at the beginning, we do this my way. I know how to play. I was pulling games when you were still just a tickle in your daddy's loins.'

'Jake.'

'No. Fuck this. There's nothing that the likes of you can teach me about working a racket. We do this my way, or you can just forget it.'

Now Wilson was smiling. 'You done?' he asked, his tone soft with menace. 'Good. Now, sit back and shut up. It's my money you're splashing around when you take a seat at that table. And you owe me, don't forget that. The deal still stands. You do this one thing and we're quits. You'll never hear another word from me again. But you screw this up, or if I get even a hint of a notion that you're not giving this your A-game attention, I'll take you apart at the seams. I'm not a man who believes in idle treats. Look at me. I said, look at me, Jake. Because I don't want any misunderstandings. Try to screw me on this and I swear to God I'll take you out to the Bronx Zoo and personally feed you to the fucking lions.'

They drove on in silence for a while. Wilson knew this area now, and there was no further need to rely on the older man's directions. When the lights turned red they stopped, even though theirs was the only car on the street. Apart from the junkies, they seemed to have the city to themselves.

Jake nodded slightly along to the music, though he had to make up a beat. When the song, if that's what it was, had wound itself out, he cleared his throat again. 'The two grand was just to hurt him. There was no serious cash in the house tonight. If there was, he'd have been power playing, trying to frighten me off with big numbers. But when I show up tomorrow night he'll be fit to spit. And he'll be packing cash in boxes. Tonight was just to rough him up a bit, hurt his pride. I needed him to get his mind working up a little vengeance.'

Wilson glanced across, and considered the words.

'Is that how you always play?' he asked, at last. 'The way you did tonight? All that talking, I mean? You hardly shut up from the moment you sat down. Or is that just part of the gag, too?'

'Depends. Some guys like to talk a lot, thinking that it'll mask any flutters. It doesn't. Not when you know where to look. Others, like our man Kimble, prefer to concentrate. In such cases, talk rattles them hard. If I can get a player spitting bullets at me then I know he'll be an easy mark. The talk tonight kept him off balance and gave me a chance to see what kind of stuff he had.'

'You definitely riled him. But even so, he didn't exactly limp away.'

'If you're worried about the hands he won, then don't. If I had gone in and cleared the table you think I could have walked out so easily? And if I did make it out, you think they'd ever welcome me back? I dare to show my face again, odds are small on me waking up in an alley with my knees broken. That's if I ever woke up at all. The hands he won were nothing pots, more or less, but it gave the game a balanced look. When it comes to cards, doubt can be a dangerous thing. The way I played it tonight, there were no problems. He was pissed that he lost, but he didn't feel like he was being torn apart. It's good to stir him up a little bit, but survival is all about recognising where the limits lie. When a man is angry he'll have his mind tied up on unimportant details. But there's a difference between anger and blind rage. That's how you get yourself shot, and that, from my perspective, is something to be avoided at all costs.'

'So you're telling me everything went according to plan. Is that it?'

'My plan was to study his game, and to see what moves would produce mistakes. The talking angered him, and then the fact

127

that he was losing angered him even more, but I had to be careful. Like I said, there was no point in playing hard when the money wasn't in the house. The important thing is that I got what I wanted. Within two hands I'd sussed out his moves. Within ten, I knew him better than he probably even knows himself. Now I know what he does when the deal is friendly to him, a little thing with his eyes, a gesture so slight that ninety-nine people out of a hundred won't even bother to notice, and I know what he does when he's out to try a bluff. The bluff hands are always the best ones to throw. With them the pot will never get too far out of control, so they are usually okay to give up. And they taste as sweet as fine malt liquor. Nothing like scoring on a bluffed hand to kickstart the confidence. You really feel like you've put a big one over on your opponent, and that's when you're ready to be plucked.'

The Honda cut across another junction. Up ahead, a late bar was spilling yellow light out onto the street. Wilson pulled in to the curb and let the engine idle. Another tune had started up, but to Jake's ears it seemed like the same mess as before. Same heartbeat bass line, same squawking chaos of horn. Some of the bar room light fell across the car's hood, and they both stared at it for a moment, as if it meant something.

'All that talk, though,' said Wilson. 'Where did it all come from? I mean, have you really got a kid, or was that just another line?'

'It's a game of confidence. Don't you understand that yet? When I was a boy, I got my Monte routine down cold. All the other kids would be out playing stickball or trying to steal hubcaps. I'd sit on a stoop and practice. Before age got into my bones there was no one the length and breadth of the country could touch me when it came to switching shells. What you see

128

is what you get only if I want it to be that way. Tonight I talked a lot, and I've got a hundred thousand stories.'

'You mentioned a girl named Molly? Does she exist?'

Jake shrugged. 'Can't for the life of me see why you'd want to know, but yeah, as it happens, she does exist. Or did. She was the daughter of a woman I used to know, back in Detroit. A long time ago. A lifetime ago. And we lost touch, the way people do. But such a sweet girl. A real peach. She wasn't my kid, though for a while I was like a father to her.'

'But why mention her? I mean, what was the point?'

'It was random chat, that's all, though maybe a psychiatrist would argue differently. I could just as easily have talked about my Second Grade English teacher or an old sweetheart from my childhood. There's no strict pattern. Sometimes the people I'll mention are real and sometimes they're not. That mixture confuses everything. If nobody can tell the difference between the truth and a lie, then surely one is just as good as the other.' He considered the bar for a few seconds. There were dozens of bars like this one across the city, nondescript and desolate, that provided easy shelter for the deeply lost. And places like this made a city just as much as its skyscrapers and traffic jams. 'I like this bar,' he said, and a smile cracked his mouth. 'It's a good place to sit and blow the suds off a beer, maybe swap a little chat with the bartender. As long as I've been coming here, I've never seen the place busy. Maybe that's what I like best about it. That and the fact that they show ballgames.'

Wilson couldn't help but laugh. 'So that was true, then? That stuff about the Giants?'

'You've just proved my point,' said Jake. 'Muddy the waters enough and truth can be just as good as fiction.' He nodded to himself, then turned to open the car door.

Wilson lay a restraining hand on his shoulder. 'I'll take the winnings, Jake.'

'What?'

'The winnings. The two grand. The money you won with my money. Give it to me. I'll add it to the stake for tomorrow night.'

Jake cleared his throat. 'Look, Wilson, can't you give me a break, just for tonight? I thought that maybe… that is, I guess I was sort of hoping I could do a little bit of business. You know what I mean? And you don't have to worry. I won't be losing. It's just that I can't get into a decent game with anything less than two grand. If you could just let me hold on to it. Tomorrow night you'll get every cent back. Every single cent of it. In fact, how about this? You give me the two grand now and I guarantee you'll get three grand back. That's a promise. You have my word.'

The shadows of the night masked Wilson's face, but added a dreadful sense of menace to his voice. 'That's the trouble with you, Jake. I never know when you're telling me the truth or spinning me some fancy lie. No, on the whole I think it's best that I take the money. These are dangerous streets. It would take practically nothing for a man to get himself mugged in a neighbourhood like this, and I'd hate to see you put in the way of danger. So, come on. Hand it over.'

And just like that, the night had gone to pot. Knowing he was beaten, Jake slipped a hand inside his jacket and withdrew the wad of won cash. He held it in his fingers, feeling its small heft and thinking of all that it could have achieved. Then he dropped it into Wilson's waiting hand, opened the car door and stepped out into the street.

He walked around the back of the Honda, keeping his hands out of his pockets to spare himself from having to acknowledge their emptiness. He was almost to the bar room's front door when Wilson cranked the car window and called him back.

'Hey, Jake,' he said, 'wait a minute. Look, I'm not a hard case.' He fumbled at the roll of notes. 'I know how it is to be on the skids. So, here.'

Jake took the offered bill and glared at it, barely able to hold back his disgust. 'What the hell am I supposed to do with fifty bucks?'

'Have a drink on me,' said Wilson, through a terrible, mocking grin. 'And make sure you have yourself a good time.'

Back in the club, the following night, it was obvious to all at the table that playtime was over. Some three hours worth of cards had already been dealt, and there was no toying with stakes now. This was a no-limits game.

Kimble eased back in his chair, considered the pot and then his opponent.

'Another five hundred? Mister, you don't look to me like you can afford to lose that sort of cash.'

Jake smiled his most winning smile. With his face so etched in fatigue, the effect was pathetic. 'Oh, that's all right, sport,' he said, softly. 'I'm not planning on losing.'

'Well,' Kimble sighed. 'It makes no difference to me, you understand. But you're already in quite a hole tonight. Bet you wish you'd stayed in some bar now and watched the Giants game. By the way, that was pretty bad luck, them going down the pan like that last night.'

Across the table, Wilson lowered his own hand. 'What? The Giants lost?'

A rumble of laughter shook Kimble by the shoulders. 'Sure as hell did. A single run, bottom of the ninth. From what I caught on the news, it was a truly deplorable thing to see Bonds choking like that at such an important moment. Who could have seen that one coming? The Angels must have made some kind of a pact, or something. These days there are turncoats everywhere. No bet is safe any more.' He shook his head, ruefully. 'But that's the way it goes sometimes. I just thank my lucky stars that I didn't have currency riding on that one. A heart can take only so much squeezing.'

Jake met the knowing smile with a snide leer of his own. 'We playing, or what? Price is five to stay in. So how about you get to it, sport?'

This was too much for Kimble. He rolled back his head and laughed, loudly and with thorough delight. 'Oh, I'm in,' he said, when he could regain his composure once more. 'Don't worry about that.' His right hand worked the large pile of chips. 'Your five and... let's see now... I got, what, two, three, four... five grand. How about we see if the pot's for sale tonight. Five thousand in good, clean notes of the realm. I'd say that's a fair price.' He glanced at Wilson, drawing him into the equation. 'Wouldn't you agree, Wilson?'

Wilson stared at the centre of the table, his eyes showing all their bloodshot whites and his mouth hanging open in the agog manner of those shell-shocked by war. 'Five grand,' he whispered. 'Jesus. That puts me on my ass. I can't do it.' The legs of his chair scraped backwards along the floor. He rose and tossed his cards face down on to the table. 'I fold,' he whispered. Then, a little more loudly: 'I'm out.' He met Kimble's stare and then Jake's. If he was looking for reassurance then he found none. Finally he staggered away across the room in search of something strong to drink.

Kimble watched him go. 'Fold, huh? Well, that's a shame. A real damn shame. But, it's true what they say, the show must go on. That means it's down to you and me, old man. So, how about it? You fancy an early night? They're probably still swinging in Candlestick, what with the time difference and all. The odds on a repeat of last night must be pretty high. I'm sure if you left now you could probably make the last few pitches. See whether Bonds can redeem himself or take another bust. Two in a row might prove fatal.' He smiled and leaned in. 'Or have you come here to play some proper cards? It's going to cost you five big ones to see my hand. You got the stomach for that, old man?'

The world seemed to have lost its spin. Jake's cards were fanned open before him, shielded from all viewpoints but his own, and yet he hardly even registered their story. He looked beat. Tiredness clung to him like a coat. His mouth was dry and it hurt to swallow. Several seconds passed, then he squeezed the cards together and lay them face down on the baize.

'You know,' he said, and the softness of deep reflection made feathers of the words. 'I saw a terrible thing once. I mean, in my life I've seen a whole stack of bad stuff, just the same as you or Mister Wilson there, or anyone else, for that matter. But this was truly terrible, the sort of horror that gets you right in the gut and leaves its worms behind to eat away at you. It happened in Vietnam. Quang Tri province, October twelfth, nineteen sixty-seven. I was about a third of the way through my tour, and even then I'd taken to counting down the days, marking them off every night on a little sweat-stained pocket calendar that my sister had sent me. You learn to get along the only way you can, and that little calendar was my way of dealing with it all. I kept telling myself with every passing day that things couldn't possibly

133

get any worse, but then I'd wade into some putrid new degree of shit and I'd have to reassess the whole damn situation from scratch. There were days, nights too, when Vietnam was hell on earth. Wouldn't expect you boys to understand, of course, you being so young, but war leaves some bad marks on a man.'

'My father was over there,' muttered Kimble. 'Sixty-nine.'

'It's a funny thing, but there are times now when I remember that calendar better than my sister's face. She was a few years older than me, had married while I was still a kid and moved out to Abilene. Her husband was Texan, and a nice enough guy, but he could never swear further than the panhandle dirt and the smell of cow shit. Well, to each their own, I guess. TJ or JD, or some kind of name like that. Dead now. Both of them, actually. Him first, in a truck wreck, then my sister, with her heart. A few years back. I should remember his name, don't know why I can't. And I can't remember her face either, not clearly anyway, though that calendar might as well be right here in my hand, the numbered days in pale red print and each done day marked off with a little black X.'

'Your way of getting through.'

'That's right. That's exactly right. But time is different in the jungle. It seems to mean less, somehow. Because the air is so still, I think, and so heavy. And it messes with you. We'd been on the trail three, maybe four hours that particular morning. There'd been some shots fired early in the week, and then nothing for a couple of days, and we just kept moving, like the map said, and it was so hot that the soles of my feet were breaking up, the flesh practically boiling in my boots. Then, on towards noon, we came across the temple. The trees thinned to a small clearing and there it was, maybe a thousand years old, ancient. The charts didn't have it, no one did.'

Across the room, Wilson slammed down his empty shot glass on the counter of the small bar. 'Jesus, old man,' he snarled. 'Can't you just give it up? No more damn stories. You talk way the hell too much, you know that? We've heard enough from you to last us a hundred fucking lifetimes.'

Kimble didn't look up from his cards.

'Take it easy,' he said, 'I want to hear this one.'

'Feel free to take a walk if you don't want to listen, sport,' said Jake. 'You folded your hand, didn't you? I reckon that about concludes your business here for tonight. But if you decide to stay, I would appreciate it if you'd stop interrupting.' He took a long, slow breath, and braced himself against some sort of reprisal, but a few seconds passed and then he heard the sound of a bottle's neck chiming once more against the rim of a glass. He cleared his throat, and continued.

'Finding that temple spooked us all pretty bad. It stood there in the clearing, you know, and after the darkness of the jungle the glare of sunlight had fire enough to put out eyes. But worst of all was the silence. Everything was perfectly still, as if all time had stopped around us. I know how that sounds, sitting here, but that's how it felt. I'd have taken a gunfight over that feeling, I swear to God almighty. Any of us would have. There was just something wrong about the place. We stood there, bunched together in a single pack, until the Lieutenant broke us up and had us fan out in threes and fours to check for traps or signs of a possible ambush. All we found at first were bones. Bones and skulls bleached white and picked completely clean. We tried to convince ourselves that they were the remains of monkeys, and when that didn't work, that we were looking at bodies of people wiped out in a napalm blast. Napalm cooks you right down, so that seemed plausible until someone pointed out that the trees

135

showed no trace of scorching. Then, twenty minutes or so later, we found two monks. They were way in at the back of the temple, eating lunch.'

Kimble looked up, comprehension breaking like weather across his face. 'What? You don't mean... Oh, Christ.'

'They probably had no other choice. When the food runs out it's survival of the fittest, isn't it? I suppose when put to the test, a man will do whatever it takes to survive. When we found them they were down to two. It was difficult to tell how many there may originally have been but it was a pretty big temple. They didn't speak, not a single word, just looked at us and then went on with their business.'

'What happened?'

Jake's mouth trembled. Finally, he cleared his throat. 'Five grand, huh? Well, I've come this far. I guess I'll see your five, and I'll raise you... let's see now. How does ten sound to you?'

'Ten grand?' Kimble couldn't keep the surprise out of his voice and didn't even bother to try.

'That's right. I fell pretty hard last night on the Giants and I've got to do something to balance the books.' He pushed his remaining chips out into the centre of the table. 'Ten thousand. Your move, sport. Ten to stay in, otherwise I'll be saying goodnight to you.'

A smile broke slowly across Kimble's face. 'You're bluffing.' He stared hard at Jake, looking for clues. 'You are. You're bluffing.'

Jake shrugged. 'Ten to you, sport. Otherwise you'll never know.'

'I know,' said Kimble. 'You're bluffing. You've got this thing you do. I've been watching you. A little pinching of your nose. You think I didn't see, but I did. Maybe you don't even realise you're doing it. Ten, huh? Well, let's see. I've got maybe three in cash. But I'm good for the rest. You can't doubt that, surely.'

'I don't doubt it at all,' Jake said. 'But I have a rule. I only play for what's on the table. It's been my experience that promises, even those made with the very best of intentions, tend to disappear like smoke on a breeze once all the shooting's done.' He rubbed his chin. Stubble whispered against his fingers. 'Still, I'm nothing if not reasonable. Maybe we can come to some arrangement. Have you got anything else to bet?'

Kimble tried to think but his mind felt sluggish, confused. He shifted in his chair, and his gaze pulled from the tight fan of his cards to the set of keys that lay on the baize beside his resting elbow. A smile pulled at the corners of his mouth.

'All right. My car. It's out front. A Mercedes, two years old. Sports model.' He held up the keys and tossed them forward into the pile of chips. 'There's not even forty thousand on the clock. It's worth fifteen grand, maybe even more. You'll be getting the deal of a lifetime, or at least you will if what you're holding happens to be any good.'

Jake considered the matter. 'You know, I only have your word on the value. But, as a gesture, I'll let the car cover the bet. In addition to the three grand you mentioned.'

Kimble began to laugh, then seemed to think better of it. 'You've got to be yanking my chain.'

'Hey, I'm trying to do you a favour. It's entirely up to you. If you can't put the cash on the table then that's your problem. Or maybe you're not so confident now in your cards. Do you still think I'm trying on a bluff, that I'm sitting down here with a handful of nothing? Maybe you're having doubts about what you saw, or what you thought you saw. Maybe you're beginning to wonder now if I might have planted the gesture in order to make you think I was bluffing.' He shrugged. 'But like I said, sport. It's entirely up to you. There's what? Forty grand in this pot? I could walk away happily with that much right now. But I'm doing you a favour, giving you a chance. You can either take it or leave it.'

Kimble thought it over. 'Okay,' he said, softly. 'I call.'

'Money first, if you don't mind. On the table. Then you can call.'

Kimble rose, crossed the room and worked open a small wall safe. The cash was a single wad of hundreds, neatly bound. 'That good enough?' he asked. 'Or do you want to count it, too?'

Jake shook his head. 'That's okay, I trust you.'

'So?' Kimble drew a deep breath and let it out in an unsteady flush. 'What have you got?'

Jake upturned his cards and spread them out with a practiced flash of his hand. 'Full house. Aces and Tens.'

The air went out of Kimble. He shrunk visibly, wilted down into a slouch in his chair. 'I honest to God thought you were bluffing.'

Jake nodded, with some sympathy. 'I know you did. What are you holding?'

'Not enough. Low straight.' He pushed back his chair but didn't get up, perhaps didn't quite trust himself to do so without staggering. 'Well played, old man.'

'Thanks,' said Jake. He thought of offering a few words of consolation, but didn't, because there was nothing to say that would make things any better. Then, as he reached out to gather his winnings, a tall, thin, black man appeared in the doorway. For an instant, he felt a stirring of fear, but Kimble must have seen it because he raised an assuring hand.

'This is Leonard. Hey, Lennie, cash these chips for Mister Tanner, will you?'

Leonard stared a moment at the pile of chips, then shrugged. 'Sure thing, Mister Kimble.' He gathered up the chips, slipped from the room and returned barely a minute later with a small black leather satchel full of money. 'It's all there,' he said, though nobody had posed the question. 'Forty-two thousand.' He put the satchel down on the table and left.

'Well,' said Jake, picking up the car keys and rattling them before slipping them into his jacket pocket. 'I guess I'll be heading on home. See how the Giants fared. I still have them down for the pennant this year, even after last night. Everyone makes mistakes once in a while, don't they? What matters is how well you bounce back, and how quickly. So try not to beat yourself up too badly over this, sport. You played a pretty good game tonight. It's just that I've been playing cards a long, long time.'

He hesitated a moment longer, then nodded to himself and moved towards the door. He was just about to open it when Kimble stopped him.

'One thing before you go. I need to know what happened.'

Jake turned. The whisper of fear was back. 'What happened with what?'

'The story. What happened to the monks?'

'Oh, the monks. We shot them. Well, can't have that sort of thing, can we? It's like our Lieutenant said. They were vultures, feeding on the weak. They deserved to die, he said. In truth, I felt bad about doing it, still do as a matter of fact, but I think maybe they were better off dead. I mean, feeding off the bones of their companions is no way to live. A man ought to be able to turn his back without feeling the blade of a knife between his shoulders. Especially where his so-called friends are concerned. I guess that when trust goes, well, everything else follows pretty quickly.' He smiled then, and cast an obvious and knowing glance at Wilson, one that would have been impossible for Kimble to miss. 'If you're not sure what I mean, Mr Kimble, you might consider asking your friend Wilson here. I'm quite sure he can explain.'

Then, without another word, he opened the door and stepped out onto the landing. He was shaking inside, but with exhilaration now as well as fear. He started down the stairs one slow step at a time, holding on to the handrail for balance. The landing below was badly lit, and the open door gave on to a very dark street. In the background, he could hear the rumble of voices, and then raised voices. Outside, the chill of the night closed around him. He found the Mercedes alone at the kerb side, got in and drove away quickly, before he was forced to hear anything worse.

KEEP WELL TO SEAWARD

THAT SPRING, the Chinese fleet were gathered in the Taiwan Strait, and war felt very close.

The room Mei and I shared every afternoon for fifteen weeks was not much, the sort of place that takes on a sense of romance only later, in the mind, in the writing, and largely because of how it held the light, the dusty electric yellow of a small watt bulb necessary even at the height of day. It helps now to focus on scattered details, the broken picture that suggests a better whole, a reality with the roaches edited out. What we really had were shabby walls, a small, caged window, and at the far end a little kitchenette with a hotplate, two-shelf refrigerator, and a cupboard for my bowls and pots. The view was concrete, obliterating all but the most determined natural light, and whenever anyone flushed the toilet or ran the shower in the bathroom down the hall, the pipes in the walls made the mournful sound of an old sailing ship surrendering to a fate of windless drifting.

But rent was low, which helped, and I had a small but sufficient income from the three or four pieces a month, mainly political anecdotes and fish-out-of-water travelogues, that I'd jot off and fax home to the *Examiner*, the newspaper to which I'd been contributing on a casual basis since my early twenties. There was a little in the way of savings too, a modest nest-egg replenished quarterly with a dribble of royalties from a short story collection I'd had published the previous summer. The book picked up a minor prize and was translated into four languages, most successfully, for reasons that defied explanation, into Dutch. Now I was working on a novel that, eighty or a hundred pages in, had already begun to stagnate. In hindsight, I recognize the problem as fear, a towering insecurity fed by the nagging sense that I'd gotten away with too much and would next time be found out, that I'd only ever been lucky rather than good. I knew half the story like I knew the blood in my own body, but what lived in my head only made it onto the page in flashes, and I kept returning to the beginning and starting over, changing tense or point of view, trying to unlock the rest.

Because I liked to work mostly by night, and because Mei had other commitments that needed meeting at home, we tended to pass the long, sweltering afternoons lying together in my unmade bed, our bodies slick with the exertion of lazy hours spent making love, talking just for the sound and soothing of the words.

'What about our future?' she'd ask, while I held her in my arms, and because I didn't want to hurt her or make her cry I'd smile at the stained ceiling and assure her that I could see only beautiful things ahead for us, that I could see us old and happy together, sitting holding hands in a garden in the sun, sipping glasses of tea and waiting, maybe wishing, for the phone to ring, for our grandchildren to call. She'd smile, longing to believe, but tears would brim and blacken her eyes to glass, and even as she pressed her face into my neck I knew she understood. Yet she continued to ask, unable to help herself. Not every day, but often. And to keep from having to see so clearly, I'd bring her mouth to mine and slip into a calming dark, promising over and back the only real truth in my possession, the words *wo ai ni*, I love you, whispered against her lips and tongue first in her language and then my own, and meant utterly in both.

But to me, then, there was no future. Not much past, either. At twenty-seven, I had yet to earn one. I had a few scars, but none that showed, and none I understood well enough to write about. At that age, I thought only of the present, and Taipei's foreignness made everything a wonder. The air was different there, the way it tasted, the way it felt on my skin, the way its heft slowed me down and forced me to look around, to see and hear and notice the city's tumult and its tales. Against all that, pasts and futures felt as indistinct as shadows on the hottest, cleanest noon, and with the Chinese cruisers amassing in the northern waters, readying their missiles to test and antagonize, the notion of hoping for anything more felt almost blasphemous.

I remember that it took weeks for her to smile.

She worked as a waitress in a small six-table restaurant, close to the National Taiwan University, a simple little walk-in, with bare gray walls and never enough light, but cool and pleasant during the early hours of day. I found it by accident my second or third week in the city while out looking for a bookstore that I'd seen recommended in the *Lonely Planet*, and quickly made it my regular breakfast stop. Always sitting at the same table beside the narrow floor-to-ceiling window that gave out onto the bustling thoroughfare of Roosevelt, a rectangular table big enough for four, big enough for my newspaper and notebooks. I kept coming back because the place offered cheap and decent coffee, and because of her. She'd take my order in near silence, her dark eyes lowered, then return to her duties, but I liked to watch how she moved between tables, the fluid way she filled space. Medium height and so slightly built, her body delicate as eggshell in a white, short-sleeved blouse and simple blue wool skirt that fell to just below the knee.

From the first minute of the first day, I ached to get inside her life and discover who she was, what fuelled her serenity and what could break it, where she went after finishing her shift and where she came from to get here. I'd sit, sipping coffee and nibbling at a few sentences that usually went nowhere, but could occasionally be coaxed into fitting together just right, and I'd snatch glances at her as she passed, or cleared and wiped down a table, or stood a moment at the window to take a breath and consider the flow of the world outside.

Eventually, after maybe a week, she began to acknowledge me with a nod, and soon after that she'd call my order back to the kitchen as soon as she saw me in the doorway. I was easy because I always ordered the same thing: the first of three cups of coffee and two thick slices of lightly toasted bread smeared in peanut butter. As we grew more familiar with one another, and as I grew more comfortable, I'd speak to her, just a few words when she brought my coffee, or my refills. Keeping the subjects light, drawing her attention to something I'd seen in that morning's paper, or complaining about the heat, which even at that time of year was clear notches above anything I'd ever known in Ireland. My Chinese was bad, but getting slowly better, and she'd look out onto the street as I spoke, her expression all angles and straight edges, not appearing even to listen, but when my words ran out she'd answer in a soft English, imperfect only around its edges and thrilling in its sound and texture, that this was nothing, that I should just wait for the heat of June and July when the air really burned. And then, one morning, when I was the only customer in the place, she put down her coffee pot and picked up one of my notebooks, leafed through the pages and randomly selected a few lines to read. And she smiled. 'So this is what you come here to do,' she said, and I wondered but did not ask if she'd happened across some bad description of a place she might know well, or worse still, the beginning or climax of some sex scene. I should have been embarrassed, but I didn't ask because I didn't care. The smile was enough.

And that was the beginning. From then on, when she'd bring my refills and if there were no other customers waiting to be served, she'd sit a while, lowering herself down onto the chair next to mine or across the table from me. I could sense her uncertainty, the feeling that she was in some way compromising herself or committing before she was quite ready to something she did not yet properly understand. She looked set to bolt, but never did, and during that first hesitant conversation she asked me in a voice as soft as smoke what I was writing about and why I bothered to write at all. Really, for the first time, gazing at me, into me, keeping me entranced with her eyes the big wide colour of molasses and watching the shift of my mouth with serious fascination, her brow knitting slightly, reefing the bone-pale smoothness of her skin, in an effort to comprehend, when I finally answered or tried to answer. I talked a little about my novel, and told her that writing was how I made a living, though a poor enough one, and was the only thing I really knew how to do, the only way I had of making sense of my thoughts. She listened, nodding slightly along with whatever rhythm she caught, and the words seemed to worry her. But then she met my eyes and smiled again, a sweet, delicate incision that hinted at gently prominent front teeth, and I felt something move inside me. And when, finally, she stood, refilled my cup and then carried the coffee pot back down the aisle and behind the counter, I knew that I'd just lived a moment never to be forgotten, one of those that inspires songs, or bigger things.

145

Our initial conversations had the purpose of buying us breathing space, and gave her natural defences a chance to soften. I'd sit back and let her lead, happy just to be close to her and be able to luxuriate in the high, airy sound of her voice. Some mornings she'd want to talk about Ireland, which she had heard of but only as a place-name and a stereotype, and I'd describe for her our scenery, music and poetry and, always, our weather.

'It rains here too,' she said, smiling again, 'and when the typhoons come it rains hard. But I think it is not the same.' I assured her with a laugh that it was not, and tried not to stare at her hand, which lay flat and relaxed on the table barely four inches from my own, her narrow fingers splayed, the skin thin enough to show spindles of bone and turquoise ribbons of vein, her neatly trimmed nails clean as pearls. The thinness of her wrist and naked forearm made me want to hold her and never let go, and I had not yet had enough experience with women to know that this was something she wanted, too.

When you fall in love for the first time, something disconnects inside you, causing your consciousness to shift. You take to living almost purely through your senses and become far more aware of your physicality. And you feel at once free and imprisoned. I have no recollection of asking her out, but I remember very well the walks we took around the city, with her as my guide and keeping so close that our bodies already felt joined. And I remember the bustling streets, the night markets, the wide open plaza and low maze gardens of Chiang Kai-shek Memorial Hall, watching the soldiers take down and fold away the flag. We visited the Longshan Temple more than once because although Mei kept no orthodox religion she felt comforted by the thought of prayer. I understood. There was something ancient and serene about the place, with its overload of light, brass and incense, the scowling dragon shapes of its carved, painted timbers, the people lining up and bowing before fat gilt statues. I stood in line, too, in silence putting heavenward the deepest question of my heart, whether or not any of this had a chance of being forever, and clutching in my cupped hands the three red crescent blocks known as *zhi jiao*, which the Taiwanese faithful used for communicating with their gods. When it was my turn, I tossed them, as instructed, onto the floor, enjoying the clatter they made against one another and the stone, but not the anxiety they induced, and tried desperately to interpret their fall as anything other than a negative.

'You can write about this,' Mei said, gesturing to the surroundings. And I smiled, knowing already that I would. Someday, when the time was right, and when I'd finished living the story.

Initially, because I lacked experience, I held back from speaking of my true feelings, afraid that I'd frighten her and ruin the friendship we'd built. But the words swelled inside me. And then, one evening, strolling with her through the university grounds, I couldn't wait any longer. The sun had just gone down, and the heavy mid-November air held and magnified the relentless percussive rattle of the tree frogs. There were hundreds of kids around, sweeping by on large-wheeled bicycles, slouching on benches or on steps, eating food from 7-Eleven, groups of laughing girls made pretty by their age, and boys leaning against walls or trees and trying hard to look at ease, waiting for a word of encouragement to draw them from the cover.

'With me?' she asked, looking up into my eyes as we passed a lamppost and stepped into its white pond of light. I stopped and she did, too. Her expression was so serious. I took her hands and said of course, with her.

We kissed then. She was shy at first, conscious I think of being seen, but I didn't care. And after a moment something moved for her and her mouth hardened against mine until there was no more air to breathe except hers. She tasted of the mango slices we'd just eaten, a thrilling accident that would never happen in quite the same way again, and even after all these years it is one of the details I hold most dearly about her and about our time together and might be part, if not all, of the reason why every kiss I've ever known since feels just a little lacking.

Without discussing the matter, we returned to my apartment. She drew the curtains and immediately began to undress. She had no other appetite. I sat on a corner of the bed, slowly unbuttoned my shirt, and watched her. She hardly acknowledged me. She slipped off her blouse, stepped out of her skirt and draped them neatly across the back of the room's only chair. Then she unclasped her bra, turned away and began to pour water from the large porcelain jug into the bowl I used for shaving and washing my face. She leaned in over the bowl and sluiced handfuls of water between her legs.

'You must wash, too,' she said, without turning. 'Because of bacteria. I don't want to get sick.'

The water was tepid from lying for so long in the sun. I took the towel that she'd been using and dried myself, then followed her to the bed. It was my first time in a long time, and when I began to hurry she put her hands on my hips and slowed me down. Her sparse thatch of pubic hair, fine as cobweb, gleamed darkly from her wash, and I kissed her neck, tasting the salt of the day on her skin, until the small puce stone of her nipple stiffened against my palm, and when I began to flick and encircle it with my tongue, she arched her body, grabbed at my hair and cried out a deep, heavy sigh. Who knows where that time went, or what we thought about. I climbed on her and she opened up to me, and my heart beat so fast and hard I could feel it in my eyes.

Afterwards she lay for a long time with her head against my chest and her fingertips teasing half a dozen inches of the skin inside my thigh. Warm tears, that I thought were beads of sweat until I felt the tremor in her breathing, caught the channels of my body and trickled down between my ribs. But when I enquired what was wrong she whispered that I please not ask, and then at last she got up, washed herself once more from the bowl and began to dress. Standing directly beneath the electric light, her skin was the pale yellow of buttermilk, and her tossed hair fell nearly to her waist, spilling in black tendrils over her breasts and narrow shoulders. With all her passion spent, she looked sad and frail. I lay on the bed and watched her, taking in the jut of her hips, the knuckles of spine and risen poke of her shoulder blades when she bent to step into her panties, her arms and legs thin as reeds. And in those few seconds I saw her as the old woman she'd one day be. I cleared my throat and asked if it was something I did, or did wrong, but she shook her head and said no, it was not me. When she'd finished dressing she came back and perched on the edge of the bed. I sat up and drew her into an embrace, and we remained like that until it was time for her to go.

Our routine shaped itself along clear lines. By eight o'clock or so, she'd have left to return home, and I'd settle down at the small window table and try to write. Four or five hours went on the novel, time spent picking through the pieces, seeking a shape that would hold and support the narrative, mainly trying to figure out what it was that I needed to say. Stopping often, to make tea or eat a bowl of cold rice, pacing to the window and back, the door and back, to sit on the edge of the bed. On good nights, finishing a page or even half a page, but moving slowly ever onward. And beyond midnight, if I still had something left, I'd put in an hour on the next *Examiner* piece, chipping away at maybe a third of my twelve-hundred word target, taking a first pass at some culture-clash article on what could be expected from the Year of the Rat, or the difficulties of the cuisine, or the Asian approach to religion or the supernatural. Sleep, when it finally came, was rarely more than an interruption. My mind was too lit, and just a few hours sufficed. Before dawn had even broken I'd be up again, scribbling notes in the margins of last night's pages, scratching out words, sentences, whole paragraphs.

Aware that the day would be a long one, I tried to time my arrival at the restaurant for nine or a little after, catching the lull following the first breakfast rush. If she was not too busy, we'd get to chat a while, and I'd read things to her from the newspaper, sometimes in my struggling Chinese, more often from the English-language papers that made it in a day late from Hong Kong. Nearly two weeks into February, a bomb had gone off in London's Canary Wharf, causing widespread destruction. Casualty figures stood at two dead and some forty injured. The IRA were claiming responsibility, bringing an official end to the ceasefire, which had held, in admittedly tenuous fashion, for nearly eighteen months. Conservative estimates put the damage to infrastructure at somewhere in the region of a hundred million pounds, and many political commentators were speculating that this escalation in paramilitary activity would prove the death knell for the Northern Irish peace process. The pictures in the paper only hinted at the true carnage, and I stared at them and read the reports, searching for something that would let me connect with what had happened. I'd been to London and could see the streets and buildings in my mind. But the story felt unreal to me. When Mei, standing beside my table with the coffee pot, asked me the reason for the bomb, there was nothing to do but shrug. I could have tried explaining the history involved, and maybe she'd have understood, but it wouldn't really answer the question she'd asked. A shrug, empty as it was, seemed the better response. And out in the Strait, the standoff continued, with all negotiations frozen to stalemate by the Kuomintang party's steadfast 'One China, One Taiwan' rhetoric. In what seemed a clear gesture of intimidation, another round of missile testing had been announced by the PRC, scheduled for mid March, just days before Taiwan's first ever democratic Presidential Election. This time, the strike zones were to be set within thirty miles of the island's busy northern and southern ports, far closer than all previous launches. Trade was already suffering, crisis point had come into view for the plummeting Taiwan Dollar, and the talk was that the United States, with carrier fleets home-ported in nearby Japan, would be faced with no alternative but to intervene.

After leaving the restaurant, I'd just walk, heedless as to my direction. This was the emptiest part of my day, the hours before I got to see her again. But I liked losing myself on the increasingly busy streets, trying to absorb the atmosphere, the colour and blaze of the traffic and the packed footpaths, keeping wherever possible to the shade. Down side streets and alleyways, men and women, teak-skinned from the sun, made slow rituals of stocking and restocking fruit stalls or laying out trays of dumplings and pork buns, and war felt not only far away but fantastic. I'd usually stop to buy something, really just so that I could chat a while, and if their questions were always the same then so were mine, and they smiled at my stumbling words and answered, in the main, with nods and waving hands.

A bookstore recommended by the guidebook stood across the street from the university, filling an entire ground floor and basement of a building within hard throwing distance of the main campus gate, and was a good place to idle away an air-conditioned hour. Day after day, from around lunchtime, I could be found there, perusing the same ten shelves of English-language books carried to serve the needs of students. I'd already read probably a quarter of the stock and dismissed a further quarter or more again as stuff that held no interest for me, but there was almost always something on hand to satisfy my mood and my compulsive need: a Dos Passos, a Simenon, a Henry Green, a George V. Higgins. Then I'd go and wander the university campus, because it was a large, wide space with a lot of old trees and the air felt clean there, and I'd find a place to sit, drink my juice, read a little, watch the girls in their shorts and flimsy tops, and try not to think about what troubles might be waiting in the waters up ahead. All of that lay beyond my control, and for those days and weeks I was alive to bigger things.

The time apart from Mei left me hollow, as if someone had taken a knife to who I was and cleaved away an essential part. I'd sit on one of the benches around the campus, and I'd read and watch the girls go by, but all of that was really just waiting, killing the hours until three or four o'clock when I could stroll back to the apartment, tidy the place a little and boil water for tea, knowing that she'd soon come. Early on, I'd asked if we could meet at the restaurant, or even outside, if it in some way embarrassed her to be seen with me by people she knew. But she shook her head. There were other things to do, she said, before she could be free for me. Her mother was elderly and in poor health, and she had a duty. And I could accept that easily enough because by five o'clock she was always at my door, slightly out of breath from the stairs, the skin of her neck a touch damp from the hot bus ride when I took her into my arms and nibbled the line of her jaw in that way she liked. Sometimes we drank tea, or ate simple noodles and some blanched vegetables. Often, though, we couldn't wait for food.

Afterwards, she'd close her eyes and sigh in a way that brought every feature of her face and frame to a complete if temporary ease, and I'd lie beside her, thinking about what it meant, and how lucky I was, to be this near to someone, to be this involved. I had fallen in love, for the first time in my life, and never wanted the feeling to end. Talk passed like breeze between us. She usually led, slipping back and forth between her own past and questions about mine. Her childhood; her father, who had died some years earlier from a rare form of blood cancer; the eighteen months she'd had at university, studying Literature and English. Real literature, she called it, lying on her back with the fingers of both hands splayed slack across her stomach, teasing me and trying not to smile, as another sweaty afternoon turned yellow and then to rust. 'Hemingway, Golding, Graham Greene. Not the stuff you write.' She'd been slowly reading my collection, missing most of what I'd meant to say, but sometimes shaping a sentence aloud to embarrass me and make me happy. And then, invariably, a little at a time, she'd bring out the questions about Ireland. What I loved about the place and the things I hated, and what it was like to live there, how it had been for me as a boy. Whether or not I thought she'd fit in, and whether or not Ireland and my family would like her in return. 'Tell me,' she'd say, opening her eyes just for a second to the ceiling and then easing them shut again. Raised up on one elbow, I'd cup her small left breast for the slow, easy bang of her heart, and run my hand the length and back of her body in order to feel that smooth, still ocean of skin and the turbulence of the life it concealed. And I'd talk, giving her the answers she wanted to hear. A good place to live, I said. Wild as a bear sometimes, especially on the coast, but calming too, once you escaped the cities. Lovely then, but always with a certain sadness holding to it. She knew a little of the music, not the lyrics but the forlorn airs. A tune that, when she tried to hum the melody, sounded vaguely like 'Carrickfergus', but also others, like 'Danny Boy', slow tunes that she'd heard played on pipes and whistles and whose names she'd either forgotten or had never caught. And she'd seen the film, *Ryan's Daughter*, with Robert Mitchum and Sarah Miles, and wondered if the villages still looked like that, with mud streets, and if the beaches were really so beautiful. In school, she'd seen pictures, in books. Of mist-covered mountains, sheep in fields. Withered old men with sunken mouths and flinty stares, dressed in wool coats and flat caps, standing in the rain. Little whitewashed houses with straw roofs, and doors painted in hard-wearing scarlet or the pleasing emerald shade of their grassy surround.

'We can go together. And in the country I want to buy a little house.'

'But won't you miss Taiwan?'

She'd sigh, and stiffen her mouth. 'There is nothing I will miss.'

'You'll miss the sunshine, I think. Try spending the early part of the year in west Cork or Kerry. The wind comes hard enough to lift you out of your shoes, and the rain is so relentless that it causes you to forget what a clear day even looks like.'

'I don't care. I can stay inside, in bed with you. We can light a fire to keep warm.'

She was like nobody else I had ever met. Gentle, soft, with a smile so beautiful it made my stomach churn, but vulnerable too, decked in a kind of perpetual and impenetrable melancholy. Even in laughter, I could feel the shiver of her wounds. And in that room, in that bed, staring wildly into my stare, wanting nothing to be missed, and then clenching her eyes shut so she could feel all the things that went unseen, she clung to me and used my body as a shield against the world, sometimes biting my shoulder hard enough to mark the skin, sometimes whispering pleas that I never let her go.

And then, a week into March, a day like all the others except for the storm raging over Taipei, she arrived at my door, wet through from the downpour. I didn't care, I took her in my arms. She had become like oxygen to me. As usual, I fumbled with the buttons of her blouse, already wanting nothing between us. She sighed at the feel of my mouth against her jaw, raised and stiffened her chin to expose her throat. I closed my eyes and could hear the water running from her, and the sound of her breathing, and the incessant drive of the rain scratching at the glass. Thunder cracked in the distance, faded to a prolonged grumble, and I slipped the blouse from her shoulders and began to kiss the part of her chest that lay exposed above the drenched white cotton bindings of her bra. My hands were everywhere, clutching, supporting, famished for her skin.

'Stop,' she whispered, but I didn't, not until she asked again, tearfully, and with force.

For a second or two she stood there, then turned away and moved towards the window. I was confused. I watched her back.

The ribbon that held up her hair had slipped with the rain and come partially undone, and strands like spider's legs kicked and fluttered the air.

'Mei? What's wrong?'

She shook her head. 'I can't. I am sorry.'

I didn't know what she was talking about, and said as much. I lowered myself onto the chair. She glanced at me and then returned her gaze to the day beyond the window, her thin arms folded tightly beneath her breasts. Lightning flashed, far off yet, but so instantaneously brilliant that its fading seemed to deepen the sense of dusk. I wanted to tell her to move back, for her own safety and because somebody was sure to see her, but in the rain-streaked glass her fused reflection fixed on me and kept me silent.

'What is it? Are you pregnant?'

'What? No.'

'Well, what then?'

'I told you a lie. About my mother.' Again, for just a second, she glanced at me. 'About everything.'

'What lie?'

She'd already slipped out of her shoes and stood barefoot and bare-calved in just her skirt and bra, a patch of floor shining beneath her. The slender inch-long earrings that I'd bought for her from one of the market stalls fish-hooked her lobes, silver filaments staggered with specks of green and yellow glass, meant I think to represent flowers, since everything bloomed here.

'I am married. I have a husband. My mother lives in Tainan, not with me.'

Her reflection watched me from the glass, the face a runneled mask. When I could no longer bear the scrutiny I stood, stooped to pick up her blouse from where it lay sodden and discarded on the floor, and held it in my fists.

'What are you talking about?' I said. Not angry yet, only confused. 'How can you be married? You spend every day with me. We make love. We make plans, for Christ's sake. Is this a joke?'

She had begun, silently, to cry. 'I love you,' she said, but it was the tears, far more than the words, that made me understand.

When she was seventeen, close to finishing school, she met a man. Wang Chenglei. He was considerably older, in his early forties, a friend of her best friend's father. But kind. They met on a couple of occasions at her friend's house, sat across the table from one another to eat shrimp and noodles. He was short in stature, with a thickset build softening to fat by a combination of settling middle-age and long days spent slouched behind a desk. His skin was poor, too, the shade and grainy texture of wet sand that indicated some indigenous ancestry, spiking blood pressure and a long-waged war of attrition with acne. A vaguely piggish face, small cocked nose, heavy lips, kept him low on any measure of handsome. But he had good, gentle eyes, and his soft-spoken manner suggested a certain strength of character, an assurance. At her friend's house, he talked a lot, probably afraid that if he stopped she'd be free to turn away, and she knew by the way he stared at her that he was interested. She was seventeen years old, and flattered. She'd flirted with a few boys her own age, and had twice in her life been kissed. Having the attention of someone so mature made her feel, probably for the first time, like a real woman. So she smiled back at him, encouraged him by showing an interest in the stories he told about the places he'd been. China, Japan, Korea, Australia. Even, once, America, a tour of Washington D.C., Boston, New York, all the way to the Buffalo side of the Niagara Falls. At the end of the second night, maybe a week after they'd first met, he offered her a ride home. She glanced at her friend, and shyly accepted. He kept to five kilometres inside the speed limit the entire way and held his stare fixed on the road ahead, but his talk came in gouts. Mainly about himself, growing up in Taichung, his family, brothers, sisters, and then about moving in his twenties, after he'd finished his national service, to Taipei. He'd found work in the accounts department of a large plastics factory, climbed the ladder to the point where he was now earning a decent salary and living a pretty good life, all things considered. He had a nice apartment in the Wanhua District, changed his car every couple of years, got away for two weeks every summer and usually for another week in January. Not wanting to interrupt, and because she had nothing much to say, she hardly spoke, except to offer directions. As she was getting out of the car, he gripped her gently but firmly by the upper arm and asked, without letting go, if she'd have dinner with him the following night. His fingers were short and thick, the nails bitten down to tiny crescents. A plain gold ring lay imbedded in the flesh of his pinky. The hard coldness of his touch frightened and repulsed her, but when she lifted her eyes to meet his gaze there was such an exposure of sadness above his smile that she felt compelled to say yes. Five months later, just a month after turning eighteen, and largely at her mother's urging, she accepted his proposal of marriage. It wasn't love, but she believed the advice she'd been given, which was that love, while nice when it came, was not among the essential ingredients of life.

My head ached. I spread the drenched blouse across the bed's iron foot-rail.

'Stop,' I whispered. 'Please. I don't want to hear any more.'

She stared out at the rain, the blinking sky, wiped her eyes with the heel of one hand and folded her arms again across her chest. 'I am sorry,' she said. 'But I have to tell.'

And then, catching time with the next burst of thunder, a rage broke inside me. It was everywhere, and sudden, unlike anything I'd ever before had reason or need to know. I pulled her around. Her face was streaked with tears and she held one side of her lower lip pinched between her teeth. She seemed to cower before me, her shoulders hunched, bracing against the blow she should have known I'd never deliver, and in that moment it became clear to me that what we had going was merely surface platitude, with just the illusion of depth. We'd shared our bodies but kept the important parts of ourselves concealed. We were still strangers to one another.

'I want you to leave,' I said.

'What? No. Please, Billy. Let me explain.'

'You've said enough. Just go.'

I sat once more. She remained standing, just beyond my reach, half-naked and statuesque, huddling against the chill suggested by the rain. The thunder came again, and another electric shock of lightning sang half a heartbeat's worth of life into the room and with the same urgency died away, leaving only its mark as a memory on the eye.

'Five years ago,' she said, 'he suffered a stroke. That was the reason I had to drop out of university. I woke with the alarm clock. At first I didn't even notice. We'd been married fourteen months. He lay on his side in the bed, turned away from me, the way he always slept. I dressed and only then tried waking him. His face had fallen on one side. I called for an ambulance. I don't know what else was in my mind, except that I was afraid. He looked like he was dead, but I could hear him breathing, making a whistling sound. Not like birds, but like the wind on a dry day beside the sea. And then I saw blood on the pillow. I remember calling for the ambulance and for a moment forgetting our

159

address. I cried, of course. I was still just a girl then. Marriage was not everything I had hoped or been promised, but Chenglei was a good man.'

Hunched forward on my chair, hands laced together between my knees, I closed my eyes and tried to keep myself separate from the words so that it would be easier for me to hold on to my anger. The day around us had begun to darken. When I opened my eyes again I saw that she had slipped on her blouse and was slowly fastening the buttons, working from navel to neck. The drenched white cotton clung transparent against her skin. And as her fingers worked, her words continued to detach themselves. Her voice, raw with tears, carried just above the heavy sound of the rain.

Doctors explained the severity of his condition, their words pitched low to hide the embarrassment of having initially mistaken her for the daughter rather than the wife. She simply nodded, too dazed to properly understand. A haemorrhage had caused the stroke, and the bleed lay too deep in the brain for them to risk surgery. Because he was fighting hard, they had placed him in an induced coma, tried to regulate his blood pressure with medication and monitored his progress with daily scans. The biggest problem was that he'd bled in his sleep, probably for most of the night. A considerable amount of time had been lost, they said, which put his chances of survival at perhaps twenty-five percent. And the quantity of blood lying on his brain had caused significant scarring, permanent damage. The first forty-eight hours were critical. All she could do was wait.

Days turned into weeks. For a long time after he'd stabilised, he didn't wake, though he'd sometimes move his hand, or mumble something incomprehensible in a voice not really his at all. But he was in there, somewhere, caught in the shell. Mei spent almost all her time at the hospital, either at his bedside or else drinking coffee in the cafeteria, returning to their apartment only to bathe and sleep. Sitting, holding his hand, gently stroking his thinning hair. His face changed shape, due to muscular collapse, and made him only vaguely familiar. His nose seemed more pronounced, and his mouth hung open beneath the plastic oxygen mask, exposing his bottom teeth and the pinkish bulge of his tongue. A faint bruise discoloured the flesh of his right temple. She prayed, for the first time in her life, because that was what people did in situations such as this. She prayed that he'd live and that he'd recover, and some nights, in her own bed, she wept and prayed for God to forgive her the moments when her heart wished him dead.

'That was five years ago,' she said. Her face looked pale and, yet again, very old.

I met her stare, wanting to hate her, and wanting, more than anything, not to.

'I told you to go,' I said, and she bowed her head and, finally, reluctantly, obeyed.

The entire night I stood at the window, gazing out at the rain, braced against a tumble of memories. Lightning flashed again and again, and at some point during the small hours I realised that I could make it to a slow count of five before the thunder broke. But the suggestion of an end was not yet a surrender. Inside me, a wall had come down, spilling loose everything I'd gathered. The things we'd said, the promises, the books I'd write, the love we'd make. All told, the life we'd have together, a world away from here. I had made a faith of those words, but now found myself weighing them for traces of performance. She'd already married once for something other than love, so her façade was set. And because my trust had been so violated, everything felt contrived. I'd been a fool not to recognise signs that in hindsight seemed so obvious, but I suppose I wanted that ignorance, maybe in some way even cultivated it. A glimpse of her, the merest murmur of her voice, set my blood running. Her kiss had breathed life into me, and I'd have promised the world and my soul combined to preserve that. But I was not thinking as far ahead as all eternity. At twenty-seven, the future for me still felt like myth.

When the storm cleared, on towards dawn, I went out, walked the empty streets. It was a Sunday, and the air had been washed clean and lay still as a toad against the early hour. The few blocks that had lost power were swamped in a turgid half-light, similar to the slow peel of a waning eclipse, and hoarded shadows for the day to come. Where the power did survive, the streetlights poured a sheen across the blackened roads. But even when the morning began to brighten, and even through the edgeless blue of the days following, I felt the weight of those shadows.

And I fell apart. For most of a week I barely ate. That was death. I've known it since. Family members, friends. My heart stopped beating, the roof of my mouth throbbed with the dry, thorough ache of withheld tears. I stopped writing, even though the novel was almost done, couldn't sleep, and spent the long hours of each day drifting around the city, trying not to think about Mei but unable to focus on anything else. Who she'd really been in those moments when I had thought her wide open. My mind functioned in overlaps, high above my own head. It was exactly the same sensation as having death close by and suffering the fallout of its aside. Like lying in five feet of ocean and looking up at the day as a colour almost within reach, but feeling the weight and movement of the water colluding to keep you flat. That same kind of pressured helplessness. And through it all, the only constant was a yearning to know that she truly had loved me, even if only for a little while, as much as I loved her.

By early afternoon of the sixth day, I found myself at the window of her restaurant. The place was a cave against the brightness, but when I peered inside I could see her, pale as meerschaum in a sleeveless white blouse and apron, wiping down empty tables. There was only one customer, a very old man seated against the back wall, bent into a newspaper. Wanting to believe that I'd arrived here accidentally, I entered and settled in my usual spot. She had her back to me and didn't notice, but perhaps some balance shifted because after a few seconds had passed I saw her stiffen. She turned and stared at me, and a single tear fell hard down one side of her face, causing her to turn away again. She finished wiping down the table, then hurried through to the back of the restaurant. I sat, trying to concentrate on the street outside, the passing traffic, so that I wouldn't have to think about what I was going to say. A few minutes later, longer than should have been necessary, she reappeared, having shed the apron. She stood at my table, without speaking and refusing eye contact, until I got up and followed her outside.

We crossed the street and walked toward the university, neither one of us risking a word. I touched her once, to warn her against stepping off the kerb into the bicycle lane. Her arm at the elbow was thin and cool, somehow hurtful in its familiarity. We still fit one another well. The campus pathways were lined and overhung with camphor, fig and ancient, twisted banyan trees, and we slowed but kept going until we found a bench that would let us sit undisturbed in the sun.

'There's something I need to tell you,' I said. 'I've decided to go home.'

She glanced at me and then away again. She looked beautiful. The brightness of the day touched her eyes, made them shine the same way it did the very first day I coaxed her outside. I tried to see if the tear she'd spilt had left a mark, but it hadn't, at least not in any way that showed, and she held her mouth knotted against more.

'Because of me,' she whispered.

I said that I was sorry.

'For what? I am to blame. Not you.'

'It's not about blame,' I said. 'All right, so you lied. But so what? The world survives on lies. My heart is broken, but this is the life you carry around. Wishing won't change it, and knowing it doesn't change my feelings. I still love you. I don't know how not to love you.'

The twist of the footpath ahead seemed to interest her, maybe for the people it carried past us and away. Girls basking in a day off from classes, boys with rucksacks, sleeves rolled up, their thin shapes and hair turned shaggy-long the only obvious indications of how far away they were from home. Her hands fell together in her lap. I watched them, the way the fingers of one hand lay across the fingers of the other. Seconds passed before I realised that even this small gesture was a reflection of the survival instinct, yet another attempt at concealment.

'My prayers worked,' she said, smiling slightly. 'But I cursed myself with them. He has some speech now, after much treatment, and he can eat a little if I make the food into liquid, but he will always be blind except for shadows. He can't walk or use the toilet. There is very little he can do for himself. And nights are the worst, when I have to lie there beside him in the dark. The air strangles him, but too slowly.'

I moved a little closer and put my hand down between us on the bench. I stared at her until she felt it and stared back. 'I want you to come with me,' I said.

'Don't say that.'

'We can be happy. I don't want to lose you.'

'His sister comes every day, to help. In the morning and again in the evening, so that I can work. Our savings went on medical expenses. Her name is Ling, his older sister. She and I have become good friends. She knows about you.'

'What?'

'About us, I mean. That we meet. That we are in love. I told her.'

'And she doesn't care?'

'She understands. I am twenty-five years old. Chenglei will not get better.'

'Does he know about me, too?'

'No,' she murmured, and she hung her head and began to cry again. Her breath came in rags, the way it had in high moments against my neck and ear. She had no handkerchief, and I had none to give her, so she wiped her eyes with her fingertips. I wanted to put my arm around her, draw her close, but too much lay between us.

At Danshui, some days later and the better part of an hour by train northwest of Taipei, we had the entire strand to ourselves apart from a horse and rider far off in the distance cantering lazy figure-eights inside the tideline. Not yet nine o'clock and still only mid-March, but already the air had the kind of sodden, dirty heat that hurt to breathe, with a thin wind from the north setting mists of hot sand scrying across the beach. I was leaving in two days and we'd already said our final goodbye, so all of this was something else. Part catharsis, I think, part benediction.

To cool down, we went and stood up to our waists in the buffeting surf. Mei had come prepared and already wore her bathing suit, a garish but modest milky pink two-piece, under her clothes, but I hadn't thought to do the same and was forced to undress there on the sand. Nakedness wasn't a problem since there was no one else around, and I smiled when I caught her watching me, which made her blush and then smile, too. I pulled on my trunks and waded, hand in hand with her, into the sea. She said that she hadn't been to the beach in years, not since she was a girl, and I felt her happiness as she squealed against every wave and lifted herself to ride the breaks. In the water, splashing one another, so much fell away and it was almost possible to forget that our time together would soon end and that we'd almost certainly never get to meet again. Because I could swim a little, and she could not, I tried to teach her how to stay afloat. She lay on top of the waves, holding to my outstretched arms, hesitant at first, afraid to release herself even though we were in less than four feet of water, until I assured her that I'd let nothing bad happen. That was an easy promise to make, and one I could keep.

Back on the sand, we spread a large blanket. Mei had prepared us a picnic breakfast, sandwiches of cheese and sliced boiled eggs, a flask of coffee, and a cellophane-wrapped bowl of pineapple and watermelon chunks, and we sat, our bodies touching, our skin still wet and warm from the sea, eating slowly, not saying much, watching the distance. The water far out was the blanched mildew of old pond stones, but in close it dulled and then ruptured in a bright spume before finally rolling clean and transparent up onto the beach. Spread out along the horizon line, the bones of three boats were just visible, ghostly against a soft background stave of cloud.

The menace of war had heightened in recent days. With the election imminent, the Chinese were undertaking a series of live-fire exercises and had just made public their plans to carry out a simulated amphibious assault, scheduled for the following week. In response, and in what the newspapers had taken to calling the most significant display of American military might since Vietnam, Bill Clinton deployed two carrier strike groups, centred around the *Independence* and the *Nimitz*, into the South China Sea.

Mei suggested that the boats on the horizon were advanced runners for the PRC fleet, and imagined aloud what we'd do if they opened up on us. I told her that the only chance we'd have would be to run. I lay back and considered the Greek blueness of the sky, then closed my eyes to everything. 'Run and try to hide,' I said. A moment later, I felt her settle down beside me.

'They're fishing boats,' I added. 'That's surely still Taiwanese waters. Coming so close would be considered an act of serious aggression, maybe even a declaration of outright war.'

She murmured something, not a word exactly but a noise of acceptance, because we both knew that I was right, that I had to be. But we also knew that just because we couldn't see them, the large, threatening Chinese fleet, did not mean they weren't out there, perhaps just beyond the water's distant edge, readying themselves, waiting on a word. And if they did decide to come there would be no mistaking them for shrimp boats. They'd fill the world from side to side, and we'd see the glinting steel, we'd smell it, even through the baked and salted air.

Now and again, people appeared at the far end of the beach, men or women either walking dogs or playing with children, but no one came close enough to disturb us. We lay in the sun, and I was happy but also conscious that time was slipping away. Twenty paces from our feet, the tide rolled softly in and back, the waves breaking in feathers to brush our footprints from the sand. And the picture was already there, in my mind, of a rainy night at home, standing at the window and gazing out over the lit street so that I could avoid for a while longer the empty bed. Thinking about her and what she might be doing, listening and waiting for the whisper and stroke of her sigh against my neck, wondering if she might at that same moment be thinking of me. When I kissed her, she kept her eyes closed and her breathing shifted only to slow. Her hand found my shoulder and drew me close, wanting not just the connection but the print of me against her, and we remained like that, touching along the full unfurled length of our bodies, craving that unity, through to the early afternoon, and then we dressed and walked back into Danshui.

Because this was a tourist town and no one knew her here, she didn't mind holding my hand on the street. She wore her hair down, the first time I'd seen her that way outside of my room, and had on a chiffon blouse the colour of peanut butter, with high sleeves and a string-drawn neck, tight blue denims that came to a fold just below the knee, and simple leather thong sandals. She'd painted her toenails the heavy maroon of newly drawn blood, and I tried not to stare but couldn't help myself.

The restaurant she chose for us was a small, whitely lit place close to the train station. I don't recall whether the food was bad or good, but I still remember how it felt to be sitting there with her facing me across a scratched pine window table. Meeting my gaze, not smiling, barely a squeeze away from tears. Breaking a promise to myself, I asked her one last time:

'Come with me.'

She just sighed.

'You feel guilty,' I said. 'I know, believe me. But you can live with guilt. There are ways. And I'll help you.'

'This is good tea,' she said.

I reached out, took a strand of hair off her face and tucked it gently behind her right ear. I let my palm rest against her cheek.

'You can't sacrifice yourself, Mei. There's a life to be had away from here. A shot at happiness.'

'He needs me,' she whispered.

'I need you,' I said.

She hung her head again. 'I'm sorry.'

'Is that a no?'

'It's an apology.'

We ate then, whatever was put in front of us. I kept seeing how she'd been in the water, happy, lifting herself up into each wave, her hair in wet trails down her back and over her shoulders the blackest thing in the world that day, emphasising the pure, cold paleness of her skin. I didn't look up because I was not ready to lose that vision of her.

'My flight is at four o'clock,' I said, making it sound like an afterthought. 'Thursday afternoon. I'll be at the apartment until around one. In case you change your mind. Or even if you only want to come and see me off.'

And that was all.

At the station, she sat on one of the platform seats and I stood beside her, holding her hand, the way fathers did with small, wild children. The train arrived, sounding like half a jazz band, and the door shunted open, causing most of the waiting crowd to scurry forward. We kept back until the platform had almost cleared, and then she stood.

'Let's not sit together,' she said, and I could see that she was close to tears again.

I took her in my arms. 'Write to me.'

She mumbled against me that she would. I was glad she said it, but knew better than to believe her. Because some promises break even as they're made.

'I don't have to go,' I told her. 'I'll stay if you ask me to. I'll only lose a ticket.'

She put her arms around my neck and we kissed. I closed my eyes, felt the last snaking flick of her tongue, and for maybe five seconds forgot completely where we were. And then she released me.

'Mei.'

'Don't speak,' she said. 'Only say goodbye.'

Then she turned away and walked up along the platform to one of the further carriages. I stood and watched her go, feeling dead inside, thinking only about whether or not I should run after her. Willing her to come back, craving one final something, a smile, a raised hand. But she just kept walking. And when, at last, she reached the open door of the third carriage along, she stepped onto the train and was gone.

I still think about her. A lot of years have passed, and I have long since moved on, but for a brief while at a very impressionable time in my life, she was my day and my night, and so it seems only right that I don't forget. For too long I denied myself those memories, but time has softened their impact and I can bear them more easily now, even on the mornings when I wake to find her fresh as oranges before me, still there after a long night and then, slowly, halved and halved again, and finally gone. Nobody makes it through wholly untouched by regret. And while thinking of her saddens me, and still hurts, I feel both proud and lucky to have survived.

After the plane lifted off, I sat hunched forward in my window seat and studied the city that lay sprawled below me, the shapes of the buildings and the well-ordered streets in the hot late afternoon, the multitudes continuing about their day, thinking their own small thoughts, oblivious to my gaze and even my existence. In the seat alongside mine, a middle-aged woman smiled. She had worried eyes and too much make-up, and a son living in Amsterdam who'd paid for her ticket. She'd never been anywhere, she said, except once, to Hong Kong, with her late husband. But that hardly counted. Her son had phoned that morning to say it was snowing in the Netherlands, had been for almost a week. I nodded, but I didn't feel much like speaking. My throat hurt when I swallowed. I felt wrenched from the world. And out over the Strait, as we climbed higher in the rough direction of the sun, dark slabs lay scattered across the water like chips of land that had slipped adrift, and I knew well enough what they were, but not yet what they'd decide to do.

In fact, war didn't come. The PRC launched their test missiles, simulated air strikes, and carried out their landing exercises on one of the small islets, and for a while the stand-off seemed certain to spill into something more, but the presence of the U.S. Fleet deterred notions of further advance. When that first historic election day arrived, the Taiwanese people, angered by so much Chinese posturing, threw the force of their vote behind the most nationalistic candidate, Lee Teng-hui, who'd already served eight years in office. Tensions continued for a while, and I suppose, on some diplomatic level, still do so today, but at least no blood was shed.

Unfortunately, the same could not be said of the situation back at home, with the Docklands bombing proving merely a prelude to further tragedy. A major explosion that summer in

Manchester left more than two hundred people hurt. The seasonal marches, in Drumcree and elsewhere, met with increased violence. And, in August of '98, a car bomb detonated in the crowded shopping area of Omagh, County Tyrone, killing twenty-nine people, Catholics and Protestants, men, women, children and even the unborn, and injuring upwards of three hundred. The Omagh blast, which came to be regarded as the single worst atrocity in the long, bloodstained history of Northern Ireland, was decried from all sides, roundly condemned. But out of such abject horror came something unexpectedly good: a new resolve, and a hunger for change that led ultimately to the enforcement of the Good Friday Agreement and the subsequent decommissioning of paramilitary weapons.

Even the darkest days pass, if you can outwait them. And nothing stops time. I lived beside the crisis in the Strait, and within spitting distance of the Troubles, but apart from the occasional flare of anger or fissuring sadness in response to some terrible headline, their details held very much to the background and remained, essentially, unreal. And while even in their resolution they continued to be stories worth knowing and worth remembering, they were never really my story. During my time in Taiwan, I never saw much further than Mei, and for a long time after returning to Cork, I continued to keep my horizons close.

Healing is a process, and a slow one, but some wounds simply refuse to close, despite the most careful nursing. Neruda had it right, I think. Forgetting really is so long. But maybe it's also true that, as people, we're not much more than the scars we wear. After Mei, there were other women, a couple who even, for a while, threatened permanence, and they hurt, too, in their passing, and left their marks on me. The pain I felt in their aftermath was just as real, though always somehow different, lacking an acuteness. I told myself it was because those relationships had enjoyed or suffered full and natural conclusions, but it may also have had to do with degrees of love.

Mei was my broken mirror. She changed the way I saw myself. She was also harder to forget, I think, because so many questions had gone unanswered. But my door for her was always held a little bit ajar. During those first few years back at home, I'd sit up late into the night, and after finishing work on the novel, or the new collection of stories, would set myself to writing letters full of long, one-sided conversations. Most of them I'd burn, or tear into confetti, but a few survived, the ones that didn't turn too maudlin. There was never really much to say, except that I was fine again after a bout of 'flu, or that my brother had decided to marry a lovely girl from Kerry, or that I'd had my manuscript accepted or some stories published in America. Empty platitudes, mostly, ways of filling air. Laid out on the page, the words looked stilted and hardly felt as if they belonged to me at all, but I'd invariably soften them by asking, in the most casual way I could, if she had any regrets. Because it didn't have to be too late. She'd given me an address that I took on faith to be genuine, but for whatever reason, the letters went unanswered. And as time passed, even after I'd stopped writing to her, I used to wonder about the husband, Chenglei, and whether or not he was still alive, or whether she might have left him for someone less willing to take no for an answer. Finding freedom of one kind or another. Part of me always hoped she did, the same part that hopes she is happy.

On a certain level, it would seem that my story begins and ends with her. But actually, I'm not so sure that even she isn't incidental. The image I've retained of her is likely idealised, and in large part imagined. That in itself says something about me, I think. Lately, though, I've been coming to understand that life really might be less about the destination than the journey. Keep Ithaca always in your mind. That's a realisation, perhaps even a kind of wisdom, which only comes with time, and may be one of the main reasons why this story took so long to write. In the end, if it amounts to anything at all, it is my attempt to explain and hopefully gain some understanding of who I was at twenty-seven, a wide-eyed child learning to swim amongst the big waves. A stranger, it seems, from the vantage of settled middle-age. Until I look closely.

THROWING IN THE TOWEL

I HAD SEEN him years before, back when he was still in something like his prime, when he was trying to make a name for himself as if that were a thing that mattered worth a damn. And it's funny, but he looks the same as I remember, more or less, anyway, except that the edges are gone, all that finesse and guile. Time, I suppose, turns everything soft. Now he has become just another old fighter, sloshed on one too many hits to the head. He looks the same, if you can see beyond the fur of bad or at least questionable living, but even from a long way off you can tell that damage has been done.

He is sitting by the window, but with his wide back to the fogged glass, and he smiles a wide open smile when the waiter finally brings the tray of food, his big, round face mangled with happy creases. Even before the plate has been set down he is picking up his knife and fork in anticipation and holding them spread apart in his huge fists, sharp ends at the ready. The white light of early afternoon pours through the window and dissects on a sharp diagonal the part of the table that lies untouched by his shadow. The tines of his fork flash a signal across the room, full of some intent, as they lean into and away from the light.

'Stop staring,' Jenny says. She is whispering, which always makes her seem harsh until you look at her and realise that she's not. Whispering, she makes the sound of rustling leaves.

I look at her, then without enthusiasm cut into my omelette. The menu had made it seem so enticing, but the reality is flat and lacking in imagination. Overdone eggs, chunks of onion diced far too thick, entirely the wrong sort of cheese for easy melting. And the side portion of ham is stringy. I poke at the omelette with my fork, rake it asunder and eat a piece for the sake of doing so.

'You're staring again,' she says.

'So, I'm staring. So what?'

'So, some people don't like being stared at. Some people take great offence to it, in fact.' She pauses here, and steals a glance herself. 'What is it? Do you think you know him or something?'

'Something,' I answer, knowing this will annoy her. But I am instantly sorry. Sorry for everything. I give up on the omelette, lean back in my chair and take to sipping wine. The food might not be up to much here, but they do serve a decent Chablis. 'I've seen him before,' I say, at last. 'In Paris. He was a fighter. A boxer, I mean. And a good one.'

His name was Doherty, and I had watched him at the *Palais*, in Bercy, as one of the opening acts propping up a bill headlined that particular night by a fighter named Mike Culbert, whose pedigree had once put him in the ring with Roberto Durán. Our man went in as the long-odds nobody against a Mexican, name of Ortiz, who was one of the most fancied middleweights of his time, a real contender. The story doing the rounds was that Ortiz had only scheduled the fight because his numbers were a little lacking and that he'd been told to pad things out if he was serious about wanting a shot. You couldn't put a penny down on him, he was that locked on. No one was expecting anything from the match-up so the entire place was stunned when it turned out to be seven and a half rounds of the most brutal fighting any of us had ever seen. A real brawl. But it was obvious at a glance that

Doherty had the stuff. He could dance when he needed to dance and could mix it up, too. He had a right jab that clipped away like a jackhammer and never let up, and a left hook capable of stopping a man at foundation level. The Mexican knew within ten seconds of the first bell that trouble lay ahead. But there's no back door in the ring. That night, he took the beating of his life, lost an eye and his career. I remember that they had to wash the ring down with buckets of water before the next fighters could come out, and after the bout most of the crowd left, figuring correctly that Culbert would have nothing left in his game to match what we'd just seen. Outside, the streets were packed, even though it was raining, and the bars and cafés along the Rue de Pommard did a roaring trade. It was one of those nights when we were all feeling something, and nobody wanted to go home.

Across the restaurant, he is eating slowly. Everything really has gone soft. He's no middleweight now; he is heavy turned to mush. He chews his food well, even though it is only beans and buttered slices of white bread, and his eyes stare ahead into a far distance. At some point, a daub of sauce seeps from his lower lip and spools across his yellow stubble-ridden ball of chin. He wipes at it but misses, his thick fingers too out of shape for neat work. He mutters something that comes loud and hoarse across the restaurant floor but which makes no sense, and the waiter who brought the food tosses him an anxious glance and slips behind the safety of the counter. I pour myself a second glass of wine, and wonder if the old fighter is a regular in this place or merely a passer-by. He looks comfortable enough at the table, and the waiter's nimble footwork seems to speak of past troubles. Time slips quickly by, but it leaves its share of scars. Most of us, maybe all of us, wear our histories as shackles around our necks. Out of some duty I don't quite understand, I take another piece of omelette and try to forget that I am not twenty any more, and haven't been for a long time.

Jenny sips coffee. At thirty-nine, six years younger than me, she has a sad sort of prettiness. Always did, actually. I don't quite mean beautiful, you couldn't exactly put her in the movies. But still, not bad. Nice. The kind of pretty that some women have without knowing it. When she was young she could smile without moving her mouth. Her whole demeanour suggested it, as if the happiness came seeping through from underneath, though it's possible that I was reading something more than was truly there. A word can mean one thing to one person and another thing entirely to someone else. We have been married a long time, my second shot at the title, her first. Now that I've long since gotten used to seeing it, the smile that is not a smile, my thinking is that it has always been just a peculiar confluence of cheekbones and chin. And whether made more pronounced by the few brief pregnancy pounds or diminished by diet after diet, it has endured. A nearly-smile that's just another in a conga-line of lies, one of those tricks of birth that works as either lucky or unlucky, depending on your point of view.

A month ago, the doctors removed her right breast; this morning they spoke of taking the left one, too. She sat in that office as though made of wood, stared them down and said in a voice that was all one flattened tone that they should go right on ahead with whatever needed doing because she had no more tears to cry. I'd felt a nearly crushing urge to reach out and take her hand when she said that, but I couldn't. For the better part of a year now, we've been fighting one another to a standstill. With this early supper we're merely killing minutes before the moment of final goodbye. We have already thrown in the towel. By eight, I'll be on a train, with a cardboard suitcase full of shirts and books, and by tomorrow I will be in another city, holding another woman's hand.

FOR OLD TIMES' SAKE

I AM SITTING at my father's table, going through his personal effects, when his address book falls open onto the floor. Glad of this distraction, I pick it up and begin scanning the list of names.

Lydia Barstow is on the second page, the third entry under 'B'.

Christ, the past is always there, waiting. In a heartbeat I am a boy again, thirteen years old, doing what boys do. The light on, the curtains split just wide enough to see. And me, tucked away behind my window, with pennies for eyes, watching. Looking back, she must have known I was there, but if she did then she never let on. Maybe she even got something out of it. We all have needs as well as wants.

Actually calling her up is a throwaway notion, but the problem is that nothing looks quite itself at dusk. Twilight has a peculiar way of condensing everything, real and unreal alike.

She picks up on the second ring, as if she has been waiting all this time, forty-something years, for the call, expecting it. Impossible, of course, but that's how it feels. There is that lovely claxon sound as I pluck out the numbers on the old-fashioned dial, followed by a bar and a half of robotic chirping as a code builds and breaks itself open. And then, into a cough of emptiness, a sultry, questioning 'Hello?'

For a moment, my mind flushes with all sorts of things and all sorts of nothing.

'Uh, hi. Could I speak with Lydia, please? Oh, it is? Lydia Barstow?'

Well, Lydia Barstow that was. Lydia Hunsecker now, and for about as long as the road to hell and back, but yeah, Barstow, too, she guesses, once upon a time anyway. But why, and who's asking?

'This is Steve Glick, I don't suppose you remember me. From next door, back when... Yes, in Laurens. That's right, little Stevie Glick. Except not so little anymore... Changed? Well, I... It's been a long time. No, no, not any more, not for years now. That's all cleared up. What? Oh right, yes. Thank God. Kenny? My brother, Kenny? He's fine. Well, I *say* fine. He lives up in Oregon now. In a log cabin way the hell out in the assend of beyond. You believe that? Well yeah, I guess he was always a bit wild. He's retired, of course. That's right, a teacher, yes, and these days he's into this whole hippy trip that he missed out on first time round. Got himself a beard down to here and a wife who's not even half his age and who goes around braless and barefoot seven months of the year. He's happy, though, which is what counts. What's that? You did? Really? Wait 'til I tell him, he'll be tickled purple. But I suppose he did have his moments. Let me guess. The curls, right? Those curls did it for a lot of girls, back in the day. No, no. Long gone, I'm afraid. Sorry. What? Oh that. No, he *is* fine. I just meant about him losing an arm. You knew about that, didn't you? Oh, he's right as spring rain now. It was all a long time ago. I guess I just assumed you knew. He always says how lucky he was to have made it back at all. Christ, we all were. A pisser, indeed. That's a word for it, all right. A hell of a word for it. Yeah, I will. Sure I will.'

Lydia Barstow, after decades of existing only as wrought-iron dreams, suddenly alive and real again, and hard and hungry as the tip of a pick hacking at the wood of my inner ear.

A lot has changed, of course. Passing years have tagged the once-pure soprano lilt of her voice with a textured addendum that evokes little cool finger snaps or pages on the verge of crumbling, and her background breath has the bobbing inconsistency of a chimney breeze. But still, my mind insists on picturing her as she once was. Forever seventeen, timeless in the manner of standing stones. The senses work of their own accord, I suppose, but I can't shake the notion that somehow, through a series of spun numbers, I have found a way of quantum leaping. I'm talking witchery of a high degree here, magic that would have made the ancients come apart in hosannas of madness. In our airy small-talk way we find ourselves traversing, not merely miles in their thousands, but time in its decades' worth. Telephones play such wicked tricks. In a single sleight-of-hand, I have exhumed and reawakened the dead-and-buried past of 1961. My past, full of sweetness and glory and even back then probably nine-tenths imagined.

'Listen,' I say, urgency hook-punching holes in the walls of my throat. 'The reason I'm calling is because I feel like a thank-you is in order. In fact, it's long overdue. Christ, I thought I could just choke this out and then that'd be it and you'd either take umbrage and hang up with a bang or else you'd find a funny side to it and we'd maybe even end up raising a few giggles. But suddenly all my best intentions seem to have gotten stuck somewhere in the back of my head. Well, all right. Deep breath and here goes. It will probably seem a bit silly to you, and actually I'm kind of hoping it will, but I just want to say thanks, you know, thanks a lot, for leaving your curtains open just enough...'

For some interminable length of time I am left to sit there, empty as a pot and feeling a little bit like the Coyote in those *Road Runner* cartoons, that wily old ever-optimistic fool crouched behind some rock with his eyes squeezed shut and his fingers jammed in his ears to at least the second knuckle, waiting for the special ACME mail-order rocket-bomb to work the way it is designed to instead of the way it will. Then, finally, a little breathy laughter breaks the emptiness, rattling like a penny in a tin box from a two-pack-a-day habit, two packs at least, and the need for words becomes redundant.

In 1961 I was thirteen years old, and knew all there was to know about the things that seem important only until your hormones take flame and fire the world into an entirely different colour. My formal education was a shoplifted and well-thumbed copy of *Playboy* that I'd procured from Timmy Swanson for the princely sum of two rather peachy forty-fives, Chuck Berry's 'Too Pooped To Pop' and Sam Cooke's 'Twistin' The Night Away'; records that had become mine by virtue of some hand-me-down inheritance law after my brother, Kenny, fell into his dyed-in-red-fur folkie phase. Timmy was a neighbourhood kid and not really a friend of mine. He had a year on me in school, and even back then you could feel the inevitability of some serious jail-time glooming up his horizon. But that extra year counted. *Playboy* was already just a shrug of the shoulders to him, no biggie, but blues and soul had become a kind of holy grail, especially since his father kept a special spastic-level of rage set aside for so-called 'coloured' music. Deke Swanson was a fair-to-middling ex-bruiser who spent big hours working his way up the rankings as a heavyweight drunk, and nothing in this world or any other could light his fuse like the holler of a black man on the radio. Timmy seemed to pleasure in cranking his old man's gears, and often came to school wearing the results of those rages like Purple Hearts, but in those days people, even teachers, could still look and look away from that sort of business. As they saw it, kids were forever stepping out of line, and the occasional upside tap was simply the world's way of packing them back in their box.

Trading with Timmy did push me forward on the page, but I was still wrestling strictly within two dimensions and had yet to find a way of successfully turning paper into flesh. For that I needed a mentor, one who not only knew the ropes but also how to play them. Step forward the lovely Lydia.

Back then, she'd been middle teens at a hard push, but already she had a Sandra Dee thing going on. She was a bonfire in a storm, blonde-bobbed and bubbly as shaken soda, with big cerulean eyes that shifted shade as the day juggled its light and the kind of permanent top-to-bottom smile that could have breathed life back into a blackened blood cell. She was firecrackers and dark ponds, burning you up and then numbing you to a standstill; she was space candy on the tongue, that alive. Cut, admittedly, from that well-visited and by then already-starting-to-bedraggle Marilyn cloth, but still not a wannabe, at least not in any kind of pathetic way. And all she had going and all she'd ever have was put on nightly display just a house's distance away from mine, the whole beautiful array within easy reach of a well-trained eye.

Nights both summer and winter would find me huddled at my window in the darkness, armed with the set of binoculars that my father had hauled through the wringers of Guadalcanal, Peleliu and Okinawa. Eventually, often after a wait that would have strung my resolve to an inch past snapping, she'd appear, delicately prancing back and forth between a wardrobe and her bed, her room backlit like a Vegas stage, her body slim as a sapling fir and loose-limbed as any dancer. On a good night I'd happen across her in her skinnies, and you could actually feel the screams of the world's brakes as they struggled against gravity's turn, desperate to make a mountain out of a moment. But on the best nights, the very best, when the stars fell into rare alignment and the elements were all in balance, I'd catch her wearing nothing at all. By some holy and magical conjunction, every dream that had ever bucked a kick inside my head came breathlessly true, and that was me, done for, boned and rolled, my limbs turned cobweb, my mind reduced to a useless, quivering mess. She was a mortal lock for stunning; cute as one of those red-assed bumblebees and sweet as ballpark pickle.

Try to understand just what kind of animal the average thirteen-year-old 1961-era boy was, with the world finally opening up like a flower for him. You had Elvis doing his thing and Marilyn doing hers. Kennedy was in the White House and drainpipe was the new hip. I was a kid fringing on adolescence, and driven by curiosity, not perversion. And Lydia was my teacher, not really all that different from, say, Mrs Hennessy, my science teacher, or Miss Barker who taught me History. Well, not all that different. In moving back and forth past the window, clad in underwear or even less, her attention fixed on folding some flimsy blouse or with a poetry book heart-unfurled in one raised hand, Lydia was actually lecturing me on the way of things, just as Smell-the-Cheese Hennessy or Bitch Barker did on the chemical elements or the Battle of Ticonderoga. She was educating me, and education is a gift. How can I be anything but grateful for that?

'I always knew you were watching,' she says, and isn't it funny how a smile can make its way into words, how it can physically or chemically change their balance? A little bending seems to lighten them, to turn them easy somehow.

I let the wind escape me, in a silent way, and smile back.

'I sort of guessed you did,' I answer. 'I mean, nobody gets that lucky that often, do they?'

A curtain has gone up somewhere, revealing the Great and Powerful for who and what she really is. This is a different kind of nakedness, like a wide open embrace. And we have at it, talking about little things, shooting the breeze. I lead, less by choice than by mutual consent, dance-floor rules, the proper thing to do, us being of an age where chivalry can still count as something other than sexist, and I spill the guts of my life only to find the contents merely so-so, with the colours strangely lacking. Not bad, handclaps rather than dynamite blasts, but dull. Marriage: tick; children: tick; nice home, half-decent job, car that looks fine in the driveway and does its duty out on the road. Et cetera, et cetera. Honest answers, but suddenly, distilled to this, devastating in their emptiness. It is some wake-up call. For years, decades, we live these lives that seem okay, but the fulcrum in that statement is the lagging verb, and to create the illusion of balance we cling to the only survival mechanism available to us: myth. The myth that we are doing enough, as if getting by is all that matters. I say my piece, without once stumbling onto a single worthwhile subject, then gust out a lungful of sigh and unfurl an ellipsis that cedes to her the ground and everything on it.

She enters the limelight a star in the making. The contrast between us is like Kansas and Oz. What she has to say is hardly the stuff of Arabian nights, but she navigates the various twists and turns with an ease worth envying. She'd married out of college, after less than six weeks of courtship. A big fucking mistake. Fucking, delivered in the loose-handed way of poets grown soul-weary from seeing their hopes so continuously torched. Officially of old-woman age, but really getting her gusto blowing, putting her shoulder into it.

Hubby was Felix Hunsecker, a travelling salesman from Bowling Green, Ohio, thirteen years her senior and the type who believed everything he uttered was a commandment dictated from on high. He was her cross to bear, and the biggest of all her many mistakes was buying so recklessly into all that sanctity-of-marriage bullshit. Because she'd have thrived in Paris, or New York. But getting free was the thing. Still is, actually. Felix has been dead a tad over two years now, and she is still unearthing little snarls of him around the house. A handkerchief here, a balled-up sock there, the diamond tongue of a necktie jammed in mid-pant by some carelessly shut bureau drawer. Plus, he'd had this fixation on writing notes, got through roughly a post-it pad a month. Two years on, those little yellow bastards continue to pop up, flapping on some draught and almost always stating the fucking obvious. *If the clock stops, it probably needs winding.* At the beginning, when she was still young and gullible enough to be blinded by the lightning notion that some man might actually want to put up with her for more than five minutes, such compulsive scribbling had seemed cute, even the pearls of incessantly moronic wisdom. But that cuteness grew warts in a hurry.

'You know, Stevie, at first I thought it was your father watching me. But that didn't fit the profile. He was too grown up for such nonsense, and too far away, if you know what I mean. And with me, he was always the perfect gentleman. I think he did like me, though. Not in *that* way, but maybe I reminded him of somebody he'd once known, some girl who'd danced off with a little piece of him, a piece he'd never been able to properly replace. That happens, you know. That's where the hollowness comes from. I remember him on the porch of an evening, sitting there sucking on that old Popeye pipe. It seems funny putting this out there now, but he was my first crush. With the likes of your father around, Tyrone Power's job was safe as the lock on Fort Knox's front door, but handsome isn't everything, is it? He was always too thin, and he had this nervous, bowlegged walk that you only get if the Lord's really itching for you, but his smile was just the ticket. Well, I guess I don't have to tell you.'

She is right about the smile. It ran clean through, like wood grain. Despite all that he'd seen and known, my father was a man made of gentle things.

I feel embarrassed, but not surprised at finding myself close to tears. The funeral has been done to dust but, even a month on, certain details still feel close enough to touch. I clear my throat and explain to Lydia that I am really just calling on a whim, having discovered her number in an old address book. It's fallen on me to clear out the old man's belongings, his personal effects. Kenny would have come, but Oregon is so far removed. Since packing in Des Moines, My wife and I live in East Peru, must be getting on for seventeen years now, and my Chevy can haul me from our front door to the Laurens town limits inside of three hours. Faster, if I feel like gunning a death rattle out of the old girl.

We hold a few breaths of stillness, Lydia slightly throaty at her end, set to tingling by some shadowy thing that has taken hold and is not for letting go, and I numb to the marrow at mine, raked out in a way that needs no explanation. You step back far enough, grief softens to fog, and the world remains real but not all the way real. But the crux of what I have just said hangs between us, and we both catch a draught of it. The fact that my father had stowed her contact details through all these years, even if he had never actually bothered to get in touch, barks with implied significance.

'He was my first crush,' she says again, and her voice flutters with a kind of giggle and turns tender, wistful. 'I pined away nights beyond counting, the way all girls do when they set their hearts on something unreachable. But looking back, I am glad beyond belief that it was so strictly one-way. Because think of how tainted my memories would have been. Think of the damage it would have caused me.'

And after a while, she says, once it became clear to her that she was simply wasting buckshot, she looked around and fixed her eye on my brother. Ken was boyish in a way that could have passed for handsome on a good day, which seemed like most days back then. But he also had something of my father's quietness about him. In the big, bad world that didn't count for a whole lot, but up on a movie screen it would have been the real deal, shoot-'em-up stuff. Looks go, but character is like the marks a chisel leaves in granite, and that's what keeps the good ones in work long after the pretty boys have passed their sell-by dates.

'That's what I liked most about Kenny. That quietness. It gave him an air of knowing himself, of understanding exactly who he was and who he'd become. So few people have that. He was skinny as a corn shoot, and his hair was always too long and too tossed, and if he wasn't swinging a baseball bat at thin air then he probably wasn't at least three-quarters the way awake. But a searching eye comes up with its own definition of what's golden. Of course, nothing came of my efforts, not so much as a handshake, but for a while it was pretty nice to dream.'

She laughs, and her breath rustles across thousands of miles of telephone line. I lean in and believe that I can almost feel that breath against my cheek.

'I know, I know. I picked the wrong Glick. Story of my life. And you were so much younger than me. Three, four years, was it? When we were kids that made us practically different species. But who can say what might have happened if I'd stuck around a little longer than I had. I always knew you watched me, though, and I guess if I'm totally square about it I must admit to being more than a little flattered. Something about the men in your family always just seemed to rub me right.'

My throat aches with a need to cry. And yet, the phone has become a kind of tether to the world and I understand that the moment I drop the receiver back into its cradle the stillness will sweep in from all sides. Being alone in this house suddenly feels too much for me, and even though it hurts to talk I know it will hurt worse not to, so I keep going, on and on. I recall things, unexpected flashbacks. My father loved baseball and thought nothing of two or three hundred mile round-trips, sometimes with Kenny sprawled out in the back but always with me up front, just to catch one of the big boys, Mantle, Mays, Clemente, Hank Aaron, or so that I could share in the tail-end of old timers like Ted Williams. Guys with the stuff, as he used to say. Even from a young age, I got that it was more than just the game itself he'd been chasing. To him, baseball was about something. The scores and the strikes mattered, but they were never what mattered most.

I had friends when I was a kid, though not many, and none that were truly close. My nature, I think, tended toward introversion. I'd been turned wrong from reading and as a result thought too deeply about things and the consequences of things. Where secrets were concerned, my head was an Alcatraz, and in this way, and in some other ways too, I was far more like my father than Kenny was. Lydia missed that, I guess because of the age difference between us, but I'm sure that even if she'd taken the time to look she still wouldn't have seen. Things can be real and yet intangible, and you either know and recognise them for what they are or else you miss them entirely as they pass you by.

My father was a quiet man, and as deep in his way as any ocean. But there were moments when the wind changed that he'd talk to beat the band. And it's all here, in my head and, I suppose, my heart, every wise and foolish thing he ever said to me. Because, right or not, it was stuff that worked. I loved him, of course, and I loved to listen while he talked. He knew the names of all the trees and birds in our neck of the proverbial, and could hit precisely on just what it was that had made DiMaggio so much a man in such a game of boys. And sometimes, when his mood turned just so, he'd even start in about the war. A little of the way in, at least, up to his shins, just talking but from out of his own depths and with an oddly stoic kind of violence.

I was always the prompt. Looking for a tree to climb or a dragonfly to snag, I'd plug gaps with a turn at the punchline scene of some John Wayne shoot-'em-up. I had the swagger down pat, too: a way of rolling my shoulders and a certain affected pelvic drag, and even if my 'Now just a darn minute, Pilgrim' catchphrase happened to fall an inflection or two shy of the ideal then it was still close enough for comfort.

My father would sit there, raking the prong of some stick idly through the embers of our campfire, and chuckle without needing to look up. Most of the time he'd let it go, but occasionally something about it would catch him like a briar snarling wool and he'd clear his throat and say no, sorry Stevie but no, John Wayne and all of those Hollywood big shots were selling it wrong, because war was nothing like the movies. What it mostly was, he said, was being afraid, even during the long stretches of boredom when you'd almost find yourself wishing for a little action, and what terrified you most was not even the idea of dying as much as the thought that maybe you wouldn't be able to measure up. That when the moment arrived you'd be too numb to move. Every soldier sets out lopsided with thoughts of heroism, he said, but he'd been through the thick end of it and had seen and done enough to know that Sherman, for all his bullshit and bravado, really had nailed the whole sordid business to a tree. War truly is hell, black as night and smoking hot.

'Think about that,' he said, and I waited the requisite moment, then nodded and said I would. The way we all do when a thing is easy to say.

This call feels like my old man's parting gift. Lydia listens, laughs, and now and again skirts against a place of tears. We talk, the way people do when they are trying to grope their way through a downpour of sudden, unexpected grief, and it feels genuine, I think on both ends. With night coming in, my childhood feels like a blush of winter sledding and summer days spent hiking out in the woods or fishing for steelies up at Pickerel Lake. It feels real, a thing that actually did happen and was not simply imagined, a thing that will leave a small but indelible mark on the roll of time. And there is reassurance to be had from that.

When I finally run out of juice, the better part of an hour has been lost. Evening is about to give out, and the last of a soft October sunlight hangs in blood-orange spatters across one pink-papered wall. I have reminisced myself hoarse and laugh a little at how unlike me it is to be so open. Lydia catches my laughter but reads it wrong, mistakenly deciphers an unwritten word for panic in amongst the mix, and asks, with genuine concern, whether or not I have anyone here with me tonight. I say no, I have the lane all to myself and am rolling this one alone.

The fact that tonight will likely be the last I ever spend in this house is one I leave unsaid. In many ways, the miscellaneous details that need tending to around here are a pretence, or an excuse.

'I am fine on my own,' I say, which is mostly true. But more than that, more than anything, it is how I want it.

Bonnie, my wife, had offered to travel up with me, but her arthritis has recently been pinching something rotten and I latched onto that as an excuse to lay down a little law and to tell her no, thanks but no, that what she needed to do was sit back and get her feet up, take it easy. Lengthy jaunts in the car are the stuff of axe-murders on her in that state. And, thankfully, Bonnie is one of those women who get the hook of a cryptic crossword. If a story has nothing going on between its lines then it holds no appeal whatsoever for her. Out of duty, she'd pulled an inevitably disagreeable face, but finally nodded to my demands and let me kiss her. Still able to pucker with the best of them, and still as always nailing me down to my boot heels.

'But don't you find it strange?' Lydia says against my ear. 'To find the place so empty, I mean?'

I purse my mouth and admit that I do, at least a little. This was a house built with life in mind, and emptiness is not at all its natural state. I laugh again, wanting to set things at ease, but the sound echoes all around me and feels uncertain in the room. Lydia tries to laugh too, but the line does not translate the gesture too well, and after a second or two she kills it with the suggestion that if I should find myself struggling to sleep then I absolutely must call her up again, time be damned. Hardly cracking a dream any more is, in her considered opinion, one of the truly great ass-aches of old age, that and all the bran you need to chow if you have any interest at all in keeping even semi-regular. But she has enjoyed the call, and the chance to dig up a few old bones.

'Don't hesitate,' she says. 'Now that you know the number, use it. I'll be bunking down for the foreseeable with a big fat Updike, so you can count on me being wide awake. The toothpicks are already in place. Three, four in the AM: it's all the same to me. Clocks hold no authority around here, these nights. So just dial, okay?'

A goodbye silence presses in. Static bleeds into the line in tiny, shapeless whispers, imprints of things long since said and done, breaths spent like easy money. Unable to think of anything further to add, I thank her once more, a composite thank you, blanket-embracing all I'd already said and all I'd been hoping to say but hadn't quite found the way. She reiterates her invitation to call, insisting that I no longer have any reason now to be shy.

'And if you really can't sleep,' she adds, her voice all the way seventeen again and soft as birdsong, 'why not try looking out your window?' Tossed into the pot as a parting joke, but perhaps meant as some small thing more, a kind of permission as well as an offer of forgiveness. I hang up on a thin 'so long', but linger at the table, until the hour grows late and a plummy darkness has thickened the entire immediate world to mud. Then I surrender.

By four or so, I am done with even trying to sleep. At my age, you understand that there are nights when sleep comes and nights when it is somewhere else, a long way off from you. My old bed feels damp in that way beds do when they have not been slept in for a long time. The sheets are clean but clammy, and the pillow still and unyielding, no longer used to a steady flow of dreams.

I lie here, playing dead, moved only by shallow breath, feeling my age but also feeling absurdly young. My life as I once upon a time lived it hangs within touching distance. Even the air tastes of it. With a cough of sadness I realise just how many hopeful thoughts I have left behind in this room, good solid longings simply abandoned. The places I intended visiting, the millions I'd make, the girls I was going to kiss, consequences be damned, starting of course with Lydia Barstow. And when I can bear these thoughts no longer, I rise and dress quickly, go downstairs, put on a pot of strong coffee and set to work.

Amid a clutter of tacky little carnival souvenirs and age-browned paperbacks that stir awake long-forgotten and most unexpected joys, the occasional photograph passes through my hands, of my father and mother young and laughing, looking too mighty, too immense for the trap of black and white. But I refuse to dwell on any one detail. Drawers and wardrobes need stripping, boxes wait to be filled.

And on towards dawn, when I hear a movement over near the foot of the stairs, an echo that has all the reedy vibrations of a father calling for a son to get up, the fish are waiting but won't wait forever, I sigh the sound away as nothing more than the rattle of pipes heating slowly inside the wall. All words echo. Every footstep leaves a mark, however vague. I seal up one box and, without even checking my pace, start straight in on the next.

ICEBERGS

THIS MORNING, after they have brought the bad news home with them, Abigail moves through the house, straightening the edges of things. Cushions on chairs, picture frames, the glossy magazines and newspapers that lie in a heap on the living-room coffee table. 'Putting the world to rights,' she says, as if from out of a dream.

For a while, ten minutes, half an hour, Jacob follows along behind her, keeping a distance between them, moving ever into the space that she vacates, but braced and ready to catch her should she fall. She seems caught in a drift, and her movement has all the grace of dance. Noon is smothered in rain, a cold, heavy fur of mist that mutes everything. It feels like weather made for whispers. Or, even better, for silence. Whenever she floats by a window, the dim light finds a way of penetrating her body. The world blurs, the way it does when tears come. But he is not quite ready yet to cry.

After she has worked through the downstairs rooms, she slips out into the hall and pulls the door shut behind her so that he can't follow. She says nothing, doesn't even acknowledge him, but the closing of the door makes everything clear. In the living-room, he holds his breath for several seconds and listens to how her footsteps carry her up the stairs. He is breaking down, and he knows it. There are things that need saying, but the words will not come. Even in his mind, they refuse any semblance of order.

He stands there, staring at the door. Overhead, she moves around their bedroom, loping to the world's slowest waltz. Then a radio comes on, muffled strains of something with a chugging bass line, and the slow-dance stops and he knows that she is sitting on the edge of their bed. In his mind, he can see her, perched on the brink of the mattress, stooped forward, elbows digging into knees. Her body all angles, transfixed by dread. Weight loss would perhaps have suggested something awry, but there is so little weight to lose. Apart from a certain piecemeal hardening of her flesh, Abby's body remains as it had been when she'd first unfurled herself for him all those years before.

But alone, she at least has the chance to think things through.

They've been expecting something like this. Doctors prepared them, in that offhand way employed by the medical profession whenever the truth becomes too big for eye contact, with particular phrases dropped in passing during the straggle of tests and scans. But even keeping the worst in mind, the sheer finality of the confirmation has still thrown them headlong into this state of matching shock. A punch in the mouth hurts whether or not you see it coming.

It is late before she reappears. She stands in the kitchen's archway, reduced to silhouette against the rancid orange background glow that seeps in from the street through the front door's fogged glass panel. At first, Jacob doesn't realise she is even there, but then, triggered by some tiny movement, something of the room's equilibrium shifts. He looks up from his place at the red slate counter, and is stunned at how much of the day has been lost to them. Full darkness has fallen. And outside, the rain is still coming down.

'Hi,' he says, uselessly.

She nods, from somewhere else. 'Yes.'

Forgetting it has lain before him for hours, he lifts the cup that he's been hunched over and sips some coffee. It washes cold and slick over his teeth and tongue. He can spit it out but doesn't. He holds it in his mouth, and swallows.

'Did you sleep?'

She shrugs. 'I'm not sure. I dreamed, but I can't say for certain that there was sleep involved. Christ, Jacob, how can I hope to deal with this?'

'You will. We will.'

Her hand reaches for the light switch. There is a click, and a quite violent flash as the light comes and is immediately lost. And this darkness feels more thoroughly pervasive, deepened by an afterglow that streaks his vision from the inside out. Grabbed in that split instant of light is an image of her face, pale, slender, elongated, with her hair tousled from the pillow and her mouth awed all the way slack. This, he knows, is the moment to speak. Now, with all the cracks exposed. He draws a breath and feels its quiver going deep.

'Can we talk about this?'

'Can we, or will we?'

'I'm serious, Abby. I really think...'

'What good will talking do?'

She steps from the archway into the room, and vanishes. And as if to demonstrate some point, the world falls perfectly still. The rain, which has been murmuring against the window, presses tightly to the glass and becomes soundless. Jacob has a sense of everything getting caught between beats, and he wonders if this might be how death feels, this same sort of deep-tissue inertia. But then a sob breaks through, a dislocated thing in and of itself but vital, and this alone is enough to tip the whole back into being.

'Sometimes,' she says, her voice small and lost in the blackness, 'the things that break us apart seem less if we keep them hidden. If we talk now, what will we say?'

'It's okay to be afraid, you know. Cancer is frightening.'

'There are worse things than being afraid, Jacob. There's being alone, for one.'

'But you're not alone.'

'I've been alone for years. We both have. That's who we are. That's what we are.'

'We need to eat,' Jacob says, after a few seconds have passed. His voice can't seem to hold any strength. 'Should I make us something or would you prefer to go out?'

'Out. Of course. Always out.'

This is not mere habit. Silence in a public place can be far more easily masked. And without discussing it, they decide on the Chinese option. Something about the bulk and fire of that cuisine appeals, something about the physical aspects of the food, the portioned variety of the bowls, the textures, the colours. And Chinese to them always means a small place on Marlborough Street, Wong's, a snug, lamplit, eight-table restaurant, rarely more than half full, that does not even bother to properly advertise its wares and which prioritises taste and quality of product above all else. They discovered Wong's quite by accident, ten years or so ago. Longer than that, maybe. Jacob had been recommended a then-new Italian place just around the corner, on Oliver Plunkett Street, but their cold-call coincided with a birthday or an anniversary party, and the noise and revelry sent them reeling back out into the night, unfed and unfulfilled. It was a decent break, one of the few in their married life.

Mrs Wong greets them on entry. A small, fat-bodied woman in her late sixties or seventies, she lowers her eyes, curtsies instead of bowing, and lets Jacob take her hand, then embraces Abigail, the way dear friends do. Her face and hair smell of spice, and for these few minutes Abby is content. Their hostess leads them to a table near the back, their table by favour and habit, and once they are settled she sets to pouring tiny, slender, welcoming glassfuls of a pale plum liqueur. Ten minutes later, she returns from the kitchen with a platter of shredded duck spring rolls, simple fired shrimp, Jiaozi dumplings and a ginger soy dipping sauce. They eat, mostly watching the other diners, listening in so as to catch snippets of conversation. The walls of the restaurant are kept a simple unobtrusive shade of pale that reflects the subtle lamplight and bear large traditional two- or three-colour prints, great empty-space paintings of vague mountain peaks, low-hanging islands of cloud, occasional trees, skeletal, contorted in a surrender of balance.

There are a few other customers dining tonight, two youngish men in suits doing more drinking than eating at a table near the wall and, over by the large blinded window, a happy-looking mixed race family. As Abigail watches, the family erupt in gouts of laughter. The man is Irish, perhaps thirty, with a very serious expression except when he laughs. The woman, slightly younger, Chinese and pretty, smiles a lot also, with huge eyes and shining black waist-length hair draped over her shoulder in a single woven rope of ponytail. Seated with them are two young children, a boy and a girl of about an age with one another. As a unit, they look mismatched, yet perfect. The man sets down his chopsticks every few bites in order to hold his wife's hand and even to kiss her, in the most gentle and adoring way. And with every kiss, the children, who are probably not more than four or five, the boy with a short bowl of black hair fringed low above his eyes and the girl with her hair long and in braids, squeal in unison and make joyful teasing sounds. The woman is shy, but happy about being kissed in so public a manner.

Jacob considers them, then fixes his attention on the shrimp. Abby, though, continues to watch. A smile sets in of its own accord, causing her eyes to narrow.

'I always assumed I'd see old age,' she says, mostly to herself. 'Funny how we delude ourselves.'

'So. You're giving up, is that it?'

The smile doesn't falter. It seems cut into her face. Her shoulders hitch, then fall.

'Call it that if you have to call it something. Anyway, maybe it's for the best.'

'What?'

'Well, you must admit, it simplifies things.'

He glares at her, but she still doesn't bother to meet his eyes.

Across the room, the little girl gets to her feet beside her family's table and begins an adorable recitation of 'Puff, the Magic Dragon'. Demurely, but in a beautiful, brittle lilt. The two men in suits also stop drinking so that they can lend the show their fullest attention, and Mrs Wong comes again into the kitchen's doorway. The girl sings, in a gentle, off-key manner, her many mispronunciations lending the song an added and unexpected poignancy. When she finishes, everyone applauds, and one of the men in the suits catcalls with a sharp, bleating whistle squeezed from between the thumb and forefinger of his free hand. Embarrassed and blushing, the girl slips back into her place at the table, but the applause goes on and at her mother's urging she stands again and issues a quick, reluctant bow.

'Cute as a puppy,' Abigail declares. 'Isn't she just the sweetest thing?'

Jacob lifts the last of the dumplings and sinks it into the ramekin of ginger soy. He eats it in three bites, taking his time. Abby picks at the remnants of a spring roll that she has torn open, fishing out morsels of meat and shredded vegetables with a kind of surgical precision, her chopsticks clacking like a reprisal of the just-dead applause.

'What do you mean, "it simplifies things"?'

She looks up. Her mouth is clenched but her front teeth work a sliver of duck.

'Forget it. It doesn't matter.'

'It does matter. Come on, Abby. If you have something to say then say it.'

'Why? To get it all out in the open? No thanks. It won't salve our consciences, it'll just make us both feel worse about things than we already do. So let's just eat, okay?'

They order. He chooses the beef satay, with a side of jasmine rice. She lets herself be guided by Mrs Wong after professing a vague interest in something fishy, and ends up with king prawns in a delicious light sweet chilli sauce. A basket of steamed dumplings arrive unordered, compliments of the house, a selection of oyster, chicken and vegetable. Jacob asks for beer, though he does not much feel like drinking. Abby takes another glass of the plum liqueur. Everything tastes good, even though there is too much of it all.

'No one is talking about an end.' Jacob keeps his attention on his food but steals occasional glances at her. 'I understand what you must be thinking, but it'll do no good to go jumping to conclusions. It's serious, yeah. Of course it is. Any cancer is serious. But no one has mentioned terminal, have they? If it was that kind of bad then they wouldn't even be bothering with treatment. That has to be a good sign.'

Abby chews slowly, but there is resignation in her eyes, in her face. He can see that the fight is already gone from her. And her voice, when it comes, is soft and empty too, almost contrite.

'You don't believe that, so why expect me to? We both know how these things work, Jacob. Did you happen to take a look around you today? If you did then you'd have recognised the scenery. We've been down this road before. Doctors always tell the best side of the story.'

He shakes his head. 'It's not the same and you know it. That was a long time ago, and an entirely different situation. The child was born with problems. That was a losing game, right from the start.'

'You heard what they said.'

'What? That the treatment will be fairly intensive?'

'Invasive was the word they used.'

'Intensive, invasive. At least they're doing it. Yeah, I heard. And I heard the rest, too. I heard them say they're holding out a great deal of hope. They said that it might be necessary to consider surgery. But that's only might, and it's not today or tomorrow. It's months from now. The course of chemo will hit the thing first. Break it down to a manageable size. These doctors know what they're doing. I know it sounds bad, it sounds terrifying, but you need to cling to the positives. They never said anything about finding out your size and taste in pine boxes. Life might have gone a bit over its quota of letdowns, but there are plenty of people worse off than us. So have a little faith, okay?'

Abby feeds herself another bite and smiles.

'Forty-eight is no age at all, is it? At least, not these days. But I feel old.' She lifts her head and takes a sip of liqueur. 'Do you remember when we first started going out together?'

'Of course I do.'

'We couldn't keep our hands off one another. And you were as bad as I was. Maybe worse. When we bought the car, you'd drive down from Dublin or Galway, Belfast even, clean through the night sometimes, straight after making a sale, just so we could have breakfast in bed together. That was love. At least, that's what I believed it to be. Why do you think we stopped doing things like that? Was it just that we grew up, or was it that we began to see things as they really are?'

Despite everything, she looks good. Even with the insinuation of the cancer. Age, so far, has barely touched her features. She might be turning all sorts of old on the inside, but in a certain light she can still pass for mid-thirties. But she's right; what once lay between them has long since faded.

He asks for another beer. Abby thinks about taking a third drink, but decides against it. Mrs Wong comes to the table and pours the beer, then empties the little that remains into an unused wine glass. Simple problems have simple solutions, she says, showing her little yellowish pebbles of teeth and resting a hand gently on Abigail's shoulder. As usual, as expected, taking sides. She and Abby have developed quite a friendship these past few years, and it is an odd, comradely association, one that thrives on weekly lunch meetings, snippets of gossip and morning cups of green tea. Widowed longer than they've known her, the old woman lives with her son, Ji, and daughter in-law, Melanie. The restaurant was opened by her husband, but Ji took over at a young age and takes almost all the credit for its modest success. She helps out, as she always did, and long hours seem nothing at all to her. She is a simple woman, wise in her way, with an earned hardness. She speaks with an accent that is heavily Chinese, and has retained that calloused external quality so common to people of her era and ethnicity. But she is possessed of a big heart, and the way she looks at Jacob makes it clear that she knows things, that she is privy to all the inner workings of his marriage.

He drinks the beer, and Abby gazes at a spot somewhere inches left of and above his shoulder. When she reaches for the other glass the gesture feels abrupt, almost aggressive, though she limits her consumption to little sips. Spumes of froth cling to her upper lip. She daubs at it with her tongue, then wipes away the rest with the heel of one hand.

'If it's any consolation to you,' Jacob says, 'I feel pretty damned old myself tonight.' Though it is somewhat out of character, he too has taken to watching the family across the room. Most of the plates and bowls on their table are cleared, and now the children, particularly the little boy, have begun to grow restless. He keeps slipping from his chair onto the floor and then clambering back up to the table. The boy's father, serious and serene, makes no attempt at chastisement. Instead, he turns, reaches out for his wife's little eggshell chin, lifts her face to an angle and kisses her again. She says something in response, lowly, the words hidden only until the ambient music breaks.

'There are people here. They can see.'

'So what?' the husband says back. 'Let them see if they want to. Maybe it'll do them some good.'

Playfully, she pushes him away. He leans back from her, smiling, and raises both hands in a gesture of surrender. Then the music comes in again, light piano, hums of violin, the same or similar to what has already gone before.

'Sweet kids,' Abby says, in a whisper. 'Kids like that would keep anyone young.'

Jacob finishes his beer, and counts some fives and tens from his wallet out onto the table, more than enough to cover their meal, the drinks and the gratuity. Suddenly, he just wants to be away.

'Say I die.'

'No.'

She comes out of the en suite bathroom, naked to the waist aside from a cream-coloured bra and wearing a pair of cerise pink silk pyjama bottoms. He steps out of his trousers and folds them into their pleats.

'No,' she says. 'I mean, speaking hypothetically, let's say I do.'

'I know what you mean, and I mean no. I don't want to do this.'

She stands there, on her side of the bed, watching him. He smoothes out the legs of his trousers, then folds the garment neatly in three and sets it out on the seat of the Canterbury that they found eight or ten years ago in an antique store in Tipperary and had reupholstered at a cost which ran to nearly double their initial outlay.

'Well, did it occur to you at all that maybe I want to do it? That maybe I need to? You're involved. I understand that. But think about me. For once.'

'I am thinking about you. Come on, Abby. You're on the edge of something pretty rough, but you're not going to die. So why torment yourself? I just don't think that sort of talk is a good idea.'

She unsnaps her bra. Her breasts slip from the cotton cups, medium-sized and slightly elongated, bottom-heavy but still firm, still shapely for a woman of her age. Her nipples lie like muddy thumbprints against the milky paleness of her flesh. Jacob stares, but doesn't react. At first, she hardly notices, then does.

'You know,' she says, her voice almost wistful, 'there was a time when you'd have capsized this bed trying to get at me. You were insatiable then. We both were. You'd come in from work, and plenty of nights we wouldn't even make it all the way through dinner.'

He grins, but as an expression it goes nowhere. 'I remember,' he says, trying anyway. 'The impetuosity of youth. Before the bastards ground me down.'

The rain has still not let up. A wind awakens and beats in flaps against the side of the house. It is weather to match their mood, yet there is something innately comforting about being tucked up safe and warm in a nice house. Not ideal, of course, given their situation, but comforting. He unbuttons and peels off his shirt, folds it with the same care shown to his trousers, and crawls into bed. But because he knows he will not sleep, he switches on the radio, keeping the volume low. Music often deters them from talk, or at least lets them feel a little easier about saying nothing. Beside the bed, Abigail is slipping into her pyjamas. But there is no hurry. Leaving her top unbuttoned, she reaches for her hairbrush. He watches her reflection in the dressing table's mirror, feeling in his heart the measured cadence of the strokes that she pulls through her long hair. When she leans leftward, the lapel of her top falls away from the swell of one breast and reveals her again to him, but this has become just another detail, a thing to notice. Even before she finishes, he sets the alarm clock, lies back down on the pillow and closes his eyes. It isn't about sleep, it's about escape.

'I might read,' Abby says, but lowly, so as not to disturb him too much. 'I'm not sure I'll be able to concentrate but it might help take my mind off things.'

He opens his eyes, then closes them again. 'Fine,' he says.

'You're tired. Won't I be disturbing you?'

'I'm okay with the light on. It's fine. Really. I probably won't get to sleep anyway.' He is tired, but already the insomnia that has so marred his recent weeks and months is causing his mind to churn. She climbs into bed beside him. They don't make contact, but he can feel a balance shift. He takes a deep breath and waits, fighting to remain calm.

She keeps a small bundle of magazines on her bedside locker, a dozen or fifteen in all, that she replaces or at least replenishes every couple of months, and she reaches for one and begins to amble through the pages. He lies there, listening to the rain and the music, trying to let it all wash over him and accept it without judgement, not wanting to disturb his rut too much. Because even an hour of sleep would be something. But within a minute she is done and tosses the magazine back onto its pile.

He waits for the snap of the bedside lamp's switch and the plunge into a deeper darkness, but nothing changes. For long seconds there is only the rain and wind outside and the murmur of Springsteen, low but audible on the radio, singing 'Stolen Car'. An old song, one he has not heard in a long time.

'Are we finished?' she asks. Taking him by surprise.

'What?'

'As people, I mean. Is this all there is for us?'

The answer is no, of course no, but suddenly it feels like such a difficult thing to say and actually mean. So he says nothing.

'I still dream about him, you know.'

The words hang almost out of reach. He opens his eyes again but resists the urge to move. His body has become a dead weight, trapping him in its cage.

'That's natural. Don't worry about it.'

All that come are whispers. He clears his throat, which helps, but only a little. The bones of her shoulders and hips can be felt through the material of her pyjamas. He knows the angles of her by heart without having to reach out a hand, though a part of him suddenly wants to, just to feel again connected in some small way.

'Is it, though?' She gazes at him. 'Because it doesn't feel natural.'

'Of course it is. He's a part of your life, of our life, and always will be. Our only child.'

'Do you think about him?'

'I don't have to. He's there. At first, he was in my mind all the time and I could think about nothing else. But I eventually realised that that's no way to live, no way to survive. The world just isn't that patient. In the beginning, and I'm talking probably the first two, three years, he was everywhere I looked. I could read traces of him in everything. So I did what a lot of men do. Probably a lot of women, too. I threw myself into work. But for weeks, maybe even months after he died, I cried twice a day. After a while, it even got so that I could handle it. It became routine. I'd feel the tears coming on and go and lock myself in a toilet cubicle. I learned to weep in a silent way. Sometimes people would look at me after I returned to my desk, but no one ever said a word. I suppose I learned how to control myself. Trial and error, but I got there. And gradually the tears came less and less, and then eventually they stopped falling altogether. But just because I no longer cry, it doesn't mean I've forgotten him. He's still with me. Even now, every single day. And I miss him.'

The space gapes between them, oppressive with insinuation. Jacob can feel it and wonders if she can, or if with time she has simply grown used to it. The thought of that awakens sudden hurt, the realisation that if he were to reach out for her, she'd likely as not pull away. Or, worse still, she'd just lie there and bear him. Because who has given up on who in all of this? What always seemed so clear now feels anything but. Nothing feels right any more.

Her smile in profile has a wretched shape to it, turning her haggard.

'In my dreams,' she whispers, 'he's nothing like I remember him. He's always older, though there's not much order to any of it. Sometimes he's a boy, sometimes a teenager. And sometimes he's a man, fully grown. And yet I always know him. It doesn't happen often, maybe a few times a year, but it's all so real. That's what gets me. I mean, I'm dreaming, and in a funny sort of way I know I'm dreaming, but it feels almost as if I am being granted a glimpse of some other world, some alternate reality. I don't know, it's as if I'm the ghost, I'm the one who has died. Saying it out loud like this, even if it's only to you, makes it all seem so ridiculous, but a part of me can't help but wonder if these might be something more than dreams.'

'Does he seem okay?' Jacob asks, when he can trust himself to speak. He is hesitant, without understanding why.

'What?'

'In the dreams or whatever they are. Does he seem okay? You said you see him at different ages, different stages of his life. Does he look happy?'

For a few seconds she is unable to answer. He watches as she bites her lower lip. The idea that their boy, wherever he is, might be anything other than happy has never before occurred to her.

'I think so,' she says. 'Yes, I think so.'

'And you're sure it's him? I mean...'

'I'm certain. I know my own child, Jacob. It's him, no question about it.'

A little 'what if' storms his mind. Half afraid, he draws a deep breath, and exhales. What if this were to be his final breath? He has juggled with this supposition before, though not for some time. And the real crux of the question is not what would he do, because what could he do, but whether he'd even know it. Is death the sort of deal-breaker that likes to announce itself, or does it prefer to work in secret so as to prevent panic until the last possible moment? He tries to focus on the breath in his mouth, but the idea arrives too late for due consideration and he finds himself too suddenly out of air. An instant later, a new breath pours through him, tidal, in and back out. His relief is genuine, but of the checked variety, tempered by the acceptance that, whether recognised or not, this is how the end will some day or some night come. He decides that, given a choice, he'd just as soon do without a warning, would much rather the flank hit.

'Good,' he murmurs, afraid to risk much more. 'That's something, at least.'

The radio works as filler. No longer Springsteen now, but something equally of an age. A little leisurely piano, plunking raindrop arpeggios and a nice thumbing bass, perfect for the lateness of the hour, the notes sullen, wringing but in demure fashion with a knowledge of grief, or at least the sadness of loss. And in time a voice comes pouring in, layering itself in close to perfect synch. Bob Seger, scratching but pent-up, battle-ready.

'Do you think there can be anything to it?' Abigail asks. She has begun to cry again.

'To the dreams?' Jacob shrugs. 'Who can say? There are things we understand and things we don't.'

'I think I'm going mad. My mind runs wild. Mostly I can bear that, but talking about it is too much.'

Tears trace a stripe of wetness to her ear. As he watches, they bristle among her lashes then spill again. Until he moves, he has no idea of what he's going to do. He turns to her and draws her into an embrace. Her hand slips under his arm and pulls her body against his, and there is desperation and terror in her grip.

'No it's not,' he tells her, in close, in a tone that he might use on a child, but speaking it first against her cheek and then the corner of her mouth. 'And you're not mad. If the dreams feel real to you then they are real. And if talking helps then talk yourself hoarse. We all need to make the best of things, Abby. All of us.'

Everything feels near, every good piece of the past. Her lashes feather the skin just beneath his eye, and her tears soak and soften his lips. He remembers all of this from before, and had given up hoping to ever know it again in quite this way, but he also recognises it for what it is: desperate, sad, necessary, a transient thing. And later, after she has drifted into sleep, her pyjama top still spread wide and unbuttoned, her bottoms bunched somewhere at the foot of the bed, he draws the tangles from her hair and kisses her face, her cheeks and her nose and mouth and chin, and when he kisses her eyes, their rapid dream movements shift and flicker behind their lids, almost as if stimulated to respond. But she is asleep and he is wide awake. He covers her with the duvet, bringing it up over her chest. Her breath whispers thinly through her nose, making the barest sound.

A *National Geographic* that he'd been reading and abandoned some nights earlier lies open on the floor, to a piece on Alaska's fast-retreating Mendenhall Glacier. Thinking about icebergs and ocean currents and how simple surfaces often belie the turmoil just beneath, he eases himself away from Abigail and slips from the bed. Without even glancing back, he pulls shut the bedroom door and goes downstairs to make coffee and watch some old movie with the sound blocked nearly all the way out. And standing at the kitchen sink, filling the kettle from the tap, what dominates his mind more than anything else is just how young her unconscious self had looked, lying there eyes-shut in the lamplight, and how beautiful. Sleep turned a trick with time, but only one shard of time. Somehow, at an unmarked point in their embrace, and as if mortality's brink really did become her, she regressed back to her fullest flowering, back to the time of their early marriage, perhaps even a year or two before that. But in that same moment, he'd felt himself thrown forward and plunged into a state of decrepit old age. Now, long past midnight, the truth has turned pale and then dissipated, leaving it difficult to tell which one of them is supposed to be dying and which of them has been cursed to keep on living.

THE THINGS WE LOSE,
THE THINGS WE LEAVE BEHIND

A mile outside the village, I pause to watch four boys kicking an orange plastic football around a field. Through a heckle of laughter and calls to attention, young legs battle the tangle of long grass, the ball looping from one to another to another with hardly a pause, their play dictated by some pattern or set of rules that is far beyond my comprehension, but which seems to make perfect sense to them. They look happy, and I try to recall how it had been for me at that age, when I too was full of running and careless as to my direction, but my old world and this one now seem like the two perspectives offered by a piece of one-way glass.

Our pasts pool around our ankles, dragging at every forward step we take, but it doesn't do to dwell too deeply on what has gone before, even if we sometimes use those past events to explain or excuse the things we've done. So much has happened to me here, enough to chase me away, enough to call me back.

I watch until the boys become aware of my presence, then I raise a hand in salute. 'Grand day, lads.'

The boy who has killed the game moves a few paces closer and stops, hands on hips, ball pinned beneath one foot. He studies me while chewing the innards of his lower lip, his head inclined ever so slightly to the left and his eyes pinched nearly shut in resistance against the washed-out glare of an April sun. He is all worn edges and scuffed knees, and his yellow hair has the same shorn, bristled look as the fields after the hay has been taken in. Short in stature and a shade too thin, perhaps, but still just right for a child of his age – seven going on for eight, if the signs match the facts. Short because it is not yet his time to stand tall, thin from so much running.

'You lost, mister?' he asks, after a minute or so has passed. It is only the middle of the day and there is no need to hurry.

The others mutter their amusement at his question, and I, for my part, feel obliged to break open a smile, but suddenly I have a lump in my throat that makes it difficult to swallow. I shake my head.

'No, boy. I'm not lost. No one can get lost on an island of this size. Out here you can see every direction coming. For lost, you'd want to try a city. Dublin isn't bad, London is better still. Best of all is New York.'

'You've been to New York?' asks one of the other boys, in a small husk of a voice that pokes up out of the pack and which knows all there is to know about the ocean, even at such a tender age. Boys grow up hard on islands.

'I have,' I say, 'and believe me, it's not all it's cracked up to be.'

The lead boy rolls his foot off the ball, drawing it up into the air. He shows me his tricks, which play out as a slow but stately magic, even in the long grass. Needing, for some reason, to impress me. His control is not perfect, but his put-on swagger of confidence more than makes up for that fact, and when the ball slips loose of its invisible leash, he shapes his face so as to pass the mistake off as intentional. It spins away but he doesn't chase it, not even with his eyes.

'You need directions to somewhere?'

Age is such a conceptual thing. Eight-year-old mouths can shape ancient expressions just as easily as they can chew gum. Boys long to be men, to say and do the things that men can say and do. Men, meanwhile, waste years of life on dreams of childish things.

I shake my head again, and wonder if he knows who I am, if he has at all sensed a suggestion of the bond that once bound us so fast. No matter. I recognise him even if he fails to recognise me. I suddenly long to use his name, to feel it from my own mouth. Jack. Spoken as a brazen sigh, put out for the whole island to hear and contemplate. A word for the wind, and an acknowledgement of sorts. Or an admission. Jack. But I can't. When a man walks away from his infant son, he gives up all claims in that direction.

'That's all right, lad,' I say, forcing my tone to steadiness. 'I think I can manage, well enough. You boys can get back to your game.'

There is a murmur of breeze, a first teasing hint of summer carrying the smell of the ocean on its breath. Hands in pockets, I move on up the road. Being back is hard to take, almost as hard as knowing that I will soon be gone again. I walk slowly, at the pace this place demands, and I know that if I were to turn, I'd find the boys still grouped together in the field, watching me. They know who belongs here on this island and they know how to recognise tourists. Fitting neither category quite right, I have triggered confusion.

The only difference in six years is the fresh coat of whitewash. Six years. Christ. Standing here now, it feels impossible that so much time has passed. Time should change things, really change them, not merely tug at the seams. Since the day I left I have held a picture of this place in my mind, a matted image that hardly deviates from any of the hundred such scenic postcards that they peddle to the tourists in every seaside town and village up and down the country. A small farmhouse cottage set back from the twist of dirt road, its thatched roof touched up with season after season of newly cut reeds and always keeping to just the right side of collapse. And five or so acres back beyond the cottage, the land finally rolls away, collapsing down into jagged spokes of shale that rake the sea. A huge cloak of sky completes the picture, a sky forever working, from minute to minute moiling to churn out yet more new tricks of the light, now the glare of a tilted looking-glass, now the deception of smoke. The ocean today is calm, another April lie in a place that has practiced such skill to perfection.

Tommy is in the kitchen, sitting hunched over in a hard chair with his elbows resting on his knees and his hands laced together in a prayerful grip. He looks up when I come to the back door, but his eyes have the watery resonance of a dream, and it takes him a moment to register my presence as something real. Then he rises slowly but not quite fully, courtesy of the hard-won lumbar kink that keeps him off balance and constantly at odds, and by way of greeting he offers a hand that is nothing but rags and sticks. I come inside and sit at the table, and he finds a bottle in the cupboard by the range.

I have known Tommy all my life, and I have known him as a father-in-law since the age of nineteen. We have plenty to talk about, but for a while it is easier just to sit and drink. The whiskey is a brand name type, nothing special, the stuff they make in big factories and sell in every licensed premises in Ireland, but here in this kitchen it takes on new properties. I can taste the flavours of the island filtering up through the heat, and stones grate inside my throat. Not molten lava, but certainly blazing dust. The old transistor radio in the corner is skipping out a fiddled reel that seems without beginning or end, but the station is slipping in and out of tune in a way that brings a wonderful and priceless sense of distortion to the piece. A happy accident, like so many of the best things in the world.

'So,' he says, at last. 'Where'd you end up, then?'

I'm not sure why I have to think about the answer, but I do. 'America,' I say, when I can. 'New York first, then some other places. But one is much the same as the next until you give up on the cities.' My voice sounds unfamiliar to me, and feels worse. The tone has dropped a notch, and become airy. It takes the better part of a minute for me to recognise the fact that we are conversing in Irish. Old words and older ways, ways that I have long since put aside.

He nods at what I have told him, sucks down the whiskey in his glass and dashes off a refill. I hold my hand across the mouth of my glass to indicate that I'm fine for the moment, that I want to take things slowly, but he waits with the bottle until I give up and then he pours anyway. I try not to stare but can't help myself. And I see that I was wrong in my earlier assumptions of time and its effects. Six years might not have touched the rocks and the dirt of this island, but people are not rocks and dirt. Time has all but torn Tommy asunder. His face is a ruin of years hard spent. Ashamed of the part I have played in making those marks, I want nothing more than to turn away, to lower my eyes, hide myself among the kitchen's thickening shadows, maybe to run again and this time never look back. But I owe him more than that.

'You got my letter?'

'I did. A week back. I'd just about given up expecting you.'

'It's been a while, all right. I never meant to stay away so long.'

He recognises the lie and drops his gaze.

The kitchen looks the same now as it did when I first sat here. Same furniture, same worn paper on the walls, same curtains on the window. But such sameness only serves to emphasise all that has been lost. Without discussing the matter, we decide to give the whiskey a bit of a beating. I have a bad stomach and hardly touch the stuff any more. But I'm not at all sure that I can bear to sit in this house without the sustenance of something strong. I suppose Tommy feels the same way, at least today.

'I was sorry to hear about Bess.'

He smiles at that, a nice, heartbroken ache of a smile that widens his eyes. 'I know, boy.'

'She was a good woman.'

'The best,' he says, then pulls again at the whiskey in his glass. 'And she was always fond of you. But it was an ease to her. The other thing had her eaten away. By the end, you'd have been hard pushed to even recognise her for the woman she once was. It's a terrible waste, having to watch something like that happen to someone who was always so strong.'

'How long has it been, now?'

'It'll be two years come June.' He empties his glass and looks at me, and I am shocked again to see the surface for what it truly is, a cracked and crumbling façade. 'I'll tell you, Bill. If it wasn't for the boy, I don't know how I'd have coped.'

Big subjects lie between us like shards of glass. Neither of us wants an argument, so we tread lightly, but the words prove difficult to come by, and when spoken don't seem nearly enough to cover all that needs saying. The picture of the Sacred Heart hangs crooked on the wall beside the window. That picture was crooked when I first entered this house, the better part of ten years ago now, to ask Elizabeth if she might like to come out for a walk along the shore with me. And it was crooked, too, on the day I left, the day I turned my back on all the sorrows and the joys and walked out, with England in my sights, but America very much on my mind. Elizabeth was already gone by then, in the toughest way imaginable, and buried to a great depth, her grave on the stony hillside marked by a name half-mine chiselled into a misshapen, mud-grey slab of granite. Yet everywhere I turned I could see her, every voice I heard shifted with her own musical timbre. America lay a full huge ocean away, and I wanted to believe that would be more than far enough for escape. But it was not. Home can be like a disease. It gets in your blood and poisons everything; it's with you in every heartbeat, hammering away until finally you have no choice but to give in. You have to come home. And this land has a way of paralysing time, because out here all you really see is rock and ocean and sky, elements that keep a count in aeons rather than years. What was real back then seems just as real now, and you have to dig deep beneath the ancient veneer before that illusion comes apart.

I clear my throat, but my voice, when it comes, feels as if it belongs to someone else.

'How is he?'

'Jack? He's grand. He's good as gold.'

Tommy licks his mouth, bunches his chin in a way that squeezes up his face, the pasty flesh rippling and then holding its folds. He is thinking of something that won't be shared, and a softness turns his mouth and sets his eyes to glistening. Outside, the sky is doing something new to the light. The sun has slipped behind the fringe of western cloud. The colours feel too raw to be natural, but the salt-flecked window frames a scene that is undeniably immaculate to a painterly eye.

*

The boy enters the house at a run, draws up with an audible gasp when he sees me. By now, the kitchen is swamped in twilight, and I recall such moments as these from the springtime days of my own childhood, the few minutes when night feels close but not yet quite here, and it is still too soon to think of sparking awake the lantern. Of course, these days it will be the electric light, but the sense remains the same. A groggy dusk, but a most comfortable pocket in the day, time enough to take a breath, maybe to whisper a prayer for those still wandering out beyond the walls and beyond the waves, the lost ones.

'Hello again.' This time I mean the smile I wear, but its edges still feel anxious.

Jack glances around, then studies me carefully. 'Hello,' he says, after a long hesitation. 'Again.'

I'm not sure what to say because I'm not sure how much he knows about the way things are. I find myself wishing for Tommy to act as our buffer, but he is outside, drawing water from the pump. 'Good day for a game of football,' I say. 'Did you win?'

Jack shrugs his shoulders. 'There's no winning or losing, it wasn't that sort of game. We didn't have enough players for a proper match.' He considers sitting, decides against it. I feel like I can read the careworn jumble of his thoughts. 'You know my granddad?'

'I ought to,' I say, 'since I'm sitting here drinking his whiskey.' I widen my smile, trying to keep things light between us, but he still looks uncertain.

'Why didn't you say something earlier? About where you were going, I mean? I could have walked up with you.'

'You had your game, and a sunny day. You had no business being cooped up with us, listening while we rattled our teeth. You'd have been bored stupid.'

He should be nothing like I remember. At his age, six years is as good as a lifetime. Details sharpen and wane, hair changes colour with the sun, and running picks away every ounce of fat even as eating piles it on. The fact that, back in the field, I had been able to pick him out from the scuffed pack of others doesn't seem quite right, somehow. He should have been just another stranger who happened across my path, but he wasn't. And now, this close and with nothing to distract, I can't help noticing that the way he squares his jaw was the way Elizabeth squared hers whenever she was trying to be strong in the face of something troubling. Or that he has her eyes, her shade of green that is nearly grey, a peculiarly coastal shade of eye, mirroring the sea but only at a certain dying moment of the day, when the light has been mostly sucked out of the sky and the surface turns reflective, hiding its greater depths. I see the details of Elizabeth in him, and if I just consider the nose or the little, crooked corner of that mouth, I will see details of myself there, too. But I know when to look away. It is the pretence that keeps this house of cards upright, and denial becomes easier with practice. Anyone who has ever run more than two steps worth of escape understands that.

In many ways, I can't quite believe he is standing here before me. I have thought of him often, of course, wallowing in my guilt beyond the tuck of its pain, picturing him as he once was, an arm's worth of flesh all sleeping smiles and wise, familiar eyes, and then imagining how he might have been with every passing year. But time's wicked trick was to make him seem less real to me, somehow, more a thing of dreams than blood and bone.

'I'm starving,' he says, at last, and twisting away into the shadows he finds a large knife in the cutlery drawer and proceeds to cut himself a doorstop slice of soda bread. Not the baby that

I had rocked to sleep or tickled to hear him squeal with laughter, but already halfway towards being a man. He uses the same knife to cut a wedge of butter.

'We don't get many visitors,' he tells me, over his shoulder. He takes a bite. 'Actually, we don't get any. I'd say you're the first. Ever.'

A pot of stew has been simmering away on the range. Another feature of my younger days, part of the smell of this cottage, the scent of onions and thyme and the thick chunks of mutton filtering into the aura of the room. About an hour after my arrival, Tommy had dropped some potatoes into the pot.

'You'll destroy your appetite,' I say, just for something to take the edge out of Jack's comment. 'We'll be eating dinner soon.'

He looks at me again, for longer than is comfortable, even with the dusk thickening walls between us. I get the sense that he is studying me too, matching details as I had done. Then he takes another bite of soda bread, chews it with a daring that will probably stoke a heap of trouble for him in years to come, but which clearly makes up a big part of who he is. I'm responsible for that chip on his shoulder.

The night passes in snatches, the essences of sleep and wakefulness so diluting one another that in short order they become two sides of the same tarnished and constantly spinning coin. After the sickly gloaming of those half-nights in the cities, this darkness feels absolute. Riptides of memory claw at my mind, and I toss and turn in the old bed and try to ignore the ghosts that whisper reminders of late-hour embraces and last broken breaths. The dreams, when they come, are time trips that deepen and dissolve, and then I am back again into the waking pit, gasping at the turgid air. I tell myself that it's the whiskey, but it's not.

A little after five, I hear movement, the croak of a floorboard, outside my bedroom door. Five minutes later I am dressed and sitting at the kitchen table. The electric light now feels like an almighty gift, as would anything that can so completely dispel the predawn heft. Tommy boils a kettle of water for tea, lays a few strips of bacon in a pan. I sit there and watch his shuffled moves as he tends to his business, and decide that this sort of hour does no one any favours. He wears yesterday's clothes, the same as I do, but everything seems ill-fitting on him. Braces hold up his trousers, his heavy grey shirt is only partially buttoned. Worse, his salt and pepper hair spools wildly from the back of his head, giving him the wizened look of the truly infirmed.

'Can I do anything?' I ask, but he doesn't answer, maybe fails to hear, and I leave it at that. Lard spatters and crackles in the pan, and the heat of the range chases away whatever little chill the early morning might carry.

We eat mostly in silence. The food won't be mistaken for gourmet, but the bacon tastes the way it should and the egg yolks run when cut apart. I'm not hungry, but that's of no consequence. Here on the island, food takes on the qualities of a ritual, another of the many duties to be fulfilled. Tommy wipes his plate clean with a piece of buttered bread, chews it thoughtfully and then sits back in his chair.

'So,' he says, barely loud enough for me to hear. 'Is this about something?'

For a moment, I am lost.

'Your visit, I mean.'

I shake my head, no. 'It's like I said in the letter. I just had an urge to come home. Elizabeth's anniversary seemed as good an excuse as any. And I suppose I wanted to see the boy.' The heat of the tea in my mouth should feel better than it does. Confession has never sat well with me.

'And that's all?'

I meet Tommy's glare, then avert my eyes in surrender. 'That's all.'

'Because he wouldn't want to go, you know. Even if that was what you had in mind. He doesn't even know you. And I'd nail him to the floor before I'd let you take him out of here. So help me Christ, I would. This is where he belongs.'

Outside the window, the darkness is splitting. Dawn isn't far off, but it is more of a feeling than anything else, and there's little proof yet to the eyes.

'I didn't come to take him, Tommy. That's not what this is about. He'd like America for about ten minutes. It's nothing like here. And besides, I know he's not mine to take, not any more. It's just that, well, after all this time I had lost the picture of him in my mind. I wanted to see him, that's all. And I needed to come home, just to see that there's still such a place.'

Tommy stares at me, reading the rest of my story in silence. Then it is his turn to look away. It's been probably three or four days since he last bothered to shave, and the blue-white dusting of stubble brings to mind a suggestion of wild horses and wind-battered sails. Tourists would pay hard-won cash for a picture of a face so full of character. He smiles at something, and I know that a memory has broken slowly across his bow. I wait for him to share the thought, but he doesn't, and it's not my place to push.

Minutes pass. We drink more tea and watch the window fill with sullen grey.

'He's all questions, you know. I can see them, piled up high in his head. They wrinkle his brow and age him fifty years. But he never asks, not when it comes to serious business. In a few days he might mention something in passing, but he's never outright with it. He's bright as a buttercup, that boy. Takes his time on things, figures them out. Does it properly. He understands, I suppose, that if I want him to know something, I'll tell him.'

'Does he know about Elizabeth?' I ask.

'Some. Not the details, though. Bessie told him things, over the years. Made a story out of it and filled in a few of the blanks, softened it up. Going on about a mother's love, and how there are all kinds of sicknesses. For now, that's enough. If he ever asks for more, I suppose I'll tell him. But I doubt it will come to that.'

We sit until the silence becomes too much, and we are stuck in the same direction. Then Tommy rises with a groan and gathers the plates, leaving the cups. It is early, and we'll drink a lot more tea yet before the time comes for me to catch the ferry. He scrapes what little waste there is, the bacon rinds and a few crusts of bread, into a small bin, and lowers the plates into a large yellow plastic basin so that they can soak for a couple of hours. Watching his back, I lift an envelope from inside my shirt. Whenever I had money, they had money too; when I was on my heels they got by without. Lately, I've been doing okay. I have learned the hard way that money only tunes the material world, but it does hit a few of the right notes, and I do what I can to help. Making a small difference is still making a difference. I set the envelope in the middle of the table, and stand.

'Sun's coming up,' I say, in a thoughtful tone that doesn't encourage an answer, but it's my excuse to step outside, to gaze westward at the sloe-coloured ocean lying pinned beneath the last of night and to feel another dawn peeling open at my shoulder. The darkness feels tempered, and crumbles by degrees even in those few moments.

Back in the kitchen, Tommy is sitting again and the envelope is nowhere in sight. We drink tea until I am sick of the taste of it, and then we keep drinking to fill the time. There is no more, really, to be said. I have a question that I want to ask, whether or not Tommy has any idea why Elizabeth did what she did, but that question is always in my mind, always, and I know better than to cut it loose. Instead I ask him to tell me how Jack is doing at school, and how he is in general, and I lean forward with my elbows on the table and make sure to absorb every word of reply. Tommy talks with ease, now that I am no longer a threat to the world that he has been holding together.

'Do you think he knows who I am?' I ask, when I have heard everything else. He is becoming more real to me now, the boy, my son, the added colours making all the difference.

Tommy shrugs. 'Hard to know. As I've said, he's a bright boy, but deep. He chews on things. I give him all the room he needs.'

'Does he ever ask about me, at all? I mean, who his father was, that sort of thing.'

'Sometimes, we will be doing something. Mending nets, say, or getting the boat ready for the season. He knows his father was a fisherman, and that he was good with his hands. Damn good. Did you see him watching you, last night? Did you happen to notice him checking out your hands? I doubt he'll ever say so, but he knows. He knows enough, Bill.'

I nod, understanding that I can't hope for any more than that.

By eight o'clock, I've had enough. The ferry is not due to sail until eleven, but I make the excuse that there are some things I'd like to do before I leave. I want to walk a while, maybe look in on a few old faces. And I want to stop at the graveyard, pay my respects. Whisper a prayer for all of us, the living and the dead. The old ghosts are waiting.

I shake Jack's hand, because a hug would be too awkward, even though it is probably something we both want. 'So long, boy,' I say, hoping in my heart that it's not goodbye. He clenches his mouth and nods, then goes to sit in the corner. Tommy looks at him for a moment, then follows me outside.

We walk out onto the road. 'It's been good seeing you, Bill,' he says. 'Take care of yourself now.'

My throat hurts from tears that are near but trying not to fall. Down in the harbour a boat has come in after two or three days at sea. The men, bone-tired, will be gutting and crating their catch for the mainland markets. A breeze blowing in breaths from the east carries the impatient screams of the gulls as they circle and perch in anticipation of the scraps.

'I'll write,' I say, the best that I can manage, and I slip my hands into my pockets and stroll away, counting the steps so that I won't look back.

Miracle Hay Oil